Praise for *Between Here*

"A page-turning good read . . . A tautly written story with sympathetic characters and evocative storytelling."

—*USA Today*

"[A] haunting page-turner . . . [A] compelling look at what it means to be a mother and a wife." —*Working Mother*

"An amalgamation of autobiography, true crime and melodrama . . . The story is so engaging . . . a credit to this narrator's wonderfully appealing voice: funny, frustrated, likable, totally candid about her desires and failings . . . The perfect book club book." —*The Washington Post Book World*

"Deborah Kogan's fearless novel interrogates one of society's last great taboos—maternal love gone wrong. *Between Here and April* is a provocative page-turner with brains and soul; it boldly exhumes the human story so often buried by scandalous headlines and family silence. Reading this book, I felt like I was being told a dangerous secret."

—Heidi Julavits, author of *The Uses of Enchantment*

"[A] provocative page-turner . . . Outstanding book club potential." —BookReporter.com

"Engrossing." —*Entertainment Weekly*

"Extraordinary . . . Fascinating and detailed . . . This is a story that needs to be told." —*Elle*, #1 Reader's Pick

"[A] hair-raising journey of self-discovery . . . Reading the book sometimes feels like four-wheeling through a war zone in a fog. At the end, you turn to your driver, Deborah Copaken Kogan, and thank her for the ride." —*The Raleigh News and Observer*

"Deborah Kogan's first novel is the work of a natural writer dealing with an unnatural event, a mother who murders her children and herself. From this most tragic of premises, she makes fiction that is heartfelt, painful, and almost hypnotically readable." —Adam Gopnik, author of *Paris to the Moon*

"The author is masterful at showing the fluid state of mothering in all its kaleidoscopic dimensions—the highs and lows, the angry moments counterbalancing affection, and the depths to which some will go to 'protect' loved ones. This exceptional, riveting novel will haunt you long after you've reached the end." —*Rocky Mountain News*

"Outstanding . . . A haunting eyes-wide openness." —*Daily Candy*

"A captivating thriller." —*More* magazine

"How could a mother kill her children? This breathtaking first novel from photojournalist Kogan attempts a heart-wrenching answer . . . [An] unflinching portrait of filicide, which still manages to find light in the darkness of a very disturbing subject." —*Publishers Weekly,* starred review

"Breathtaking . . . Heart-wrenching." —*The Baltimore Examiner*

"Startling revelations . . . Chillingly told."
—*Birmingham Magazine*

"A bold, haunting, honest, and wholly original journey into the darker, unchronicled terrains of motherhood."
—Katie Roiphe, author of *Still She Haunts Me*

"Bracingly honest and poignant, *Between Here and April* is a novel I will read again and again. It's that good."
—Ayelet Waldman, author of *Love and Other Impossible Pursuits*

"Deborah Copaken Kogan has written a haunting work of ambition and dimension. Vivid and lively, disturbing and funny all at once, it captures not just one era but two, taking a keen look at the strictures and innocence of 1970s suburbia and the freedoms and pressures of present-day urban family life. This is a big, rich novel that tackles the ambivalence of motherhood full-frontally." —Meg Wolitzer, author of *The Position*

Between Here and April

Between Here and April

a novel by Deborah Copaken Kogan

ALGONQUIN BOOKS OF CHAPEL HILL   2009

Published by
ALGONQUIN BOOKS OF CHAPEL HILL
Post Office Box 2225
Chapel Hill, North Carolina 27515-2225

a division of
WORKMAN PUBLISHING
225 Varick Street
New York, New York 10014

First paperback edition, Algonquin Books of Chapel Hill, November 2009.
Originally published by Algonquin Books of Chapel Hill in 2008.
Printed in the United States of America.
Published simultaneously in Canada by Thomas Allen & Son Limited.
Design by Anne Winslow.

While April Cassidy is based on an actual person once known to the author, and the basic building blocks of her fate (the *who, what, where, when,* and *how*) are largely pilfered from real life, the mortar of this tale — the *why* — is purely a figment of the author's imagination.

LIBRARY OF CONGRESS CATALOGING-IN-PUBLICATION DATA
Kogan, Deborah Copaken.
  Between here and April : a novel / by Deborah Copaken Kogan. —
1st. ed.
      p. cm.
  ISBN-13: 978-1-56512-562-9 (HC)
  1. Women television producers and directors — Fiction. 2. Missing
persons — Investigation — Fiction. 3. Conscience, Examination
of — Fiction. 4. Motherhood — Fiction. I. Title.
  PS3611.O3654B48 2008
  813'.6 — dc22   2008021165

ISBN-13: 978-1-56512-932-0 (PB)

10 9 8 7

For Paul

✳

In memory of
C. H.

"Midway in our life's journey, I went astray from the straight road and woke to find myself alone in a dark wood."

—DANTE ALIGHIERI, *The Inferno*

CHAPTER I

APRIL CASSIDY WAS my best friend from the first day of first grade in September of 1972, until a couple of months later, when she failed to show up for school. During the weeks following her disappearance, as leaf-littered lawns succumbed to snow, and eighteen and a half minutes of White House chatter were lost into the ether, I rubbed a pink eraser over the memory of my friend and wiped the loose leaf clean. So clean, it took thirty-five years and a production of *Medea* to unleash her. And when she emerged, thus began my descent.

"Where are we?" Mark whispered, too loudly, as he slipped into the seat next to mine twelve minutes after curtain.

"Corinth," I said.

He took off his coat and stole a peek at his BlackBerry. "No, I meant who's he and why's she yelling?"

Mark had bought us the tickets to see *Medea*, to get us out of the apartment and away from the kids. Maybe, he'd joked, we'd even hold hands. But he'd been held up late at his office again, though we'd planned to meet for dinner before the show.

"That's Jason," I whispered. "And she's yelling at him because she's angry."

"Sounds familiar," said Mark. "What'd he do?"

"Broke his promises." I wrapped the wool coat I'd draped over my chair around my shoulders. I was feeling slightly feverish, chilled. Tess had been sick with the flu, and I'd been up with her every night, pouring sticky, pink cupfuls of Motrin down her throat, which she would then throw up into my lap while I held a cold washcloth to her forehead to bring down her temperature. I'd suggested to Mark that maybe we should sell our tickets, postpone the date, but he'd said, "No, let's just go. It'll be great. I promise."

"Broke which promises?" he said.

"Shh," said the woman behind us.

I took a pen out of my purse and wrote on the back of my program, "He promised to meet her for dinner and didn't."

Mark's smile was weary. "Very funny, Lizard." My name is Elizabeth, but Mark only uses it when he's upset. He calls me Liza in bed, Zab from another room ("*Za-ab!* Have you seen my glasses?"), and Lizzie-bean when he wants to make light of my grumblings. "Oh, is my little Lizzie-bean lonely at night?" he'd said recently, rubbing my cheek with the back of his finger. "Poor Lizzie-bean." After which I told him to go fuck himself. After which he suggested we go see *Medea* together. Just the two of us. On a date. Lizard is kind of his catchall, covering the bases from appreciation to contrition. "Look, I'm sorry," he whispered, "I tried to call, but —"

I put my finger to my lips, not wanting to hear another excuse. "He's leaving her," I scribbled, "for another woman."

Mark let loose a tiny laugh-grunt and grabbed hold of my hand. Then he whispered, barely audibly, "Well at least you can't complain about *that* from me."

True. He didn't have a mistress, in the corporeal sense, but he did have a mistress of a different sort. He wasn't having sex with her. He was poring over data in her. Writing formulas in her. Typing emails in her. Until eleven, twelve o'clock every night.

Like many of his former colleagues, Mark had been lured away from the math department at CUNY when Lortex, a Texas-based insurance firm, called and asked him to consult on their latest project, using neural networks to fine-tune actuarial charts. The idea, he'd explained to me, his voice all aflutter, was to completely shatter the paradigm of risk management. Instead of assessing risk for various groups of people, he was going to try to figure out a way to predict the actual hour, within a plus or minus range of seventy-two hours, of a single individual's demise. If it worked, we'd have the first financial cushion of our working lives. If it didn't, we wouldn't be any worse off than we were now, which is to say, like anyone making a go of New York without funds modified by *trust* or *hedge,* struggling to keep up with the rent. "It'll mean a few late nights," he'd said, offhandedly, "nothing major." He estimated six months before a working prototype could be built. Seven at the most. But three years and several hundred late nights later, his model, he'd recently admitted, still wasn't correlating with reality. "Oh really?" I'd snapped. "Well neither is ours."

I focused my attention back on the play. The actress playing Medea was beginning to cloy, playing the role like a put-upon housewife, her shoulders sloped inward, her delivery mousy. Medea should have been strong in her fury, full of bluster and brawn. Or at least worthy of her spotlight as a Greek hero. *"I will kill,"* she kept muttering. *"I will kill."* But she didn't seem capable of icing a cake, much less her offspring.

"Remember you started this war of words," Jason was now shouting, from stage left. *"As for your complaints about this*

marriage, I'll show you that in this I'm being wise, and moderate, and very friendly to you, and to my children."

My mind wandered off the stage and back to our narrow floor-through on West Eighty-fifth Street: to the vestibule overflowing with mini-coats and solitary mittens; to Tess's stuffed animals flung across the parquet like bodies at Antietem; to the forlorn ticktock of the kitchen clock once the girls had been tucked into bed. A few days earlier, Daisy had taped a new drawing to the refrigerator: three figures, a mother and two daughters, with the words MY FAMLY stenciled in block letters across the top. "You forgot the *i*," I'd said, "between the *m* and the *l*." It didn't seem fair to point out the other omission. The missing *i* could be easily replaced; the missing *we* not so easily. I suggested, perhaps too nervously, that Daisy put the drawing in her special box, to keep it safe from the ravages of sticky fingers and spilled grape juice. "Don't worry, Mom. We can keep it out," she'd said. "Daddy won't notice."

The curtain fell. The houselights came up. I extricated my now clammy hand from Mark's. "You're right," I whispered, "at least I don't have to worry about you and another woman."

Because I'd waited for Mark outside the theater before the play, instead of going to the bathroom as I'd needed, I spent intermission waiting my turn to use one of the three stalls available, watching the men move in and out of their facilities with the efficiency of cars on an assembly line. I pictured the inside of their bathroom, the wall of urinals like stops on a conveyor belt, the swift zip-release-zip motion of fingers and genitals, the hands washed and dried or perhaps not, with nary a glance in the mirror, while on our side precious time was lost to spreading toilet paper over seats, pulling down hose, hiking up skirts, tugging on tampons, locating flushing mechanisms, pulling up hose, straightening out skirts, and fidgeting with locks which never seemed to want to close. "Can you hold this door for me?" we'd ask each other. Or "Does anyone have any paper? Mine's out." And wads of paper would pass from stall to stall, and this one would hold that one's door shut, and more time would be lost, more minutes wasted.

And as I stood there in line and waited, mentally transforming each woman in front of me into a giant uterus, giving birth to other girls, other uteruses, telescoping out one by one from the original like the matrioshka dolls Tess used to love to split open and toss about the living room floor, heads rolling under couches, torsos under chairs, which every night I carefully gathered and reassembled, so she could scatter them once again, I thought about all those mothers and mothers-to-be, chugging along, finding detours around all those inconveniences and compromises that would have to be weighed and measured and fought over and swallowed while the men went about their business, zip-release-zip, unhampered and unfettered, along the conveyor belts of their lives.

"You were in the bathroom this whole time?" Mark said, with a slight tone of annoyance, as the houselights blinked and the bodies hustled back into their seats.

"No," I said. "I was in Stockholm. Fetching my Nobel. Want to see it?"

"I thought we were supposed to talk."

"Yes, that was the plan." But now we'd have to rush home after the play to relieve the babysitter we could ill afford, and I'd check my email or maybe read, and Mark would plant himself in front of his computer to surf the porn sites he thought I didn't know about, and I'd check on the girls and probably pass out on the couch watching the end of Jon Stewart, still in my clothes, and Mark would try to rouse me but fail, and I'd awake with a start, maybe two AM, maybe three, and hit the power on the remote and stumble my way in the dark to our bedroom, liberating breasts and limbs from straps and buttons and saying to hell with the toothbrush, and I'd see Mark passed out on top of the duvet, a chalk outline of himself, and I'd slip in under the covers on my side of the bed, wishing I'd remembered to grab a glass of water, diving into dreams about sinking ships and quicksand sidewalks, and then the window would lighten, the alarm would go off, another day would begin. "Maybe we can talk next week," I said.

On stage, Jason and the children departed to deliver the poisoned robe and crown to Creon's daughter. Medea paced around the stage, finally gathering strength now, like a tropical storm. And then, just as Medea began to slaughter her children (tastefully, behind a scrim), just as the lamentations and wails began to echo throughout the house, and the blood began to splatter across the scrim, crimson Rorschach blots arousing the sleepy unconscious, April Cassidy, wearing a pair of red shorts, burst forth into my mind's eye.

Come play! she was saying, or so it seemed, or so I thought, *It's been so long.* And I saw her blue lips and heard the phantom words spoken as clearly as if they'd been uttered by Medea's children themselves, who were shouting, pleading, begging to be saved: *"Yea, by heaven I adjure you; your aid is needed! Even now the toils of the sword are closing round us . . ."*

I rubbed my eyes, thinking the hallucination a trick of exhaustion, of a flulike fever now palpably mounting and no longer possible to ignore. But the harder I rubbed, the clearer the vision became.

"Mark," I said, tugging on his shirt, "I'm having a . . . I think I'm hallucina . . . help." This last word was spoken feebly. My heart beat inside my chest like a sneaker in a dryer.

Mark looked at me, genuinely concerned. "What is it, Z?" He put his hand on my forehead. "Oh my god, Lizzie. You're burning up."

I felt the theater closing in on me, the stage lights pulsing and swirling as if the psychedelic pyrotechnics were about to kick in. I needed a blast of January air, space to breathe, light. "I've got to get out of here," I whispered to my neighbor, "I'm so sorry," and I stood up and held onto the seat in front of me for balance. Which is when, according to my husband, the woman behind us yelled, "Jesus! Sit down and shut up already!" and Mark's BlackBerry went off, and the actress playing Medea flubbed her line about feeble lust and ruin, and I fainted, hitting my head on the armrest on the way down.

—∿— CHAPTER 2 —∿—

DR. KAREN RIVERS sat on the Eames chair in front of me, a yellow notepad resting on her knee. "So," she said. "Why are you here?"

If I knew that, I thought, *then I wouldn't be here.* "It was my internist's idea," I said, relieved to have the excuse. "I've been fainting, a lot, and nobody can find any physiological reason why that should be happening." I'd blacked out seven times altogether, if you counted the afternoon I was standing in the yard of my daughters' school, waiting for them to emerge, and was able to catch myself on the chain-link fence, my fingers clinging to the metal diamonds like claws, before everything went dark. Six times if you counted only the episodes in which I awoke to find small crowds gathered around me, staring down or trying to rouse me with newspaper fans.

I'd gone for a CT scan at Mount Sinai. Normal. I was tested for Ménière's at New York Presbyterian. Inconclusive. My blood pressure was in the normal range, so it wasn't, explained my internist, run-of-the-mill vasovagal syncope. "Vase-o-bagel what?" I'd said, and he'd chuckled and said, "No, it has nothing to do with bagels, but it can have to do with stress. How's your mental state of late?"

"And how did you answer his question?" Dr. Rivers now asked.

"I said I was fine."

"Are you fine?" Her expression was inscrutable. I wondered if she practiced it in the mirror.

"What do you think?"

She cocked her head. "What do *you* think?"

"Is that how things work in here?"

"More or less."

"Okay. I guess I'm not sure, then. If I'm fine."

"You're not sure." She jotted down a note on her pad. "Would you like to elaborate?"

"I guess part of me feels a little . . . lost." This wasn't the right word exactly, but it wasn't the wrong one either. How else to describe the sense that my life had gone off track?

"What do you mean 'lost'?"

I shrugged. "I'm not sure."

"You're not sure." She waited, in vain, for me to continue. After a long pause, in which I could sense her disappointment in my inability to plumb the depths of my subconscious, she flipped over to a fresh page in her notebook. "Let's back up. Start with some easier questions. How old are you?"

"Forty-one."

"And have you ever been treated by a psychiatrist before?"

"No."

Thus we spent the next half hour, delving into the world of verifiable fact, but even to some of Dr. Rivers's simple queries I found myself responding with addendums, caveats, and apologies. When asked, for example, how to spell my last name, I said it was Burns, but if she was asking for purposes of insurance, she should write down Elizabeth Burns Steiger, my legal name ever since that rainy afternoon in 1999 when a particularly unpleasant US postal worker told me I couldn't retrieve the baby present that had arrived for Daisy because the last name on my ID did not match the last name on my daughter's package.

"How about your work?" said Dr. Rivers. "Dr. Leland told me you're a journalist, right? A TV producer?"

"So to speak."

"So to speak?"

I chastised myself for not answering at least that one succinctly and in the affirmative. I was a journalist, after all: eighteen years and counting, the last six of which I'd focused, out of financial necessity, on television production. It's the word I always scribbled in the blank following "mother's occupation" on the emergency forms for the girls' school. I should have just said yes and been done with it. But I knew, even when filling out those forms, that to call what I did "journalism" of late was generous. My most recent assignment, from *Entertainment Now,* had been to stake out the entrance of the W Hotel waiting for an actress whose ménage à trois with a Brazilian hooker was making the rounds of the blogosphere. The one before that, for a failed pilot called *Real Women, Real Beauty,* had me interviewing random women on Madison Avenue on the subject of their nails.

"Meaning, I guess sometimes I feel like I'm just treading water these days," I said to Dr. Rivers. "The work feels empty."

My career, prechildren, I explained, had been going along a fairly normal trajectory, with various internships and wireservice gigs which lead to postings in *Newsworld* magazine's Rome bureau and then New York. But by the time Kosovo was imploding, so was I. It wasn't burnout per se, although I was definitely burned out. "It was . . ." I paused. Dr. Rivers remained silent, waiting for me to continue, but I let it drop. I could never even explain any of it to Mark. I was pregnant with Daisy at the time, and it was just easier to blame the months of crushing fatigue and confusion that followed on that.

I returned to work faithfully after each brief maternity leave, taking a more deskbound position as an editor after Tess arrived, but it didn't take long for me to grasp the economic realities of American parenthood. An old colleague of mine, who lived in Paris, would gasp when we'd swap stories. Clem was given a year-long paid maternity leave and placed Sophie in a state-subsidized *crèche* the day she went back to her job which, by law, she could only perform thirty-five hours a week. A doctor checked Sophie's ears, nose, and throat every Friday afternoon, doling out free antibiotics to her and her classmates whenever necessary. "But I don't understand," Clem would say when I'd complain about our crushing childcare expenses, the five-figure preschool bills, the uncovered well visits to the pediatrician which I had to sneak out of my office to attend. "How can you afford to live like this?"

"We can't," I'd say.

"What about daycare? Surely there is an affordable *crèche* nearby, *non*?"

I laughed. There was a daycare center on the outskirts of my neighborhood which, while not affordable, was at least more reasonable, at least for one child, than a full-time sitter, but to get in I would have to have applied Daisy while she was still in utero.

"*Incroyable*," said Clem. "No wonder all those American girls are dropping their babies in dumpsters."

Since uprooting the kids to France was not in the cards, Mark and I decided that I would switch from my full-time magazine job to freelance television producing for a few years, figuring we'd reassess the situation and our finances once the girls were in school. Then, just as Tess was getting ready for kindergarten, just as I was getting ready to "ramp back on," as the social scientists were now calling it, the news divisions of all the major networks announced massive layoffs. A month later, my old editor at *Newsworld* took me out to lunch to inform me that not only was my former position there no longer available, it no longer even existed on the masthead. "We're down to one foreign editor," he said, mumbling something about falling ad revenues, the rise of online media, the lack of general interest in international news. The only magazines with any real budgets to burn, he said, were either lifestyle/consumer or celebrity ones, but if I wanted, he could definitely set me up an interview with the editor of a new venture called *Scoop,* which sounded promising, until I got to the interview and blew the job within the first five minutes of sitting down. "What do you mean you've never heard of Pratesi?" squawked the editor.

But I'd never heard of Pratesi. Or Frette or Crème de la Mer. And I couldn't bring myself to care, either about the products or the celebrities who used them.

And so I fell deeper and deeper into journalistic purgatory, writing press releases about antifungal medications and a new brand of sneakers for a viral marketing firm, comparing the suction strength of various breast pumps for an online parenting site.

Dr. Rivers jotted down another note on her pad, crossed her left leg over her right. "What about your marriage? Everything okay on the home front?"

"It could be better," I said.

"Meaning?"

"Well, my husband and I hardly ever see each other these days, for one."

"And for another?"

"I don't know. I just said, 'for one' as an expression. I don't really have a 'for two.'"

"I see." She glanced at her clock. "Look, Elizabeth, I think we should focus, before our time is up today, on the blackouts themselves." She wondered aloud whether there might be anything to unite them: a thought process; a feeling; a circumstance; a trigger. "The first time you fainted, for example, where were you? What was going through your mind?"

"I was at the theater," I said. "Watching the last act of *Medea*. Then I suddenly remembered this girl April. From elementary school."

"She was a classmate?"

"A friend. My best friend, actually. In first grade."

"And what happened to her after first grade?"

"She . . . I don't know. She left. Never came back to school."

"She moved?"

"No, I think she . . . actually, I really don't know. I never found out. And I haven't really thought about her since. Until that night, I mean."

"I see." She was now scribbling furiously on her pad. "And what about the other blackouts? Same questions: where were you, what were you thinking about?"

I lined all the other episodes up in my head, a row of dominos: the time at the grocery store, when the girls were playing ring around the rosie in the aisle; the one at the school yard, when I was able to catch myself on the fence; the Saturday when we rented a car to visit friends who'd moved out to the suburbs, and we'd stopped off at an Exxon station to fill up on the way back; the time I was riding on that crowded crosstown bus with Daisy, the two of us sandwiched in the aisle between two other women, one who was nuzzling her nose against the fragrant head of her infant, the other who was ignoring her crying toddler. "They were all totally random," I said, listing each one, fall by fall. Picturing the dominos tumbling down. "And there's no pattern to what I was thinking about beforehand. I mean ring around the rosie? A bus ride? A gas station? One has nothing to do with the other."

Dr. Rivers glanced at her clock and sighed. "We're out of time today," she said. "But I'd like you to do something for me this week. A little writing assignment, if you will. I'd like you to jot down everything you can remember about that friend of yours. The one who disappeared. I'm not saying she has anything to do with your blackouts, but I have a hunch, if she preceded the first episode, that this disappearance may somehow be significant. At the very least, it'll be a useful exercise. To focus on your memories. From the past. To try to figure out the significance of their sudden emergence into your present. Especially when it involves a close relationship that was severed."

"I never said my relationship with April was painful."

Dr. Rivers's eyes widened. "Neither did I." She scribbled another note. "*Was* it a painful relationship?"

"No," I said, looking down at my hands, noting the prominence of the veins, the cracked crevices of their surface, like a dinosaur's. Whose hands were these? "We were children. Good friends. Nothing painful in that."

Dr. Rivers stole another glance at her clock and gathered her papers, her demeanor calm but expedient. "I'll see you next week," she said, standing up. Then she showed me, cordially, to the door.

— CHAPTER 3 —

THAT NIGHT, UNABLE TO SLEEP, I trained my eyes on the ceiling, trying to conjure April anew. Her significance to my present? What could that possibly mean? We were best friends for two months tops. When we were six. I could barely even remember how we met. I closed my eyes again, trying to will myself into a state of unconsciousness, but my mind kept drifting—to the dentist appointment for the girls I would have to reschedule; to the sheet music that had to be located in a music store in midtown and purchased before Tuesday's lesson; to a three-by-five-inch piece of wood, jelly beans, and tube of fabric glue that Daisy's teacher required for god only knew what. And then, just as I was remembering the note Tess's teacher had sent home, asking me to please replace the extra clothing in her cubby with February-appropriate gear, an image appeared: a young girl standing in front of a wall of cubbies, her arms crossed over her chest like a dare.

I grabbed my laptop from my bedside table and turned it on, anxious to transcribe the ghost before she disappeared once again. Then I opened a new file and started to write.

April Cassidy, I typed, feeling a slight jolt from just the shape of her name on the page, *was my best friend from the first day of first grade in September of 1972, until a couple of months later, when she failed to show up for school. During the weeks following her disappearance, as leaf-littered lawns succumbed to snow . . .*

That's a start, I thought, finishing the first paragraph.

Because her last name began with a C and mine with a B, we shared a cubby, into which we placed our lunch bags and our brown grocery bags full of accident clothes. April's bag contained underwear, socks, pants, a shirt, and a pair of red shorts, and I remember being impressed that first day when she reached into her bag, pulled out the shorts, and slipped them on under her dress. Bell-bottomed, braless girlwomen may have been marching against the war and for their rights just down the road on the steps of the Capitol, but we suburban DC dainties, whose mothers had learned a thing or two about fashion from Jackie O, were still made to wear dresses and Mary Janes on our first days of school, rendering all hopes of climbing trees and scaling monkey bars moot.

"I was supposed to be born a boy," April said, by way of introduction, "but God made a mistake. He's sending my boy parts with Santa. Do you do Christmas or Hanukah?"

"Hanukah," I said, suddenly fretting over how I'd get my boy parts delivered.

April, I would learn, never fretted. About anything. If her mother forgot to pack her lunch, she'd forage from others. If she found a knot in her hair, she'd snip it out. If she needed a permission slip signed, she'd forge it. Her pigtails were always uneven, her socks unmatched, and the day Miss Martin asked us to draw what we'd eaten for breakfast that morning, April's was the only picture containing a can of SpaghettiOs and a can of TaB.

"Come on," she said, reaching into our cubby and removing the shorts from my own stash of accident clothes. "Put these on, and let's go outside."

I'd never had a best friend before April, let alone one who was female, but because April professed the same aversions to Barbies as I did, because her favorite book, too, was *Where the Wild Things Are,* because when she scraped her knee she not only never cried, she rejoiced in the anticipation of a new scab, I grew enamored of her.

By the end of that first week of school, we had already fallen into a comfortable twosome, having chicken fights on the monkey bars, playing ring around the rosie in the rain until we were mud-caked and dizzy, searching for four-leafed clovers for April's massive (so she claimed) collection. April was the first person to show me that a worm, unlike us, could be cut in half and still survive. I showed her how to capture a frog, by cupping your hands over him like a dome. We created our own friendship oath and secret handshake, whose motions I can no longer recall, aside from a fluttering up of fingers, like birds, at the end.

The only problem with our newfound paradise was its inevitable dissolution at the sound of the school bell. April couldn't come over to my house after school because it had temporarily become a zoo, filled with me, my three younger sisters, an infant brother, and a postpartum mother drowning in laundry, diapers, and spit-up. And I couldn't go over to April's house to play because, well, I wasn't sure. "Why can't I come over?" I'd ask.

"You just can't," she'd say, and I wouldn't push it. Even at that age, I must have understood that a house which served SpaghettiOs and TaB for breakfast might have difficulties absorbing guests. Besides, April and I didn't live close enough to each others' houses to walk anyway. In fact, her subdivision was more than a mile from mine, separated by two busy thorough-fares. I had about as much chance of finding my way there solo as I had of rocketing myself to the moon.

A few weeks before Halloween, we were sitting on top of the monkey bars, discussing costumes. I couldn't decide between Batman and Cousin Itt. April said anyone could be a superhero. Monsters were much more interesting, because underneath their fur was a creature just like us. Or sort of like us, only different. Like Max in *Where the Wild Things Are.* We decided we should both be Cousin Itt, one for her neighborhood, one for mine, but we would definitely need a lot of yellow yarn for the hair, even though April was certain Cousin Itt was blue. "But never mind, yellow's fine," she conceded after only a minute, because even though she was pretty sure she was right, April had no interest in proving it. Or anything. The one time she was chastised for making noise in class, she didn't even defend herself. She just said, "I'm sorry, Miss Martin, I won't do it again," and moved away from the guilty party.

Then, one day in October, about an hour before lunch, a woman in a frayed housedress and flip-flops lumbered into our classroom. Her short, gray-blond hair was matted down on one side, making her appear slightly askew, while the housedress was stretched beyond capacity across her swollen bosom.

"Look at that woman," I whispered to April, who was sitting on the floor next to me, her eyes glued to the filmstrip on mammals. "I think she's lost."

April tore herself away from the image of nursing baby mice, narrated by a baritone voice which was explaining how, if the infants were touched or licked or handled by another creature, the mother would consider them contaminated and eat them. When April's gaze came to rest on the new visitor, her bottom lip started to quiver, and then her shoulders caved inward, as if she were trying to turn herself inside out.

"April?" our teacher, Miss Martin, called out from behind us.

Then, suddenly straightening, April whispered, "That's my mom's friend. My mom couldn't take me to the dentist today, so her *friend* is taking me."

"Why couldn't your mom take you?" I'd never heard of anyone being taken to the dentist by an adult other than her mother.

"She's busy."

"Doing what?" I thought of all the things that could occupy a mother's time: going to the grocery store, folding laundry, making dinner.

"Fighting her inner diamonds."

"Her inner what?" I cocked my head.

But before April could answer, Miss Martin called out once again. "April, sweetheart? Your mother's here to pick you up."

April reddened as she stood up. Then she shrugged and raised her eyebrows in confusion, as if to say, *Hmm, how weird. I could have sworn it was my mother's friend.*

The next day, when I asked her about it, she blamed her confusion on the dust whipped up from the slide projector.

"But I thought the dust was already there, and the light just makes it twinkle," I said.

"No. The light actually *makes* the dust. I read it in a filmstrip book."

And then, exactly one week before Halloween, April didn't show up for school. The first day, I assumed she had a cold or a sore throat and gave it no further thought. But four days later, when she still hadn't returned, I cornered Miss Martin by the reading lab. "Where's April?" I asked.

Miss Martin's already thin lips pressed together into a single line. "She's not here, Lizzie."

Well *of course* she's not here, I thought. I figured that one out all by myself. "Does she have the chicken pox?" I'd had it the year before, and the memories of soaking in oatmeal and wearing gloves to bed were still fresh. Plus I'd missed the class picture, an absence I was certain would result in the annihilation of my existence from my classmates' memories. But to miss Halloween? Now that would be tragic.

"No, she doesn't have the chicken pox."

"Is she sick?"

"No, she's not sick."

"Did she switch schools?" I'd known two kids who had been siphoned away from Sycamore Hill Elementary in such an unfortunate manner.

"No, sweetheart, she did not switch schools."

"Well, when is she coming back?"

"We're not sure, Lizzie. Did you finish—"

"But where is she?"

"—your handwriting assignment?"

"Yes, but . . ." Now I was totally confused. April wasn't sick. Nor had she switched schools. And yet, despite these facts (oh to be Nancy Drew!), there remained the issue of her absence from school. To complicate matters, Miss Martin, a woman who in every other domain knew all things about everything, did not know when April might be coming back. *But Halloween is just around the corner!* I thought, beginning to panic. Did she have problems gluing the pieces of yarn down to the grocery bag with the eye holes cut out of it, as I had? I wanted to tell her she should glue the yarn to a piece of cardboard first and *then* stick the whole thing to the top of the grocery bag, to keep it from drooping. ". . . but I need to tell her something."

"Well," Miss Martin said, but then she patted me on the arm and fell silent for a moment. "If you're done with handwriting, why don't you go work on your subtraction problems?"

But I don't want to subtract! I thought, fretting as usual, wishing I could be more blasé about everything, like April.

And then, the day before Halloween, Miss Martin sat us down on the floor, all three classes of first graders, and told us that April and her older sister, Lily, would not be coming back to school. Ever. "We'll all miss her," she said, "but we'll always hold her in our hearts."

I raised my hand. "Will she be trick-or-treating somewhere else then?"

Miss Martin shook her head and began to blink more than usual. "No," she said. And then the bell rang.

Afterwards, and for many years hence, I'd believe that the human form could spontaneously disintegrate, like Mr. Spock or Mike Teevee, only without the molecular reintegration on the other side. I wondered if April might have simply slipped through a looking glass, like Alice, and would reemerge years later the same person but somehow altered, the way the girls in the sixth grade always showed up in September tall as skyscrapers and wearing bras.

I hunted lions by myself that day. I tried playing chicken alone. I picked a scab on my elbow and watched it bleed. I made a valiant attempt to join in with the boys, who were playing a game of tag on the blacktop. "Cooties! Cooties!" they all screamed, running away from me as fast as their knobby knees would allow.

"I hope a killer bee comes and stings you all," I muttered under my breath. I wondered how far away Canada was, how high their fence was to keep the bees out. April, I was certain, would have known the answer to that.

That afternoon, on the bus heading home from school, I sat alone behind two third-grade boys, classmates of April's sister, Lily, one of whom was drawing small lines onto a piece of paper, his Ticonderoga No. 2 casting long shadows onto his lap. "How do you turn these into a bad person, using only three diagonal lines?" he asked the boy next to him.

I peeked over the seat to eavesdrop. The boy had drawn a few lines and a circle on the page, like this:

I II\OI I

The other boy stared at the paper, then drew two arms coming out of the circle, then erased them. "I don't know," he said.

"Think!" said the other.

"I'm thinking."

"No you're not." I'd seen Billy Nussbaum show Randy Hays the same puzzle. It had taken Randy the entirety of recess before he finally gave up, but the boy on the bus waited no more than a second or two before giving the whole thing away. "Okay, here's a hint: who's the president of the United States?"

"Nixon?"

"Yep." The boy with the pencil drew a diagonal line between the first and second lines, crossing the fourth line to form an *X*. The fifth and sixth lines he also turned into an *N*. Like this:

NIXON

The other boy rolled his eyes, claiming the puzzle was stupid since Nixon wasn't really a bad person. Not like Lily's mother, Mrs. Cassidy. My ears suddenly pricked up. "I can't believe she did that to them," he said.

"And to herself," said the boy with the pencil, switching to hangman.

"I heard they were already unconscious when they found them," said a large kid a few rows back.

"Fucked up, isn't it?" said his seatmate, and the bus driver chewed him out for cursing.

I felt a panicky tightness in my chest, as if someone had suddenly turned off the world's oxygen. The next few minutes slipped out from under me, like the floor of a spinning Gravitron, while other kids weighed in on the matter. Someone said April and Lily had been eaten by the Loch Ness monster, not killed by their mother. Another kid claimed the whole family had drowned in the JCC pool. An older boy behind me mentioned something I didn't understand about gas and carbon monoxide. The girl in the seat across the aisle from mine, who was in sixth grade, told everyone to shut up, there were *children* around. Then she tilted her head in my direction.

"What's 'unconscious'?" I asked her.

"Don't worry about it," she said. "It's just a fancy word for dizzy." Then she stared out the window.

"Oh, like when you play ring around the rosie," I said.

"Yeah, the black plague version," said a boy.

"Shut up," said the girl.

"What happened to April?" I asked.

"Ask your teacher," she said, shaking her head and catching the eye of the boy behind me as if to say, *I told you so.*

But I did ask my teacher! I wanted to yell, *and she wouldn't answer!* But my voice was suddenly stuck in the back of my throat.

When I arrived home from school, I paused to eye the gas-tank cover on our Dodge Coronet wagon and then quickly ran past it, as if it could reach out and grab me, like the trees in *The Wizard of Oz.* I rushed through the door to find my mother standing in the foyer, a baby bottle in hand. "Lizzie, please, can you feed Josh? I have to get ready to take Ellen to Daddy's office. She has another ear infection." I heard my younger sister Ellen in our shared bedroom, screaming from pain. I saw Josh in his plastic infant seat, his reddened face scrunched up like a prune. I spotted Becca—whom everyone was calling Josh's Irish twin, even though they looked nothing alike and weren't Irish—scribbling with an orange marker on the living-room wall, while *her* Irish twin, Lisa, which I figured made the three of them Irish triplets, spun Cheerios projectiles off her Sit 'n Spin. I wondered what it would take for a mother to feed her children gas.

Surely less than this.

I sat down on the shag carpet next to Josh's infant seat and fed him a bottle. *"Rock-a-bye baby . . ."* I sang, echoing my mother, pulsing his chair gently up and down with my free hand like I'd been taught to do. "I've finally got an heir!" my father kept bragging whenever people came by with presents for the new baby. "A real heir." Ellen and I were the only ones old enough to understand that whatever an heir was, it was probably good, and we weren't. *I was supposed to be born a boy, but God made a mistake,* April had said, that first day we met. Which was why, it suddenly struck me, we might have become friends. We were both mistakes, both missing some essential part, like the way Lite-Brites come packed without bulbs. I watched my brother's cheeks suck in the milk, his needy eyes probing mine with a mixture of relief and "What took you so long?" If I put gasoline in his bottle, I wondered, what would happen?

No! I thought. It made no sense! A mother wouldn't feed her child gas.

". . . *and down will come baby, cradle and—*" I stopped singing.

And then, very quietly, so my mother wouldn't hear, so she wouldn't have one more child to worry about that day, I gave in to the pressure building behind my eyes. By the time Mom was out of the shower, Josh had been fed and burped, my head cleared of all vapors gaseous and grotesque.

The next day at school, I noticed that April's accident clothes had been removed from our cubby.

I LOOKED UP from my work. Mark was snoring. A streetlight outside my window gave way to a conical mass of swirling snowflakes beneath it, through which an ambulance sped by, lights ablaze. I watched the flakes twirl around in the wind, twinkling in the light like the dust from that filmstrip long ago, and I could see why April would claim the light made the dust, rather than simply illuminating it. It's hard for anyone to know where illusion ends and reality begins, let alone a small child.

— CHAPTER 4 —

AFTER UNSUCCESSFULLY TRYING to locate Miss Martin and finding nothing about the story on Google, I sent off a FOIA request to the Montgomery County police. While waiting for a response, I decided to try my luck digging through stacks of microfilm. A six-year-old child's death, I reasoned, even back in that slow-news-cycle era, could not have been a tree falling in the forest. Someone must have made some noise about it. Somewhere.

The air was frigid, the steps of the New York Public Library glazed with ice as I ducked into the microfilm reading room stamping my feet, jingling a pocketful of dimes. I would need, as it turned out, only two dimes that morning: one to photo-copy the original article, buried on page C3 of the *Washington Post* the same day H. R. Haldeman was prematurely—if cor-rectly—fingered on A1 for his involvement in Watergate; the second for the next day's follow-up, a short rehash of the first. But while I may have overestimated the number of stories I would find, I underestimated my reaction to them.

At the sight of the words "Cassidy, Adele," in the microfilm index, I could actually feel the surge of blood and adrenaline exploding outward, wound up grabbing onto the edge of the bookshelf for balance. Steadying myself and taking some deep breaths, I sat down at the microfilm reader, loaded the spool, and watched the buzzwords of my youth whiz by. *Kissinger,* flashed the screen, as I slowed down the machine to check page numbers and dates. Then *Playtex Cross Your Heart* (vroom), *Secret Fund* (vroom vroom*)*, *You've come a long way, baby!* (vroom), *Roe v. Wade* (vroom), *Thieu Orders Cease-Fire* (vroom), until, finally, simply, there it was:

Maryland Mother, Children, Found Dead

BY JOHN SEYMOUR

Washington Post Staff Writer

A 39-YEAR-OLD POTOMAC WOMAN and her two children were found dead yesterday in the back of the family station wagon, a 1967 Plymouth Fury, which was idling in the woods in western Montgomery County when police were summoned to the scene.

While the autopsy has not yet been completed, Montgomery County police are reporting that all three of the passengers appeared to have died of asphyxiation, approximately eight hours before they were found, in a double homicide and suicide committed by the mother, Adele Levine Cassidy. The children were identified as Lily Ann Cassidy, 8, and April Noreen Cassidy, 6.

They are survived by Mrs. Cassidy's husband and the girls' father, Shepherd ("Shep") Cassidy, a vice president of sales and marketing for Pipeline Industries.

Officers John Malatesta and Vincent Polenta, the first policemen to arrive on the scene, said they discovered the bodies at around 11:20 AM after receiving a call from a resident of the area to investigate a car parked in a clearing of dense underbrush in the woods near his property, not far from the intersection of routes 28 and 107 in Gaithersberg.

According to witnesses, a vacuum cleaner hose had been retrofitted with duct tape to the exhaust pipe, the open end of which had been fed into the passenger compartment through a crack in the window, which was then sealed off with plastic sheeting.

The police report stated that Mr. Cassidy had last seen his wife, a former nurse, at 8 AM Saturday. The report also stated that the couple had been having marital difficulties and that Mrs. Cassidy had recently sought out the care of a psychiatrist.

"I checked all the pulses as soon as I arrived," said Officer Polenta. "The woman was curled up on her knees in the compartment behind the rear seat, between the two girls." Polenta said that the station wagon was located approximately one-fourth mile from the nearest road. Officer Malatesta said Mrs. Cassidy had one arm wrapped around each of her daughters. The two girls, he said, were lying on pillows, their feet toward the tailgate. They were dressed in flannel pajamas.

Dr. Angus Lord, county deputy medical examiner, said traces of codeine, of the type found in cough syrups, were found in the girls' bloodstreams.

Malatesta, who said there were no signs of a struggle in the car, said it contained two large suitcases, one filled with Mrs. Cassidy's clothes, the other with clothes for the girls, and that the car's gas tank was still one-eighth full upon his arrival.

Mrs. Arnold Traub, a neighbor, said the two girls attended Sycamore Hill Elementary School. "They were lovely girls," she said, "and their mother was a lovely person."

But for every blank now filled, every question answered, I thought of ten more. What secrets had Adele Cassidy confided to her shrink? What had finally pushed her out of her house and into her station wagon? I wondered about her husband, Shep, about the vacuum hose itself (did she bring it from home or purchase one on the road?), about the logistics of the act and the contents of the suitcases and the thoughts in Adele's head as she turned the key in the ignition, all the while circling back to the most obvious, least answerable, and most terrifying question of all: *How could a mother kill her children?*

The microfilm room was hardly crowded that day. Those who were there were immersed in their own journeys backward, leaving ample space between us, but even so once again I started to feel faint. I tried containing the inner thrum, to focus on making the photocopies, dating them, placing them into a clear plastic folder. But the heaviness grew oppressive, the staccato contractions of my chest more pronounced, the tear ducts in my eyes now quietly swelling.

Get a grip on yourself! I thought. It wasn't as if I hadn't heard this story before. I'd interviewed several experts on postpartum depression after Andrea Yates drowned her children in a bathtub. I'd helped edit the coverage of Susan Smith. This was not unfamiliar territory. What was wrong with me?

"Ma'am, are you okay?" a librarian said, bending over. She looked to be in her sixties or so, her gray hair held back from her forehead with a velvet headband.

"Yeah, I'm fine." I wasn't fine. "It's nothing." How the fuck do you rewind this thing? "I think it must be jammed."

"Jammed? No, look." She leaned over my desk, flooding my nostrils with Chanel N°5, and placed one hand on the rewind button, the other on the back of my chair. "You have to push it to the left."

"Oh. Thanks."

"Doing research on Watergate?" she asked, adding, with a knowing smile, "It's a popular spool."

"No, I was just looking up . . ." But I couldn't finish the

sentence. I could feel my face tightening, lips, nose, and eyebrows all converging together. "I'm sorry," I said. "I have to . . . I'm late to . . ."

The librarian's demeanor suddenly softened. "I can put it back in its box for you," she said.

But can you put April back in her box? I wanted to say. Because that's where I suddenly needed her to go.

Outside the library, I pulled out my cell phone and dialed the number on the business card Dr. Karen Rivers had handed me a week earlier. "Hi, Dr. Rivers. It's Elizabeth Burns," I said into her answering machine. "You were right. It probably did have to do with April. The fainting episodes, I mean. Watergate, the gas station, that mean mother on the bus—they're all related to her disappearance. I'll tell you all about it when I see you on Friday."

I hung up the phone. Continued down the icy library stairs, staring down so as not to slip, then across Fifth Avenue at Forty-first Street, glancing up barely in time to see the taxi speeding toward me. A bad corner. I accidentally ran through it once myself. As I leapt toward the curb, I imagined the impact, the crunch of bone, the body flung off the grill into a pile of twisted limbs and blood. It took so little to erase a person. It was a wonder any of us could remain standing.

CHAPTER 5

DRIVEN BY A DESIRE to delve deeper into the story I couldn't quite, at the time, understand, realizing I would need research funds to do so, I typed up a proposal and emailed it to Lucy. Lucy had just been named the director of reality and documentary programming at FemTV, a new women's cable network that was positioning itself as a darker, more cutting-edge alternative to Lifetime.

I was in Central Park near the swings in the Pinetum, walking Daisy and Tess to their rescheduled dental appointment, when she called. "Well, I hate the name April, and you'll need to figure out a way to ramp up the community outrage," she said. "But . . ."

"But?"

"Well . . ." It wasn't a sure thing, like the Britney Spears biopic she'd been trying to get me to produce, but it was, she ventured, a maybe. "Where are you anyway?" she said. "It sounds like you're in a playground."

"Because I'm in a playground," I said.

I could almost feel the disapproval oozing through the cell phone. "Irma's day off?" she said, her words glazed in a fine veneer of sarcasm, her teeth working a piece of the Nicorette I knew she kept stashed in her purse.

Lucy and I both had children around the same ages—we bonded in a Gymboree class, in fact, after she walked up to me, looking haggard and milk-stained, and asked if she could borrow a clean diaper and a shot of vodka—but we had, I'd come to realize, slightly different notions about raising them. Lucy, whose father died when she was still young, who still felt the sting of moving from a large house in Rye to a one-bedroom rental in Queens, believed providing upper-class trappings and financial security for her children was the highest form of maternal sacrifice one could offer. I, because of the vagaries of my own upbringing, believed children could handle a teaspoon of financial instability so long as their emotional needs were sufficiently met, even if it meant jerry-rigging the scaffolding of one's career around them for a little while in order to do so. But while I knew neither of us had found an ideal solution to an intractable dilemma, Lucy had staked the entirety of her persona on proving she had.

"Yup. Irma's day off," I said, brushing some snow off two swings and lifting Tess onto one so I could continue the conversation. I held my hand over the cell phone's receiver and whispered, "Mommy has to talk to her friend Lucy, okay? Give me five minutes, just five."

"But it's freezing, Mom," said Daisy.

"So put on your mittens."

"I lost one."

"Here, put these on." I handed her my gloves. "You can hold the chain that way."

"But they're too big. Aren't we late for the dentist?"

"Who's Lucy?" said Tess.

"The girl who always makes Charlie Brown miss the football," said Daisy.

"Yes, sweetheart, something like that." Then, removing my now frozen hand from the receiver, I spoke into the phone. "I'm sorry," I said. "I think I've got the girls occupied for the moment. So what's the next step here? Should I go down to Potomac, shoot some interviews?"

I felt Tess tugging on my pant leg. "Is she friends with Linus?" she said, her words punctuated with puffs of condensation.

I covered the phone again. "Tessie, please!" I said.

Tess's bottom lip began to quiver behind the tendrils of dark hair that had come loose from her ponytail. "Well is she?"

I sighed and squatted down, swing level, to speak to her. "No, she doesn't know Linus. This is a different Lucy. Caleb and Ella's mommy, remember?"

"The ones with the guinea pig?"

"Yes, the ones with the guinea pig. Give me five minutes, okay, sweetheart?" I uncovered the receiver. "Sorry, Luce," I said. "I'm all yours."

"Can we get a guinea pig?" said Tess.

"Honestly, Elizabeth," said Lucy, exasperated. "I don't see why you can't just get yourself a full-time sitter. Look, if this is a bad time, we can just talk on Monday."

"Right now's fine," I said, not wanting to get into it with Lucy, who insisted on — and could afford — twenty-four-hour childcare coverage at all times, hiring a rotating fleet of Irish nannies ("I do not want my children turning into racists," she'd said, without irony) to help her achieve it. The one time she did find herself stuck at home with her children on a weekday, she filled a bowl with candy and placed it on her desk, which was situated at the end of a long hallway, so that every time a business call came through, she could lob a handful down the corridor to send them scurrying. "So you were saying you think maybe it's viable?"

"Yes, I was saying, I think you might have something here—*might*—but there's one part I don't understand. This monster of a woman does something like this, and all you found were two newspaper stories buried in the metro section? Where's the outrage? The magazine covers? Wasn't there anything else you could find? It doesn't make any sense."

"You have to put the story into context," I said, pushing Tess on the swing to get her started. "It was 1972. Private lives stayed private." And, I added, there weren't twenty-four hours of cable news to fill. And we could still get worked up about presidents who lied. And reality TV consisted of Allen Funt and his hidden camera, and no one read—or at least would admit to reading—tabloid papers, and celebrities were famous for their performances, and publicists stayed off the front pages, and blogging wasn't a verb, and nobody gave a fuck about which yogi or bikini waxer or hairdresser anyone used. "It's different today, Lucy. Totally different." That very morning, in fact, with a suicide bomb in Baghdad thrusting the extended members of another thirty-four families into mourning, the Western press had narrowed its eyes over the corpse of a *Playboy* pinup.

"I'm cold," Tess was saying.

I took off my scarf and wrapped it around her neck. "I still don't buy it," said Lucy. "How could two girls just disappear from a school, and no one notices?"

"Daisy, let's go make snow angels!" said Tess. My daughters ran off to find virgin snow.

"That's just the point!" I said, keeping one eye on the girls, the other on the homeless woman digging through a nearby trash can. "We did notice. And we asked questions. But no one ever answered, and they didn't have grief counselors like they do today, and everyone was too busy with Watergate and Vietnam and the elections, and so the whole thing gets swept under the rug and repressed to the point where I go to see *Medea* last week with Mark, and poof, there she is. Like Beatrice in *The Inferno*."

"Who?"

"Beatrice? The girl who leads Dante through purgatory to divine love? You know, his childhood friend. The one who died."

"I have no idea what you're talking about."

"Forget it," I said. "Just trust me on this one. Look, even my mother, when I called her last week from the hospital? She couldn't remember anything about it. 'Do you remember April Cassidy?' I asked her. 'My best friend whose mother killed her?' You know what she said? 'Boy, Lizzie, you have an active fantasy life.'"

Lucy paused for a moment before speaking, which was unusual. "Wait a minute, Elizabeth," she finally sputtered. "There was actually a girl named April, she was your friend, and her mother did kill her, right?" I could hear her gum crackling, impatiently, in the receiver. "This would be reality-based, right? With stuff that actually happened?"

"Jesus, Luce. Yes."

"Because otherwise we have no show. I'm not even sure we can sell historical documentaries anymore, unless they have sex in them, like a Profumo Affair–type thing, or they're docudramas about rich people dying. Everyone's still looking for the next *Titanic*. You wouldn't happen to have anything like that up your sleeve, would you?"

I swallowed hard and took a deep breath. "No," I said, now feeling Daisy's fingers tugging at my shirt. "Daisy, what *is* it?"

The verb burst forth with more ferocity than I liked. Even the homeless woman stopped her rummaging to stare.

Daisy looked stunned. Then hurt. "Tessie tried to go against the tree like a boy again," she said, all pout. "And now her pants are starting to freeze." Then she crossed her arms over her chest and marched away in a huff.

"Oh, Jesus, not again. Look, Lucy, I'm sorry to bother you. I'll call you later." The homeless woman was now shaking her head in disapproval. "Oh, like you could do it any better," I said, running off to where Tess now sat in a patch of yellowed snow, crying.

"Childcare, Elizabeth," Lucy was saying, as I fumbled with the tiny buttons to hang up the phone. "Chi-yeld-care."

—⁓ CHAPTER 6 ⁓—

LATER THAT EVENING, when Mark came tiptoeing into our bedroom just after midnight, I flipped on the bedside light and showed him the photocopies of the articles as well as the Montgomery County police report that had just arrived in the mail. He sat on the edge of the bed, skimming the pages. "So you'd never found out what happened to her?" he said.

"No. I mean, yes, I'm sure on some subconscious level I'd figured it out, but without any details, you know? The car, the woods, the fact that April's mom was around my age when she did it, that her kids were the same ages as ours."

Mark was staring at the tiny bandage that had replaced the white tape and gauze on my forehead from my latest fall. "How's the head?"

"Fine," I said. *Physically,* I thought.

I watched Mark remove his undershirt, the tips of his shoulder blades rising up and down as he yanked it over his head. Once upon a time, he would undress facing me, the rise and fall of his chest a prelude instead of a punctuation mark. "You're built like an oak," I'd blurted, idiotically, when I first saw him do it, first saw the angular clavicles stretching from shoulder to chest, the long arms reaching up, the lean trunk of a torso branching out at the rib cage, the mop of auburn hair atop his head and under his arms. In every way, even physically, he was the opposite of the man who'd come before him: broad and linear where Renzo had been wiry, light of skin and of spirit, able to mine the humor and absurdity from under even the darkest of rocks. "An oak, huh?" he'd said, blushing. Then he molded his arms into craggy limbs. "So climb me."

But now, a decade later, he was mumbling good night from across the gulf of our king-sized bed, his back a Jersey barrier blocking the entrance.

"Good night," I said. A few minutes later, I called out in the dark. "Mark?"

"Yeah?"

"I know it's late, but . . . You wouldn't by any chance feel like taking a quick stab at sex, would you?"

He turned to face me. "Well, that depends. What kind of sex are we talking about?"

A NUMBER OF months after Daisy was born, after the episiotomy had healed and my libido was back, in spirit if not precisely in strength, Mark pulled a pair of shiny metal handcuffs out of his bedside table drawer and dangled them over my head. "You've got to be kidding," I'd said at the time, trying to make light of the gesture. He seemed serious though, and a little embarrassed by my reaction. I felt guilty for having taken his prelude in jest. He'd toyed with the idea before—on our honeymoon he'd tied me to the bed with the terry sash from the hotel robe, and I'd giggled, slightly mortified, through the whole thing—but it had never gone beyond playacting, a hyper self-aware metabondage. But ever since Daisy's birth, after the mandated six weeks of postpartum celibacy, followed by several tentative trysts which felt not unlike penetration by a large dowel wrapped with sandpaper, we were both growing frustrated, restless.

"Ow!" I'd said, as the metal dug into my skin. I maneuvered my wrists around, trying to find a comfortable position, realizing I'd never find one. "Actually, I don't like these. Can you take them off?"

"Aw, come on, Liza. Just try them. Just once."

"No."

"Please?"

"Mark . . ."

"Please?"

"Can't you at least loosen them a bit?"

"Sure."

And so he loosened them. And I tried them. Just once. And then just once again. And then just once another time, and then another time on top of that for good measure. But with each successive effort, I kept arriving at the same conclusion: not only did I *not* like being restrained, I was starting to hate it. Nevertheless Mark, ever the optimist, refused to give up hope that one day the intersection on our Venn diagrams of desire would somehow enlarge to include this. Every third sexual congress or so, he would ask, politely, to restrain me. And, feeling guilty about not being able to satisfy his needs, craving intimacy, I would give it another try. "Just please make sure it doesn't hurt this time," I'd say, which is how metal handcuffs gave way to red fuzzy ones, red fuzzy ones to leather restraints, leather restraints to rope, rope to scarves, and scarves to the softest white satin sashes by which one could ever hope to be bound, but still it hurt. Not on the outside anymore, but someplace deeper.

I tried discussing it with him, attacking the issue from a

psychological angle. Why did he like bondage? What was it about control—having it, ceding it—that turned him on, and could he find a different manner in which to explore it? What was it about Daisy's birth that had perhaps intensified these needs? Was it in any way related to some childhood loss, his early sexual awakening, easy access to online porn? Could he ever imagine foregoing it all for the sake of marital accord? Was there any explanation he could offer to help me understand it, please, really, really, pretty please?

"I just like it," he'd say. "Always have."

I tried to put it in Aristotelian terms, to appeal to his mathematical, logical side, inventing a syllogism that went something like this:

Major premise: Socrates enjoys bondage.

Minor premise: Bondage makes Socrates' wife feel bad.

Conclusion: Socrates enjoys making his wife feel bad.

"You keep looking at this through your own prism," he'd say. "But I can turn it right back on you." What was it, he asked, about being tied up that I didn't like? Why was my reaction to simple role-playing in bed so negative, when all he was asking me to do was to relinquish control? Why couldn't I just pretend to like it, at least once, *once*!

"I just don't like it," I'd say. "It turns me off. Isn't that enough?"

Some nights I'd simply resort to tired polemic, going off on a diatribe against the objectification of women, the dangers of pornography, the dehumanization of the body. But what I felt was less militant, more specific, and far more elusive than that.

"I just don't like it," I'd say, once again.

And Mark would reply, "Well I do."

"WHAT KIND OF sex do you think I'd be talking about?" I now said, my eyes skimming, for perhaps the twentieth time that day, the newspaper article on my bedside table: *"Maryland Mother, Children, Found Dead . . . a vacuum cleaner hose had been retrofitted with duct tape . . . the couple had been having marital difficulties . . . one arm wrapped around each of her daughters . . ."*

"Um, vanilla?"

"I told you," I said. "I hate that word." One time, when Mark was working late as usual, and I was trying to understand his newfound fervor for bondage, I set out on a virtual tour of the S&M world: Listservs, Web sites, scientific papers, chat rooms, blogs, anything I could find that might shed some light on my husband and his new obsessions. It was no different, in many ways, than trips I'd once taken to Amazon tribal areas, or to rural Mozambique, for as little as I understood the culture, costumes, or language upon arrival. There were women on leashes, women as stools; there were men in leather masks, men in pink robes; there were whips and chains and ball gags and harnesses; there were shorthand descriptions, acronyms, names—sub, dom, slave, master, BDSM, Krafft-Ebing, Sacher-Masoch, and always, always that word: *vanilla.*

"Why do you hate it?" he said. "It's an apt description."

"No, it's a judgment, implying inferiority, banality."

"It does not. A lot of people like vanilla ice cream."

"Yes, and some people prefer hamburgers to steak. You know what I mean. Anyway, if I'm so 'vanilla' these days, what does that make you? Pistachio? You used to like normal sex. For years you were okay with it. God, sometimes I feel like I bought a car without looking under the hood."

"A lemon," he said, turning away.

"Yes, that's the flavor." I pulled the covers tightly over my shoulder.

Five minutes later, Mark sat up in bed and flipped on his bedside light. "I have an idea," he said.

"It better not involve handcuffs." I yawned.

"It doesn't," he said, his voice tinged with injury.

"I'm sorry. That came out wrong. What's your idea?" Now I sat up and faced him.

He jumped off the bed and from the depths of his sock drawer produced a small package wrapped in pink tissue paper. "Here," he said, smiling, handing it to me. "I bought it last week, but I was waiting for the right moment to give it to you."

"What is it?" The sticker holding the package together was marked with the name of a store and an address on West Twentieth Street. "Mod Sade?" I read, tearing the tissue paper slowly, dreading its contents.

"It's a new store. In Chelsea." Mark was smiling, hopeful, as if he'd actually convinced himself that the object within, which I'd finally unearthed, was the solution to all of our problems. "What do you think?" he said.

What I thought, staring at the black leather corset studded with tiny silver spikes, was: *Why me?* What I said, when I found my voice, was, "Did you really think I would like this?"

"No, but I knew I would like seeing you in it, and I was hoping you could maybe tolerate it." He was holding my hands now, rubbing them tenderly. "Please try it on, Lizzie-bean. It would mean a lot to me."

"There are a lot of things you could do that would mean a lot to me," I said, thinking, *And none of them involves leather.*

"Such as?"

"Oh, come on!" I yanked my hands out of his. "Do I really have to list them?"

Mark sighed. "Don't confuse the drudgery of domestic chores with sex. You can pay someone to help you with that stuff."

Now I was furious. "Jesus Christ, Mark, I'm not talking about housework! And as far as paying someone to help us with 'stuff' . . ."—I made air quotes with my fingers—". . . why don't you just go ahead and pay someone to help you with yours? I give you full permission. Go find yourself a willing sub who's STD-free and takes Visa."

"So you *are* comparing sex and housework."

Only insofar as both of them feel like drudgery these days. "No! I'm just saying, if you want me to relinquish a piece of myself, you have to be willing to do the same. I can't just keep giving. You're already way into overdraft at this point."

"What exactly do you want, Elizabeth? Tell me."

"I just want . . . you."

"And I want you, too!" He was practically shouting.

"But I want the old you. The one who wasn't obsessed with this . . ."—I ran my fingers along the spikes of the corset—". . . stuff."

"And I don't want to 'do' my so-called 'stuff' with anyone else. I want to do it with you." He took my hands back in his, as serious as I've ever seen him. "Please."

"No."

"Please!" he said, and an edge of desperation had now crept into his voice.

I considered my options. If I turned away from him now, we'd be one step further down the road to separate lives. If I gave in, Mark would perhaps one day see his way clear to doing the same for me. *It's just a corset,* I thought, *no big deal,* but only because *It's just a marriage* was too loaded. "Fine," I said, wearily. Hating myself for giving in, but also granting myself the clemency to move forward. "Just don't cut off my circulation, okay?"

"Really?" Mark had the face of a kid whose mother had just told him to pick out any cupcake in the glass case.

"Yeah. Really," I said.

Mark tied the corset around my rib cage and yanked it hard. "Okay?" he said.

I could hardly breathe. "Fine."

"Now the bottoms," he said. I stepped out of my pajama bottoms and let them fall into a puddle by the side of the bed. "No," he said. "Wait." He went to the dresser and pulled out the red lace thong he'd bought me for Valentine's Day the previous year. "Here, put this on. I'll help you." I stepped into the underwear, feeling the uncomfortable tug of Lycra and lace in that furrow where such materials have no business tugging. Several years earlier, I'd noticed that many of my friends, smart women with high-pressure jobs, childcare responsibilities, and better-than-passing exposure to feminist theory, had started wearing similar types of underwear, claiming it felt fine, not like dental floss or cheese wire or a knife. You get used to it, they'd say. Husbands love it. And I'd think, *What Kool-Aid are these people drinking?*

Mark lit a candle for better illumination and went back to the dresser to fetch a garter belt. Then a blindfold. "Now let me look at you," he said finally, stepping back from his Galatea.

"Now kneel," said Mark. "Here." He tapped the bed and led me to the desired spot.

I did as I was told.

The tops of my breasts were nearly at my chin, thrust outward, shelflike, from the squeeze of the corset. I had to take short, shallow breaths just to suck in enough air not to pass out. *Just get through this,* I thought, *and you'll never have to do it again. Think of it as a necessary mortification, like standing in line at the DMV.*

I could feel Mark kneeling now across from me. He kissed my neck, then the tops of my breasts. "Now put your hands behind your back, as if you were tied up."

"Huh?" I said.

"Put your hands behind your back. As if you were tied up."

"That wasn't part of the deal."

"Oh, come on, Lize. Just play along. Pretend."

I felt the room start to spin. Put my hands behind my back, *as if I were tied up?* "That's it," I said. I yanked off my blindfold, untied the corset, and removed the garter belt and scratchy thong in a manic flurry. "I can't do this anymore. I hate it." I threw open my drawer and found the pair of sweatpants I'd kept around since summer camp, 1979, hearing Mark, as if he were under water, muttering, *But it doesn't work if your arms aren't tied.* I found a long-sleeved T-shirt and a sweatshirt, and I put them both on, hyperventilating now, scanning the room for a tissue, feeling not unlike the inside of a food processor. "I *HATE* IT!" I screamed, now crying, now grabbing a pillow under my arm, now slamming the door to our bedroom behind me.

"Mommy?" It was tiny Tess, outlined by moonlight, standing at the door of the bedroom she shared with Daisy. "Mommy, what's wrong?"

I sat down on the floor next to her. "Nothing, sweetheart. I was just having a bad dream. You know how you sometimes have bad dreams?"

"Was there monsters in it?"

"Only little ones, but they're gone now . . ." *He's still in there! What the hell am I going to do? Leave him? Where does that leave you?* ". . . and I'm okay, see? I just needed to get a glass of water."

"You slammed the door."

"I know, peanut. I'm sorry. I didn't mean to. Sometimes I

forget how strong I am. Here, let's get back into bed." I scooped her up in my arms and set her down into the still-warm indentation on the bottom bunk. I lay next to her and stroked the strands of hair out of her face, ran my fingertips along the contours of her nose (Mark's) then lips (mine), marveling at her porcelain dollness, the odd miracle of her existence. What would happen if I told her I was leaving her father? Into how many shards would she break?

"Spoon, Mommy, spoon," said Tess, turning away from me, thrusting her back into the empty space where once she floated in oblivion. And because she was still buoyant, and nothing else was, I pulled her toward me.

CHAPTER 7

"DON'T QUOTE ME on this, but I think Adele was seeing someone else, and things got messy," said the Cassidys' former neighbor, Mavis Traub. "Wait. You're not shooting yet, are you?"

"No, not yet." I was still setting up the camera I'd rented
for the day, wishing I'd taken the time to read the instruction
manual more thoroughly the night before, instead of passing
out in Daisy's bed with a copy of *Green Eggs and Ham* on my
face. "I'm just fiddling with the white balance." After swearing
to Lucy that April's story was real, I was able to convince her
to finance one day of shooting in Potomac—"Expenses only,
and nothing outrageous!" she'd said—in exchange for a first
look at the material, although she couldn't see how a crime that
had happened so many years ago had any relevance at all to the
present moment.

I'd run a mic up through Mavis's silk blouse and seated her
on the large sectional in her living room, beneath an eight-by-
ten-foot rendering, in acrylic and glitter, of her and her husband, Arnie, their preternaturally youthful faces surrounded by

smaller scenes of the two of them playing golf, tending a bar-
beque grill, eating Chinese food, and strolling along the Dela-
ware shore in front of the orange Dolle's sign. The painting,
Mavis told me, was commissioned by a local artist who drew
his inspiration from either Roy Lichtenstein or LeRoy Neiman,
she could never remember who.

Beneath the painting, in various crystal frames, were photographs of Traub children, stiffly posed in hotel lobbies on their
wedding days, as well as younger Traubs, presumably the grand-
children, whose chubby heads were floating in seas of school-
portrait blue. On the opposite wall, directly across from the
painting of Mavis and Arnie, looming almost as large, stood
a massive wide-screen TV, tuned to a morning talk show but
muted, as per my request.

"So anyway," said Mavis, "when everything went south with
the new guy, well, you know."

"No, I don't," I said, finally turning on the camera. "Please,
tell me."

"*Oy gevalt*," she said, suddenly standing up. "I forgot to put
out the pecan ring. You want some? It's Entenmann's."

I shut off the camera. "No, thanks."

She sat back down again. "You girls these days. Such will-
power. Coffee?"

"That's okay. I already had a cup at the airport this morning."

"The airport?"

"I live in New York."

"*New York?* Your poor mother. Mine stayed." Mavis beamed.
"All three of them. Well, one's in Gaithersburg, the other's in
Rockville, but close enough. You have children?"

"Two daughters. Six and almost eight. But I was wondering
if we could talk about—"

"Well, isn't that interesting . . ." I flipped on the camera once again, hoping Mavis would follow up with a comment about April and Lily having been the same ages as my daughters when they disappeared, a detail which struck me as not insignificant. "My Debbie has two, six and eight." She pointed to a photo of two nondescript boys wearing soccer uniforms. "That's Dylan, and that's Drew. They're all *d*'s. Dylan, Drew, Daniel, and Debbie. Can you imagine?" I couldn't tell if Mavis was amused or embarrassed by this fact. I vaguely remembered Debbie Traub from high school, a slightly zaftig girl who wore dense layers of Indian Earth and blue mascara and gave head to Sean Graham, or so went the story, in the mimeograph room off the teachers' lounge. "She stays home with them, though. Her husband's in finance."

"That's nice," I said, picturing Debbie shuttling Dylan and Drew back and forth to soccer practice in her SUV, armed only with her wits and a giant frappuccino, before coming home to blow Daniel. I made a point of picking up the questions I'd prepared and rustling the pages to keep us on track. "But let's get back to Adele. You knew her well?"

"Did I know her well? We were like this." She stared into the camera, crossed her fingers, and held them up in the air.

I turned off the camera again. "Actually, Mavis, you shouldn't look straight into the lens. Just talk to me as if the camera weren't here, okay?"

"Oh, I'm sorry. Like this?" She turned her gaze toward me. "I'm just so used to all of these reality shows, you know, where they look at the camera and confide in you."

I pressed the record button once more. "Okay, let's start again. And if you don't mind, since my questions are off camera, I'll need you to rephrase each one at the beginning of your answer.

Like if I say, 'What color is the sky?' don't just say, 'Blue.' Say, 'The sky is blue.' Got it?" Mavis nodded. "Okay, so. When did you first become aware, if at all, of Adele's depression?"

"After April was born."

"No, you have to—"

"Oh, sorry, I mean, I first became aware of Adele's depression after April was born," she said. She was fiddling with an errant string on a needlepoint pillow that said, *Orthodontists do it with braces!* and staring up into her cathedral ceiling. "Or maybe it was a few years later. Anyway, Adele had gained a lot of weight with the pregnancy, and so she hired this guy, this diet guru, to come over. You know, one of these guys who comes to your house and helps you plan meals and do sit-ups. None of us with small children could get out back then. We didn't have nannies or, what are you girls calling them these days, caregivers? So people came to us."

I'd decided to speak to Mavis, who was quoted at the end of the *Washington Post* article, first. I had a lead on Adele Cassidy's sister, whom I'd since located in College Park and was planning on shooting later in the day, as well as the name and address of the psychiatrist in Rockville who, according to the police report, had once treated April's mother. "And what was the diet guy's name?" I said, resigned to simply keep the camera rolling no matter the digression.

"Well, let's see, I don't remember, but he wrote that book, *Blendercize for Thinner Thighs*? You know, with all those recipes that were just, well, let's face it, they were just air with a little bit of fruit juice and ice thrown in. What was his name?" I vaguely recalled seeing a copy of the book on my mother's kitchen counter, wedged like a rebuke between the *Joy of Cooking* and *Your Jewish Table.* "Morton! Lenny Morton. Anyway, after his divorce, he quits his job—I think he was in medical supplies or something—and he starts going door to door—I kid you not, I got a knock myself—and he asks everyone in the neighborhood, 'What's missing from your life?' Well, none of us really knows what to say. We're fine, we say. We've got husbands, lovely homes, beautiful children, washer-dryers. We had everything a woman could want. Oh, sure, maybe if we could lose a few pounds, that would be good. Thinner thighs, now *that* would make us happy. Three months later, he's got a new business card and his first clients."

"Adele?"

"Yes, Adele. She was one of his first. I'd go over to her house afterwards. Her older one, Lily, was the same age as my Jessica, and they played together nicely, you know, not like some kids where you have to always be watching to make sure they don't whack each other over the heads with the Lincoln Logs."

"And what year was this?"

"Oh, let's see. April was still a toddler then, so it must have been around, what, when was she born again?"

"1966."

"So this must have been sometime around 1968. I remember we were sitting there watching Ethel Kennedy, pregnant, crying on that kitchen floor, and we just couldn't believe it. Another Kennedy. Anyway, I'd go over there to let some light and air in that place—she always kept it so dark!—and one day while I'm doing this, just to make conversation, I say, 'What'd you do with Lenny today?' and Adele's face turns beet red. 'Nothing special,' she says. 'We blended some meals,' or 'He sat on my feet while I did sit-ups,' but I could tell something else was going on. And who could blame her, really, with that husband of hers. Shep. So *goyisha* and serious, and that cross over their bed, can you imagine? He was in plumbing supplies or something like that, but he made a decent living at it because they had some nice things. Oy, but a temper. You've never seen such a temper. And he didn't get that a girl needs to play football like she needs a hole in the head. Some ballet lessons maybe, I told him, a little piano, but football? He kept treating his daughters like sons, but you get what you get, right?"

"Wait," I said. "*You* told him he shouldn't be teaching the girls to play football? When did you say this? How did you phrase it?"

"Oh, I don't remember," said Mavis, with a dismissive toss of her hand. "It was so long ago. I think I must have said something like, 'Shep, those girls are going to have a hell of a time finding husbands who can outthrow them.' Anyway, whatever Lenny was doing with Adele on the diet front, let me tell you, it was working. She. Looked. Fabulous. She lost something like sixty-five pounds that first year, and she kept it off for a long time, at least a year and a half. I remember going to Loehmann's with her one Saturday, and we were trying on clothes in front of that giant mirror. Two old ladies were there with us in their bras and underpants, and Adele was standing in front of the mirror looking, well, not svelte, but thin enough to try on tens. She was trying on this burgundy wool skirt, with a row of tiny gold buttons up the front, so stylish, and the waist buttoned beautifully, and one of the ladies looks over at her and says, 'Very slimming. If you don't take it, I will,' and the other one says something like, 'Oh, *bubelah,* if you can fit your *tuchas* into that one, I'm paying for lunch,' and then they were both laughing, and so was Adele, and I remember thinking, that's right, laugh all you like, sweetheart. You deserve it."

"I'm sorry, Mavis, hold on a sec." I'd been taking notes while she spoke, marking the time code for possible sound bites, and I now flipped back through the pages, searching for a statement I felt needed clarifying. "You said before that Adele blushed when you asked her about Lenny. But did you know for a fact that she was having an affair with him? Did she ever tell you, 'I'm having an affair with Lenny Morton'?"

"Of course not. No one ever comes right out and says such a thing." She rolled her eyes, shook her head. "You just know. You're a woman, you're married, you have eyes, you know."

I flipped back further, to the beginning of my notes. "And what did you mean by 'things got messy'?"

"I mean messy. Who knows what actually happened inside that house, but you've never heard such a racket coming out of it. Linda Deligdish, down the street, she heard it, too. A *whore,* Shep called her. As well as other things I shouldn't mention in front of a camera. A week later, Lenny was gone.

"Adele went downhill after that, especially after the girls were in school. She'd go for days without a shower. Started walking around in that pink *schmatte* and the flip-flops even in winter. Like she just didn't care. Of course the skirt we'd bought together, the one with the gold buttons, stopped fitting. I saw it in her closet the day I went over to bring a kugel to Shep after the funeral. It was just sitting there in her closet, gathering dust."

Mavis stopped talking for a moment and stared off into the distance. "Oy, those girls." She pursed her lips, shook her head and dabbed at the bottom of her eyelashes, heavy with mascara. "Those beautiful girls."

～ CHAPTER 8 ～

I DROVE MY RENTAL CAR, a gray Taurus, along Poplar Road, abutted on either side by thin patches of grass intersected at regular intervals with paved driveways, delineating the property lines of the many modest, late-sixties-era houses in shades of white, yellow, and olive. This was April's territory, a neighborhood I'd driven by and through many times after her disappearance, on a school bus, in a carpool, in a battle-scarred station wagon packed full with teenagers and Schlitz, too busy trying to figure out my own life to stop and think about hers.

The neighborhood itself hadn't changed much in the intervening years, but like the bathroom stalls from one's kindergarten, the houses, which had once seemed to me such massive and imposing structures, with enormous pilasters and grand Doric columns holding up roofs the size of God's hand, now revealed themselves to be what they'd been all along: not small, exactly, but too small to have been burdened with the architectural flourishes they'd been given, like children playing dress-up in their parents' clothes. Driving past them, I had the sudden sense of having remembered everything wrong.

What am I doing here? I wondered. What had seemed like such a good idea back in New York now felt oddly impulsive, misguided. Plus Mavis's interview, I could already tell without screening it, had yielded very little in terms of clean bites I could use.

I meandered my way by feel onto Thorn Apple Way, April's street, until I reached her old house. Seeing no signs of life inside, no car in the driveway, no telltale exhaust spewing forth from a dryer vent, I parked on the street and turned off the engine. The cement on the driveway was crumbling slightly where it met road, and the mailbox, dented in spots with two of its numbers missing, looked as if it had been smacked around by bored kids with a baseball bat.

Sliding over to the passenger-side window, I slipped my hand through the mailbox's black metal mouth, hoping for a clue, a name, someone I might call and ask what he or she had heard, if anything, about the former owners of the property. But when I pulled out the letters, I felt a sharp dip inside my chest, roller-coaster style.

They were addressed to a Mr. Shepherd Cassidy. April's father.

I'd been meaning to find Shep, but I'd wanted to wait until I knew more, or at least until I'd made a preliminary visit to Potomac. Never once had I considered he'd stayed put. What was he doing still living in the same house?

Surely Adele must have considered the aftermath of her decision when making it. Surely she must have thought about the kind of void she'd leave behind. Was that why she did it? To spite her husband, like Medea? But no. Medea had not killed herself. She'd spared her own life, experienced firsthand the frisson of retribution. Adele, by offing herself along with the children, could not have been driven purely—if at all—by revenge.

I quickly shoved the letters back in the mailbox and shut the lid. I'd have to be careful. Now that I'd found him, there'd be little point in scaring Shep off with an unplanned visit. The question was how to approach him. A phone call? An email? No. A letter. Handwritten, on good stationery. Like a condolence card, only thirty-five years late.

I slid back over to the driver's side, turned the key in the ignition, and rolled forward twenty yards until my cell phone began chiming. The caller ID showed a Manhattan exchange followed by a familiar-looking arrangement of digits. "Bernie!" I said, picking up the phone.

"Bad time?" he said.

I pulled over to the curb. "No, no, totally fine. What's up? Whose number do you need?" With Bernie, there was never any need for niceties. Conversation was purely for the expedient exchange of information, a habit born early on in his career, back when long-distance talk was anything but cheap.

"No numbers this time, Elzy." He sounded excited. I could almost picture him in his office, sitting on the edge of his chair, his desk covered with newspapers and used coffee cups. "Just a proposition." He waited a long beat before saying it: "How'd you like to go to Baghdad for us?"

It took me a long moment to find my voice. I was hurtled back to 1991, my first and last trip to Iraq. I'd written a fairly long story at the end of that war about collateral damage, starting off with the Iraqi I found lying facedown in the desert, his body charred beyond recognition, ending with the toddler I'd seen, wandering alone amid the debris. The piece never made it into print, however, as *Newsworld* had opted for a feel-good piece about cheering Kuwaitis instead. Bernie had been incensed by this, at the time, but he hadn't had the power to change it either. "I don't know, Bernie. I'd have to really think about it."

"Oh, come on, Elzy. Your girls are in school now, right?"

I adjusted the rearview mirror, stole a glimpse of my increasingly lined and haggard-looking face. "That's not really the issue, now is it?" How could my daughters possibly handle their mother's departure for a war zone? How could I, at this point in my life, handle it? "Look, Bernie, I don't know. From everything I hear, it's almost impossible to do any street reporting these days. Don't you already have people with more experience already on the ground?" Bernie had been nominated for a Pulitzer Prize for his coverage of Vietnam the same year Halberstam won; he'd also been maimed and blinded in his left eye by an errant grenade, marking the beginning of his reliance on a wheelchair and the end of his sight in three dimensions. "Plus let's not forget the whole Jew thing."

"They'll never know. Burns doesn't sound Jewish."

"Neither did Pearl."

"Oh, come on Elzy. You can do this. I know you can." Bernie had once claimed to understand why I wanted to leave combat journalism behind—why anyone would want to leave it behind—but because his own career was cut short involuntarily, he couldn't accept the concept of voluntary departure, mine or anyone else's. "What a pussy," I once heard him say of my former colleague, an *LA Times* writer who traded street reporting in Rwanda for a career teaching journalism, after his son's school counselor told him the boy's fear over his father's job was exacerbating an already acute anxiety disorder. "Look, I know," he was now saying. "I know it's out of left field. But I've got Renzo calling me, saying he can't work with anyone else, and because of our new budget constraints, we've got to double up teams to save on vehicle and bodyguard expenses, and—"

"Wait a minute. This was *Renzo's* idea?"

"Yeah, so what?"

I'd loved Renzo once, or thought so at least, until the night in early spring of '93, when we were holed up in the apartment we'd rented from a Bosnian family, eating stale granola, dry, and burning our last two candles. I'd just filed a story about Admira Ismic, a Muslim girl, and Bosko Brkic, her Serbian boyfriend, who'd been shot while trying to escape the city over the Vrbanja Bridge. Bosko was shot first, by sniper fire, ". . . dying instantly," I'd written, "the blood spurting out of his skull in rhythmic bursts, like water poured too quickly from a jug." Admira was only wounded, but she crawled over to her childhood sweetheart, wrapped her arm around his corpse, and inhaled her remaining breaths in his arms. Romeo and Juliet, I'd dubbed them, not very originally, as it would turn out, but Renzo was appalled by the description. "It's a war, not a love story," he said, rubbing a chamois over the glass filters of his camera lenses, as he did every night before bed. "They died, like all the others. She should have run for help instead of bleeding to death in his arms, silly girl." He held the filter up to the light and sighed. "*Merde.* A scratch." In Renzo's world, nothing was more disagreeable than a less-than-pellucid lens.

"Well . . ." I was a bit dumbfounded by his reaction. "Isn't that the whole point? What do you think *Romeo and Juliet* is about anyway? It's about love. Specifically love that transcends tribal hatreds."

"No, I understand this, *bien sûr.* This is not why I take offense. I take offense at sentimentality. At the whole idea of love."

"What?" I said. "You take offense . . . at love? How can you say that?"

"Well . . ." Wiping the last bits of dust from his longest lens and placing it gently back into his bag, he began a lengthy diatribe, calling love a "mythical construct" foisted upon us by clergymen and poets who needed to believe in transcendence.

"And Dante never loved Beatrice either," he concluded, wrapping up a list that included Adam and Eve, Paris and Helen, Tristan and Isolde, Kitty and Levin. "He loved the idea of her. Of something outside the realm of hell."

At this I blurted out the one question to which I'd only assumed to know the answer: "But don't you love me?"

To which Renzo replied, in English, "If I were to love anyone, I would love you."

The tinny rat-tat-tat of random sniper fire echoed in the hills to our west, far enough away that neither of us flinched. When it grew quiet again, I congratulated Renzo on his excellent use of the conditional tense—his English had improved markedly since we started sleeping together—but he didn't get that I was making a joke, that the joke wasn't funny, that he'd just lost me to a verb.

The last time I'd seen or even spoken to Renzo was eight years earlier, when he was in New York for work and showed up at our apartment with a baby gift for Daisy, along with a bouquet of yellow tulips, my favorite, and a copy of Stendhal's *The Red and the Black,* which he'd inscribed with, "*Pour toi, mon Eliza, aujourd'hui et toujours.*"

The two of us had once spent a rare weekend of decompression and museum-trolling in Paris on our way back to Rome from Bucharest. "I don't know, she's kind of unimpressive in person," I'd said in the Louvre, after we'd stumbled upon its most infamous smile.

"But you look like her," said Renzo. Then he smiled—only slightly, no more or less than La Gioconda herself—and said it: *"Mon Eliza."*

"Right. Ha ha. I get it. Very cute. *Mon Eliza,* Mona Lisa. And I'm not sure if I should take that as a compliment. She's a little homely, don't you think?"

"Homely? What is this word? Like *jolie-laide*?"

"Not really," I said. "It's, well, it's . . ." I pointed to the painting. "It's like her. Not beautiful. But not ugly either. Someone you might pass by without a second glance."

"But she is not homely," said Renzo. "She is *magnifique*."

Renzo, as it would turn out, found many things to be *magnifique* which I did not, but which, through his lens, I did: the tail of a scorpion, as seen from up close; the day after a flood, which he shot with a large-format Deardorf; the hundreds of corpses and near-corpses he photographed without cease, one of which, a portrait of a Chinese student lying dead on Tiananmen Square, had so enraged the photography critic of *Il Corriere della Sera* when it was included in a group show in Milan, she devoted her entire column that week to its condemnation. "When we beautify evil," she'd written, after calling Renzo everything from a hack voyeur to a pornographer of death, "we lose our ability to understand it."

"As if we ever *could* understand it," Renzo had snapped, tossing the paper into the trash.

"WHAT THE HELL does Renzo want with me?" I was now practically yelling into the receiver.

"I don't know," Bernie was now saying. "But he insisted on working only with you. And since he's on contract, well, you see the pickle I'm in . . ."

"Huh," I said. "Let me just digest that for a minute."

"I'll give you a whole hour if you say you'll go."

I laughed. "Oh, Bernie, I miss you. I really do."

"So go to Baghdad for me."

"It's not that simple."

"Elzy—"

"Bernie, come on. I've got the kids to think about, and—"

"The girls will be fine. Any other excuses?"

My phone beeped. "Mark Office," it said on the tiny screen, and I was struck, as I nearly always am still, by the wonder of that. The world changed so quickly. One day you're typing a story into a grouchy Telex, the next you're sending an email from the palm of your hand. One day you're grabbing hold of a man's body, the next you're grabbing six seconds of his disembodied voice.

"I'm sorry. Hold on another sec. It's Mark. Let me just see what he wants." The call clicked over. "Light of my life," I said. We may have grown distant, but that didn't keep me from trying, daily, to bridge the gap. Our first summer together, for corny reasons I can no longer recall, we started greeting each other with lines from *Lolita*.

"Blight on your what?" said Mark. His voice was pixelated, echoey.

"No," I spoke slowly, deliberately. "I said, 'Light of my life.'"

Whatever he said next was unintelligible.

"Never mind," I shouted. "Must be a bad cell. Hold on." I pressed firmly on the gas. "I'll drive through it." Were only marriages so easy to fix. "Better?"

"Better."

"What's up? And take me off speakerphone, please."

"Okay." Then, still on speakerphone: "You didn't by any chance pick up my shirts today, did you? I've got a meeting with that guy from Simtech tomorrow."

"Take me off speakerphone."

"What do you have against speakerphones?"

"What do you have against picking up the receiver?"

"I can't type with one hand."

"That's what I have against speakerphones."

"But I have IMs coming through."

"Take me off speakerphone, or I'm hanging up."

"Okay, okay. Jesus. It's off," he said, the hollow buzz of detachment momentarily remedied. "So?"

"Mark, where am I right now?"

"Um, home?"

"Wrong."

"Come on, Elizabeth. Stop playing games. I'm busy."

"So am I. Where am I?"

"I give up. Where are you?"

How could he forget? We'd just had an argument—over speakerphone, no less—about my trip two nights earlier. "We can't afford the extra hours of babysitting right now," he'd said dismissively. "You know that." As if his coming home to relieve Irma at 6:00 were not even up for discussion.

Lately, watching my daughters tackle their homework, imagining the future plot points of their lives and careers, I'd start to think about all the hours I'd spent as a young girl pondering the shape of things as they are—the circumference of the sun, the area of Nebraska, the atomic structure of zinc—with nary a minute devoted to imagining the shape of things as they might be. For all the pledges of allegiance we gave to a piece of cloth, why didn't we ever discuss the implications of pledging allegiance to another person?

Marriage is the one institution I know which doesn't require preparation for matriculation. There are no essays asking us to predict the number of children we will have, if any, and who will take them to the hospital if they bleed. There are no multiple-choice tests forcing us to envisage how our financial partnership might look, or late-night field trips to love's inner sanctums (which from syntax alone—*master* bedroom—reveals a lot) to witness sexual politics in action. There are no textbooks offering tips on what to do when the baby is sick, the sitter's on vacation, and both spouses are on deadline; no four-page syllabi containing his-and-her primary source material.

In fact, the only primary source material we're given comes from the most unreliable of sources possible: our own parents. No wonder half of us flunk out.

When Mark and I met, at a quant conference in Rome, I wasn't thinking, *How will our bond be altered by the addition of children?* or, *What is his relationship to money?* What I thought was, *He smells good.* This was the summer after the first World Trade Center bombing in '93, when *Newsworld* had us out working every angle. Mine was an analysis of the latest technology being used in counterterrorism: cryptography, mathematical epidemiology, face and voice recognition software, the modeling of terrorist networks as graphs. Mark was there to watch his thesis advisor present a lecture, which he'd helped prepare, on the idea of framing the probability of terrorist acts within a valid statistical model.

In that sweltering lecture hall, I was trying to pay attention to the topics under discussion, but the heat and the subject matter made it nearly impossible. The troika of professors kept throwing out concepts for which, like marriage, I had no background or contextual framework: data mining, complex systems theory, infrastructure vulnerabilities, Zermelo-Fraenkel axiom, Zorn's lemma, the latter which I'd written down in my notes as "Zorn's lemon."

"No, it's Zorn's *lemma*," whispered Mark.

Which is when I stared at the broad-jawed, lanky stranger perspiring so fragrantly next to me and thought, *He doesn't look like a math geek.*

"Lemma. Like dilemma, without the *di*. It has to do with making an infinite number of arbitrary choices simultaneously.

Like all left shoes or all right ones, only for socks, which are all the same." He grabbed my notebook from me and wrote the phrase correctly.

"Oh, Zorn's *lemma*," I whispered, placing the notebook back on my knee and wiping the sweat off my brow. "Now everything's perfectly clear."

Mark smiled widely, his olive eyes catching the light from the podium as he grabbed the notebook and pen once again. "If you can help me find a good restaurant near the Trevi Fountain," he wrote, "I can explain it all to you over dinner."

"Trevi = tourist trap," I wrote back. "I can take you to a trattoria in Trastevere instead."

"Tra-riffic," he wrote.

Later that night, as the candles between us dripped skeins of wax, Mark made a heroic attempt to teach me a doctoral thesis's worth of applied math in just under an hour. Then we traded life stories: mine the standard fare of suburban angst and ennui, suffused with hints of patchouli and *eau de mère déprimé*, his a wild, nostalgia-soaked tale of picking grapes and singing Israeli folk songs under the frangipani trees on a kibbutz, where his mother had fled after finding herself pregnant during her senior year of high school. The two had thrived in this fragrant garden, this bubble-*à-deux*, until the day before his Bar Mitzvah, when the bus his mother had taken to Haifa to do some last-minute shopping was hijacked and redirected to Tel Aviv, during the Fatah attack of '78. "Everyone on it was killed," he said, "either shot or burned to death. My mom, her boyfriend, Dov, the bus driver, everyone."

"Jesus. I'm so—"

"Yeah. It was . . . But I'm sure you're used to . . . You know, with your job and all . . ."

"No," I said.

"Really? I would think it would stop affecting you after awhile."

"No, it just gets worse."

"Huh." He paused for a moment to take in the thought. "Anyway," Mark continued, "the party, of course, was cancelled. Instead I flew back with the body to Boston, where my grandparents were waiting for us. We buried Mom that afternoon, out in Newton. Then, a few months later, both of my grandparents died, one right after the other. Mom never knew who my father was—he was just some lifeguard she'd met at a clambake, she never even bothered to learn his name—so I was suddenly on my own. That's when I first became fascinated by statistics. What was the likelihood of my mother and my grandparents, all reasonably young and in seemingly excellent health, dying within a seven month period?"

"Slim, I would imagine," I said.

"In a word, yes." He smiled, close-lipped, and let out a little puff of laughter through his nose.

I followed his lead, marveling at his resiliency, at his facility for seeing the comic striations in grief's granite. And it suddenly occurred to me that I might not need anything so complicated as Zorn's lemma to make an infinite number of arbitrary choices simultaneously: out of all the men in the world, I could love this one. We could build a life, a family together. All of this had crystallized, in the arbitrary way such real-life choices do, in that one moment of shared mirth.

"I'm in Potomac, Mark, remember?" I now said. "And I'm actually on another call, so let me—"

"Oh, right. I forgot. Your dead friend thing. So did you get my shirts?"

I breathed in and counted to ten, which was Dr. Rivers's idea. You cannot begin to work on your own issues, she told me during our second session, until you stop jumping down your spouse's throat every time he opens his mouth. A thousand years of female oppression are not his fault, handcuffs or no. "No," I said, with a new, practiced calm. "I did not get your shirts. I dropped off the girls at school early, then ran to the airport to try to catch the 8:30 shuttle." And then, just as I was congratulating myself on my extreme maturity and reserve, just as I was about to remain silent and let Mark have a turn like a proper grown-up, I couldn't stop myself from throwing in, "Which I missed, by the way, because I couldn't find a taxi, so I got here late for my first shoot. Not that it matters to you." *Ugh!* I thought. *No wonder he never comes home.*

"Of course it matters to me. Jesus, Lizard. I'm sorry you were late for your interview. I could have taken the girls if you'd asked."

"I did. Yesterday. You said you had to get to the office by seven to run some numbers before your meeting with what's-his-name."

"Anderson. That was cancelled, actually. I could have taken them."

"Now you tell me." I suddenly remembered Bernie again on the other line. "Oh shit. I'm sorry, Mark. I've got Bernie on the other line. Lemme call you ba—"

"Zakowski? What does he want?"

"Nothing," I lied. "I'll give you a call back in—"

"Wait! Will you have time to get my shirts tonight when you get back?"

I tried to count to ten again, to think of fluffy clouds and furry kittens and big sweaty glasses of ice-cold pink lemonade,

but by the time I hit three I was already screaming, "NO I
WILL NOT HAVE TIME TO GET YOUR GODDAMNED
SHIRTS!"

I took several deep breaths and hit the green button once
again.

"Sorry, Bernie," I said. "Listen, about that assignment . . ."

"Yes . . . ?"

"Can you give me a few days to decide?"

What was I doing?

I couldn't go to Iraq.

"Oh, Elzy, this is great. I'll—"

"No, Bernie, I just said I'd think about it. Not that I
could."

Or could I?

"Of course, of course. Yes. Sure. Hold on. What's today's
date?" I heard a fluttering of paper on his desk, the flipping of
pages in a date book. Bernie had no use for electronic calendars.
He needed to turn pages to mark time, he once told me, his
life—or at least the life his reporters were living for him, the
one he thought was passing him by—recorded for posterity in
pen and ink.

"The thirteenth."

"Yes. February 13." More turning of pages. "I can even give
you a week, as long as you get your passport to me tomorrow.
Visas are tricky, as you can imagine . . ." I could feel my blood
coursing, the once-familiar cocktail of adrenaline and corti-
sol surging through it like so many volts through a high tension wire, shocking to anyone not wearing protective gloves, as
Bernie's words—*messenger, cash advance, Hep-B shot, satellite
phone*—blurred together into the notes of an oft-played song,
the kind you once loved and overplayed until you could no

longer hear it, but now triggers waves of syrupy nostalgia. "Oh, and Elzy? Renzo's coming to New York tomorrow. To buy new camera equipment or something. He asked me for your cell phone number. Can I give it to him?"

I had to pause for several seconds before answering. "Yeah, sure. No problem," I said.

CHAPTER 9

MY MOTHER SPENT her mornings on her knees, the bathroom tiles carving bas-relief tic-tac-toe boards into her skin
as she scoured them, and the afternoons on the floor of her
bedroom, blowing smoke signals from her Carltons up to the
ceiling. Sometimes when I'd get home from school I'd lie with
her there, on the shag carpet, careful to keep my arm from
touching hers, lest she recoil, leafing through old *TV Guides*
and catalogues stuffed with smiling mothers in floral prints to
match their daughters'. The room, reeking of Oil of Olay and
old ashtray, was always silent and dark, except for small smoke-
streaked cracks of sunlight between curtain and window, and
then one kid or another—waking from a nap, maybe bumping into the corner of a table—would start to cry. Mom would
sigh, sit up, and pull herself up from the ground. "I'll go!" I'd
say, "I'll take care of it," but my mother would just crush out
her cigarette with three heavy taps and then trudge down the
hallway toward the noise.

When my father would come home, he'd hand each of us a

tongue depressor, or a plastic syringe, or sometimes a small pad of notepaper with the name of a new drug stretched across it, like Enflucare or Pedia-Zilox, always in red, which drug companies would send to his office to remind him to use their drugs, even though he was a Dimetane man himself. Then he'd say, "What's for dinner?" and Mom would answer, without removing her eyes from the stove, "Fish," or "Burgers," or "Spaghetti," which she'd kind of drop-slide onto the table, so that a burger might slip out of its bun, or the spaghetti would hop in its bowl, or the fish would shift on the serving platter, leaving an inch-long buttery streak behind it, before she either walked out of the kitchen, saying she wasn't hungry, or stood at the sink, filling dirty pots with water and lobbing tiny grievances over her shoulder.

"You think you could maybe pull your car into the garage a little less tight, so I can get to the trash cans for once?" Or, "Elizabeth Claire, if I see one more wet towel on the floor, *no one's* getting new Keds, not today or ever."

Dad would ignore her, pretending he didn't hear, which would infuriate her even further, until she'd stomp her foot or slam the refrigerator door or empty the ice tray with a sonic boom. "Goddamnit, Herb," she'd scream, "are you listening to me?" followed on many nights by, "Kids, if I'm not in my room tomorrow morning when you wake up, you'll know I've finally left!" and then the five of us would start crying, the verbal ones begging her not to leave, the preverbal ones throwing spaghetti off their high chairs, and then she'd turn to my father and say, "See what you're doing to them, Herb? *See what you're doing?*" before grabbing a new pack of Carltons and a lighter and heading back up to her room for the night.

"You're mother's having a hard day," Dad would say, or he'd

make some joke about how the Kotex box had reappeared on the bathroom floor, and we should all be on our best behavior.

Those ominous purple signifiers were long gone now, as were the mood swings they presaged, but even so visits with my mother these days were like cloudy days with a slight chance of rain: you never knew whether to carry an umbrella.

"So did you figure everything out?" Mom asked, as I involuntarily hung my coat from the now empty, waist-high rung of pegs that had once held yellow slickers and school backpacks. It was Daisy who accidentally let slip that I'd be coming down to Potomac for the day, and my mother had insisted I swing by for lunch. I tried explaining to her that my schedule would be too packed, but I didn't have the energy to argue. Or to deal with the inevitable repercussions of turning her down. "What are you doing?" she was now saying, seeing the hem of my coat hit the floor. "You'll get the bottom all dirty." She took the coat and grabbed a hanger from the closet, eyeing its frayed sleeve and torn lining and making a face like she'd sucked on a lemon. "I can sew the missing button on, if you have it."

"I lost it. But thanks."

"They have button stores, you know."

"Not in my neighborhood," I said.

"So would it kill you to jump in a taxi?"

I smiled a weary smile. "No, Ma. It would not kill me to jump in a taxi. And no to your first question, too. I did not figure anything out. I figured nothing out. Did you know Mavis Traub?"

"With the new house off Tupelo?"

"Yes, her."

"No. I don't know her. But her husband moved his practice into the same building as your father's a few years ago and paid seven times the rent for the same amount of space, can you imagine? And she wears that mink coat just to go to the Giant. I told your father he should have gone into orthodontics."

"He liked being a pediatrician."

"And look what it did to him." She turned away from me to walk into the kitchen and opened the refrigerator. "Chicken salad okay? Or we could heat up some meatloaf."

"Either's great. But, Ma . . ."

She dropped her head onto the crook of her arm, still holding the refrigerator open, and began to cry. She did this so often now, I sometimes suspected she did it more out of habit than grief. And each time it happened, each time she crumpled over, she seemed more and more diminished.

"Aw, Mom. Come on. Stop it now . . ." I tried to put my arm over her heaving shoulder, which felt even bonier to the touch than usual. She shrugged it off. I sat down at the kitchen table. My father had passed away over three years earlier, but she had yet to reconcile herself to this fact. She still listened for his car in the driveway. She'd cook two pieces of meat for dinner instead of one. For as turbulent as their marriage had been when we were young, by the time my baby brother left for college, the two of them had settled into something resembling an amicable truce. They bought a condo on a golf course near Chestertown, so he could spend the day whacking balls while she browsed the shops in the quaint villages along the Chesapeake. Once, when they were visiting us in New York, I even saw them holding hands, in their matching L.L.Bean fleeces, as they rounded the corner, a sight as shocking to me as if the two of them had suddenly stripped naked and started dancing the frug. "Ma," I said now, "you can't blame pediatrics for his death. He had a heart atta—"

"Oh, yeah?" She turned abruptly and slammed the refrigerator door shut. I noticed her eyes were dry. "You weren't here for all those three AM calls, for all those *mothers* with their croupy babies. 'Oh, Dr. Burns, help me, please. I think my baby's dying!'"

"Ma, stop it. Dad didn't die from being on call. He died because he was out of shape, overweight, had high cholesterol and a family history of heart disease. You yourself said that after the last bypass he kept sneaking those Krispy Kremes. So one day, his heart stopped beating. End of story."

"At sixty-three?"

"Yes, at sixty-three."

"Who dies of a heart attack at sixty-three?"

"Lots of people, Ma. Even healthy ones who don't kill themselves with Krispy Kremes."

"He didn't kill himself with doughnuts. Don't you say that about your father, Lizzie Claire."

"Sorry. You're right. I forgot. He killed himself with brownies and chocolate chip cookies, too."

"Lizzie!"

"Okay, okay. I'll stop. Anyway, you know that's what Mark's working on right now. Mortality rates."

"Is that so?" She was distracted, speaking by rote. Still standing immobile before the shelves of diet sodas and Tupperware.

"Yeah, he's trying to figure out a way to predict the precise hour of a person's death, using neural networks to . . ." I could tell she wasn't listening to me. "You sit. I'll fix lunch." I stood up to take her place.

"No," she said, now suddenly switching into high gear. "That's okay. I'll fix it. I'm still your mother, I can fix lunch." Filled with a newfound vigor, born of feeling needed, she spooned the

chicken salad onto two slices of rye, laid some pickles out on a
bread plate and poured us each a small paper cup of soda, their
domes of fizz threatening to spill over the sides. "I'll tell you one
thing. Mothers of kids with broken retainers don't call Mavis
Traub's husband at three AM. Here. Eat."

"So. Mavis . . ." I took a bite of my sandwich, the mayonnaise
eclipsing the chunks of chicken by a ratio of two to one.

"Oh, Lizzie." My mother took a miniscule bite of hers then
pushed it aside. "Why do you want to dig into that awful old
story? It's so depressing." She took a sip of her diet soda. "Are
you sure it's even true? I don't remember this Avery—"

"April."

"April, Avery, what's the difference? I don't remember her,
and I knew all your friends."

"No, you didn't, Ma. Josh was an infant, and Becca wasn't
yet one, and Lisa was about to turn two, and Ellen was still
in preschool, and you were barely coping, let alone asking me
about my friends from sch—"

"Oh, so now it's my fault your friend was murdered."

I shook my head and took a deep breath. "No. I was just saying that everybody was focused on Watergate, and you had all
these kids underfoot, and postpartum depression—"

"I did NOT have postpartum depression."

I stared at my mother, incredulous. "Right. You just preferred
to lie in the dark on the floor of your bedroom all afternoon
with the shades drawn and a cigarette dangling."

"Everybody smoked then."

"That's not my point."

"I did not have postpartum depression or any depression of
any kind. End of story."

"Okay. Fine. You weren't depressed." I took another bite of
my sandwich. My mouth still full of mush, I muttered, "And

you don't smoke anymore, either." I could smell the cigarette smoke that must have been blown out the window five minutes before my arrival, even though my mother always insisted she'd been smoke-free for over a decade.

"What did you just say?"

"I said, 'And you don't smoke anymore.' "

"I *don't* smoke anymore."

"I said you don't. And anyway I don't care if you do or not. I was just making a point about denial. Let's drop it."

"You brought it up." She grabbed the pickle off her plate and held it suspended in midair, pretending to study it so she wouldn't have to meet my eye. "My window guy smokes, if that's what you're talking about. He was just here this morning."

I rolled my eyes.

"What, am I supposed to make him go outside in the cold? No. I say, 'Here, take an ashtray. Enjoy yourself.' "

"That's very nice of you."

"I'm a nice person. You might not think so, but I am."

"I never said I didn't think you were nice."

"But you did say I smoked," she said, sliding her right hand, with its nicotine-stained middle finger, into her lap, like a child hiding a cookie she'd just snatched. "Anyway, what were we talking about again?"

I choked on my tiny cupful of soda, the fizz rising up into my nostrils and making them burn. "Suicide."

"Right." She placed the pickle back down on her plate, untouched. "You're not eating."

"Neither are you."

Over the next half hour, in between bites of chicken salad sandwich and more digressions, asides, and the airing of old grievances too numerous to mention, I was showered with the following unconfirmed facts and unsolicited advice:

1) My mother's best friend, Shirley Seymour, told her that Maureen Kupferberg once told her she'd seen Mavis Traub leaving the Holiday Inn in Rockville with a man, not her husband, one day when she was parking her car in the lot of Shay's Hardware. I should call the hotel. Maybe they have a record.

2) Lenny Morton, of *Blendercize* fame, divorced his wife when he realized he was gay, not because the two weren't getting along. My mother saw him interviewed on a *20/20* story about AIDS a few years back, "the one where they were talking to that angry guy, the playwright, what's-his-name, Larry Something-or-Other." As far as she could remember, Lenny was living in New York, HIV-free and alone ("His boyfriend who died," Mom said, "the AIDS activist-slash-lawyer, used a condom when they were, you know . . ."), and currently working as a personal trainer. Although she wouldn't personally want to be trained by someone who could potentially have AIDS, because even though they say it can't pass through the sweat, you never know.

3) None of her friends had ever known Adele Cassidy, although Shirley Seymour had had a "little flicker" when my mother mentioned her name and seemed to recall that Adele Cassidy had been murdered by her husband, not taken her own life. Which could have just been gossip, granted, but she thought I should know what people were saying when she mentioned April's mother's name in polite company.

4) And finally, if I was so interested in mothers who kill their children, why wasn't I doing a documentary about that crazy woman who drowned her kids in the bathtub in Texas, the one with the five kids, just like her, *kunna hura,* instead of digging into an old story that may or may not even be true?

"It's true, Ma."

"How do you know?"

"Because I have a police report. And some newspaper clippings. And as of this morning I now have Mavis Traub, who remembers it happening."

"I just cannot see how I would not have heard about this kind of thing when it happened. A mother who kills her children and commits suicide in Potomac? In 1972? It doesn't make any sense. Are you absolutely sure?"

"I'm sure."

In the twenty minutes before my next appointment, I went up to my old bedroom, looking for anything to jog my memory. The room had been turned into a gym/guest room after I left for college, with a treadmill and a blue foam mat. All traces of Scotch-taped drawings and field-day ribbons had been scraped from the walls, which were now covered in a cool shade of gray. In the corner, by the window, was one of my mother's ashtrays. Left there for the window guy, no doubt.

In the closet, shoved in the far corner, were two large moving boxes full of my childhood mementos, which my mother had been bugging me to go through and "throw out already." But I don't want to throw them out, I'd say, to which she would respond, so take them back with you to New York, what do I care? But I have no room for them, I kept telling her, with my two daughters shoehorned into a tiny bedroom and my dining room table pushed up against the living room wall. I don't know how you can live that way, she'd say, because she grew up "that way" in deepest Brooklyn and escaped, and I'd say, I like the city, I'm willing to give up space to live there. And she'd say, mark my word, your children will move to the suburbs when they're adults, that'll show you, and I'd say, perfect!, then you can hand down my boxes to them.

Sitting on the closet floor now, I pulled back the packing tape sealing one of the boxes and opened up the flaps. Inside was a ragtag time capsule of my youth: my stuffed animal dog, Dog, his once glorious coat of synthetic brown fur all but gone; a Lucite piggy bank, Lucite hand, and a Lucite jewelry box with a never-worn star of David necklace still inside. Atop a pile of books sat my dog-eared copy of *Island of the Blue Dolphins,* the novel I was rereading at the dinner table one night, instead of eating, when my father called to say he'd been held up late at the hospital again, which sent my mother into a rage that ended with a lukewarm hot dog being shoved down my throat. At the bottom of the box, buried under a thick layer of camp photos, taken with an Instamatic camera that required an endless supply of Magicube flashbulbs, were various diaries covering the years from 1973, when I first became interested in recording the details of my life, through 1979, when all those disco Bar Mitzvahs and Lucite presents and hormones kicked in, and I happened to catch my mother reading my November 12, 1979, entry about going to second base with Darren Ekholtz behind the Yahrtzeit wall at Beth Shalom. Which lead to the final entry of the diary, November 13, 1979, in which I wrote, eighteen times, as there were eighteen lines to fill—a *chai,* I remembered thinking—"I hate my mother."

The words were placed there not only because I felt them at the time, but so my mother would read them, too, and when she did, she punished me not in the usual way, like taking away TV privileges or sending me to my room, but by never letting me forget my transgression. "I was going to take you shopping for a new diary," she said one Sunday, "but since you *hate* me, I guess you wouldn't want that." Several months later, when I wrote her a Mother's Day poem, she read it, folded it back up, and placed it on the kitchen counter without saying a word.

"Why are you crying?" I'd said, eager for a bone. I was proud of myself for having rhymed "mother" with "another," as in, "You are my lovely mother / I'd never want another," which felt as honest as the final diary entry at the time I composed it, but Mom just sighed and said, "Well, since you hate me, I don't know how much of this I can believe."

I vowed, from that day forward, never again to put my true feelings into writing. Love, hate, they were simply too danger-ous, especially if you felt them both in tandem. Cool objectivity became my new god; the school newspaper office my new place of worship; black and white the only two shades of truth.

"Lizzie, sweetheart?" It was my mother yelling from the bot-tom of the stairs. "Isn't your next interview sometime soon? You should get going. College Park's at least half an hour away."

I looked at my watch. Shit. It was 1:45. Adele's sister was expecting me at 2:00. I must have lost track of time. "You're right. Thanks." I shoved my first-grade class picture inside my purse and ran down the stairs two by two, instinctually reach-ing for my coat on the low-lying pegs before remembering its placement, with a reprimand, in the closet. "Bye, Mom," I said, giving her a kiss on the cheek that made her flinch. "Thanks for lunch."

"Drive safe," she called after me, which was, I was learning to accept, as close as I was ever going to get to an expression of love.

CHAPTER 10

I ARRIVED LATE to Trudy Levine's apartment, part of a 1970s-era, warrenlike complex near the University of Maryland campus. "I'm so sorry," I said, referring on one level to my tardiness, on another to my sudden intrusion into her life.

"Are you kidding?" She laughed, undoing the chain. "In my world, you're on time. Do you know how many of my students run here, panting, weeks after a paper is due?" She opened the door wearing a patterned green caftan, which hung like a tent over her plumpish frame and made her look not unlike a bunch of grapes. Her gray hair was cut short, her eyes framed by wire-rimmed bifocals. "Come in," she said. "Don't mind the mess. I'm a bit of a pack rat."

Trudy was a bit of a pack rat in the same way the Marquis de Sade might have been a bit of a sadist. Bookshelves were placed like topiaries in a maze, Xeroxed articles lay scattered over the floor, and stacks of old newspapers and magazines lined every wall and covered every surface, filling in each available crevice and nook. Even the two windows looking out onto the parking lot were almost completely covered by piles of old *New*

York Review of Books and recycled food containers, blocking out
nearly all natural light. A single clamp-on lamp gripped the lip
of Trudy's desk, illuminating the corner like a shrine. "Wow," I
said, "You must be a prolific . . ." (hoarder!) ". . . reader."

"Oh, yeah," she said. We paused for a moment in front of the
desk, as she rummaged through papers and a stack of video-
tapes. "I read a lot. You know, the whole interdisciplinary thing.
You have to keep up. I also monitor several hundred blogs and
watch a hell of a lot of TV. If I'm going to rail against the status quo, I have to know what the status quo is now, don't I?"
She winked. "I found an old segment of yours in one of these
piles, in fact." Trudy was the Elsie W. C. Parsons Professor of
Sociology in the Department of Women's Studies, where she
was teaching a course on violence and gender. ("We start out
with Freud, Plato, Foucault. And then we basically rip them
to shreds," she'd said with a snort.) "Here it is!" She picked up
off the floor the story I'd produced on Shirley Lipscomb, who
had recently been pulled from life support after years of unre-
sponsiveness. "Shirley Hart Lipscomb," she read off the Post-it
she'd attached to the cassette. "Devoted mother, PTA treasurer,
Planned Parenthood volunteer, walked around for fifteen years
with bruises on her face before being beaten into a vegetative
state by her husband, Brian."

"She told people she was clumsy," I said.

"And of course everyone believed her." Trudy shook her head
and laid the papers back on her desk. "Never underestimate the
powers of denial," she said. "So where do you want to shoot
this? The last crew that came through here thought the kitchen
had the best light."

Oh, good, I thought to myself. She'd done this before. I
wouldn't have to waste time training her. "What were they
shooting?"

"A BBC series on castration. I'm an expert," she said, leading me around another bookshelf and through a narrow hallway, also lined on either side with books.

"Oh?" I said, my eyes widening.

Trudy started to laugh. "No, not on the physical act. On placing the act in a sociohistorical framework. I teach women's studies, honey. Not pruning." We arrived in her small galley kitchen, miraculously devoid of all literature save the morning's paper. "How's this?"

"Perfect," I said. I pulled out my tripod and camera.

"You know," Trudy said. "I have to say I'm glad you're doing this research. I've been meaning to do it myself, but I haven't figured out a way to stay neutral. I guess I'm still angry."

"At your sister?"

"No. How could I be angry at her? At her husband. At the patriarchy in general. At the kind of society that would leave a woman no other choice than to do away with herself and her children. Cookie?" She held out a tin.

"No, thanks." I attached a microphone to the neck of her caftan, positioned her chair out of direct sunlight, pushed her gray hair slightly back from her face, and turned on the camera. Then I brushed some crumbs off my own chair and sat down. "For the slate, this is an interview with Trudy Levine, Adele Cassidy's younger sister. Trudy, why don't you tell me about your sister?"

"Okay, let me think of how I want to phrase it . . ." She paused, considering her words carefully and taking a deep breath before speaking. "My sister committed suicide when I was twenty-nine years old. I was a doctoral student in sociology at the time and unmarried, which meant I was already considered an old maid. In fact, I remember April and Lily once playing that card game. We were all in Dewey Beach together, and Lily started crying when she got the old maid card. 'What's so wrong with being an old maid?' I say. And Lily answers, 'It's not normal.' 'Not *normal?*' I say. 'And just who do you think decides what constitutes "normal"?' And Lily answers, without missing a beat, 'My father. He says you're not normal.' Well, I laid into Adele after that, asked her what kind of judgmental hooey that husband of hers was feeding to my nieces, and I expected her to defend him, like she was always defending him, but instead she started to cry.

"My sister was a nurse before she met her husband. I'd visit her sometimes, during school breaks. I'd come down on the train with boxes of banana bread and cookies from Schrafft's that my mother would stick in my bag, for her 'working daughter.' Everyone at the hospital loved Adele, and she reveled in their affection. Shep, in fact, was one of her patients. The family joke was that he was admitted with a hernia and walked out with a bride, which lost its humor quickly. Everyone could see she was better off before he showed up. He was the one who made her quit after Lily was born. He said it wasn't 'normal' for a mother to work, and she caved to his wishes, even though the hospital had offered her a reduced schedule. Anyway, so she starts crying that day, and I ask her what's wrong, and she says, 'My life is a sham.' 'What do you mean?' I say. And she tells me she and Shep haven't had sex in two years. Shep has been drinking more, visiting strip clubs. She thinks he's having an affair with that neighbor of theirs, Mavis."

"Really?" I said. "I just spoke to Mavis this morning. She claimed it was your sister who was having the affair, with Lenny Morton."

"Ha!" Trudy expelled a great guffaw, causing the flesh on her upper body to undulate. She plucked the mic off her collar and spoke directly into it. "My sister was NOT having an affair. I repeat, NOT having an affair." Then she reattached it. "Although I guess you could make the argument that Lenny—who, by the way, was just figuring out he was gay—filled an emotional void in her life, and she filled one in his, and in that sense their relationship could have been interpreted as a betrayal. I don't know. I wasn't actually paying attention back then. I was too busy writing papers attacking the institution of marriage as fundamentally corrupt. It's *still* corrupt, as far as I'm concerned, the last form of socially acceptable slavery. Oh, sure, we pay lip service to equal opportunities for women, and we cite statistics—60 percent of women with small children are presently in the workforce, 80 percent of women with school-aged children are working—and we have all those shows on Lifetime with sensitive fathers helping to bathe the kids and fold the laundry. But unless we're looking at people in the top echelons, somebody still has to stay home when the kids get sick, and do the dishes, and sweep the floor, and meet the school bus, and cook the dinner, and shop for the food, and buy the shoes, and cut the fingernails, and though I have no statistics on the division of fingernail-cutting duties in middle-class, two-working-parent households, I'm going to go out on a limb here and say I'm fairly certain that at least nine times out of ten it's the mothers wielding the clippers. And pouring the detergent. And mopping up the vomit instead of putting the finishing touches on that project that could have catapulted them from underling to boss, or at least from underling to less-than-underling, if only they hadn't had to stay home to mop up the vomit. Anyway . . ." Trudy sighed. "I don't think Adele ever adjusted to motherhood. Or to marriage. She was just going along with what she thought she was supposed to do, what our mother raised her—raised us, God help us—to do. That's not to say she didn't love those girls. She did, with all her heart. Have you ever heard of 'altruistic filicide'?"

Actually, I had once run across the expression, while doing research on Andrea Yates, but I wanted to hear Trudy's take on it. I shook my head.

"Well, it's a theory that's been bouncing around since the late sixties, but only recently designated as a classification for maternal filicide in conjunction with suicide. Meaning, mothers since the dawn of civilization have been murdering their children for all sorts of reasons, right? Revenge against the spouse. Jealousy or rejection. Discipline gone awry, self-defense, an unwanted child, which of course now, thank God, is mitigated, at least for some, by access to abortion and birth control, unless, of course, those assholes in Congress get their way and turn us back to the stone age. But mothers who kill themselves and their children simultaneously are in a separate category altogether: these women actually think their children will be better off dead, rather than spending the rest of their lives without a mother. Narcissistic? Of course. Delusional? You bet. But if you really think about it for a moment, it makes sense. Did you know Adele had left instructions for how she wanted the girls to be buried? She'd picked out the music, the flowers, the caterer, even the clothes she wanted the girls to wear. As if she were planning a wedding. Lily she wanted buried in a yellow and white plaid dress, which she'd picked out herself for the high holidays, even though Shep used to throw a fit every fall when Adele would suddenly remember she was Jewish and want to take the girls to shul. April—well, you knew April—she was supposed to have been buried in a pair of shorts and her Redskins jersey. As if in death Adele could finally let April be who she actually was, not who Shep or her teachers or society wanted her to be. But you know what that man did? He buried April in her First Communion dress. And my sister? Cremated. A Jew, cremated! Shep said, and this is a direct quote, 'That woman doesn't deserve a place in the earth for what she did.' Now, granted, he was in mourning. And mad. But in her note, Adele had asked that she and the girls be buried together in that Jewish cemetery out in Olney. Instead, Shep buried the girls at Our Lady of Mercy under headstones engraved with crosses. At least he had a last-minute change of heart and sprinkled Adele's ashes over them. I'll tell you one thing, I made a decision early on that I would never get married, but until that morning I got the call about Adele, I was still on the fence about motherhood. That idea died the day she killed herself. I knew, I mean I know: motherhood did her in."

I furrowed my brow. "You don't think her depression had anything to do with it?"

"Her depression?" She threw up her hands before landing them palms-down on the flimsy table with a bang. "Come on. You know as well as I do that her depression was a direct result of the tedium of her life. She wasn't depressed before Shep and the kids. She had a good life. A productive and fulfilling life."

I decided to try another tack. "What was your own mother like?"

"She was fine. Adequate. The 'good enough mother,' if you want to categorize her. She may have spanked us now and then, and sometimes she screamed and threw pans and threatened to do herself in — my personal favorite, for the sheer purity of its neurosis, was when she shouted, 'I'm going to throw myself out the window, and on the way down, I'm going to yell to the neighbors that you pushed me!' — but she was a slave, okay, my father turned her into a slave. Did she love us?" Trudy shrugged her shoulders. "In her own way, sure. She loved us. She never said it, but we knew. Deep down we knew."

"How?"

"Well, she never killed us, for one . . ." Trudy had meant it as a joke, and she started to laugh but then abruptly stopped. "Oh, I don't know. How does anyone know she's loved? She made us soup when we were sick. She showed up at our piano recitals. She, she . . ." She seemed to be struggling to come up with another example. ". . . She made us put on hats to go out in the snow."

"You said your mother threatened to throw herself out the window. Did she ever try it?" I said.

Trudy was silent for a moment. "Don't think I'm not wise to your methods. You're trying to establish a psychological precedent for my sister's behavior, as if there ever could be one event that were the root cause of anything. You have to understand, her suicide had nothing to do with finding my mother that day. Nothing."

"What day? What are you talking about?"

"Oh. I thought you knew," she said. "I wasn't born yet, so I just know what my sister told me, but Adele was, I think, around five or six at the time. She walks into the apartment after school one day, thinks it's empty, and goes into her bedroom and starts bouncing one of those rubber balls against the wall. It was something my mother wouldn't let us do. So she figures if her mother's not home, she might as well take advantage. So she's bouncing this Spalding against the wall of the bedroom, and this is the wall that's shared between the bathroom and the bedroom, and suddenly she hears someone yelling on the other side of the wall. 'Stop it!' she hears, 'For God's sake, stop it!' So Adele calls out, 'Mommy?' and then she runs into the bathroom and finds my mother, naked, with her wrists slit, in the bathtub. You know, with the blood in the water and everything. 'Can't I even kill myself in peace?' Mom says. Can you imagine? 'Can't I even kill myself in peace.'

"The doctor called it a cry for help, not a real suicide, because she cut across the veins, not down them, like you're supposed to if you're halfway serious, but of course it was scary enough for Adele. She starts screaming, 'Don't die, Mommy! Don't die!' but she said the only thing she kept thinking as she was trying to shake my mother awake was who was going to put her hair in braids every morning. She goes running down the hallway to get our neighbor, and the neighbor calls the police, and Mom's rushed to the hospital, but she's fine, right? And then a week later she's back home, back braiding Adele's hair, back at the stove, and she's cooking kasha or something, and Adele drops a plate, and it breaks into a thousand pieces on the kitchen floor, and my mother says, 'You should have let me die. Why didn't you let me die?' And Adele starts crying and picking up the pieces of broken plate with her hands, and says, 'Because I need you, Mommy.' Look, my father sold children's shoes. He was no stranger to children, but he certainly didn't know the first thing about taking care of us. Was Adele thinking about this that night in the woods in the car? About the week she ate cereal every night for dinner? I don't know. Maybe."

"But getting back to your mother for a moment. Clearly there was a history of maternal depression in the family—"

"Well **now we**'re splitting semantic hairs. You want to call it maternal **depression**? Go ahead. Blame the woman! Add to the canon of 'hysterical' females! But just think about this as you do: when a man kills, we say he snapped. We call it a crime, an aberration, an abomination, but we also consider it within the normal range of what men are capable of doing. As if a propensity for murder were encoded into their DNA, right next to pattern baldness and erectile dysfunction, just sitting there, waiting to express itself. When a woman kills, we call her crazy. Mad. Hysterical, which as I'm sure I don't have to tell you comes from the Greek *husterikos,* 'of the womb.' Just think about *that* for a few minutes before you sit down in your editing room." She pulled off her microphone and stood up. "I'm not saying her actions are excusable. They weren't. But there are other explanations, societal influences, if you will, that lie beyond the realm of psychology." She glanced at her watch. "Look, I've got to go. I have to teach a freshman seminar in half an hour. Misogyny in Literature. I'll walk you out."

"Oh?" I said, packing up my equipment. "Which novels do you study?"

Trudy grabbed her keys and shook her head, either in defeat or at my ignorance, I couldn't tell. "All of them."

CHAPTER II

A HOMECARE NURSE, with an ample bosom and Caribbean accent, answered the door at the Bethesda home of Adele Cassidy's psychiatrist. "May I help you?" she said. A strong smell of eucalyptus and coffee grounds emanated from the doorway, which was cracked a polite but defensive body's-width.

"Yes, thanks," I said. "My name's Elizabeth Stei . . ." I caught myself. Elizabeth Steiger would never try to steal a quote from a psychiatrist. Elizabeth Burns would. "Burns. I'd like to see Dr. Sherman, if he's free."

"Oh, he free, alright," the nurse smiled warmly, opening the door all the way now. "Free as a bird until eternity. Would you like to speak to the wife instead?" She motioned with her hand for me to come in.

"He died?" I'd feared as much. Thirty-five years between the crime and the investigation tends to do that.

"Yes, ma'am. He passed away three years ago. But don't be sad . . ." The nurse was mistaking my anguished look over lost opportunity for grief. ". . . he lived a full life. Ninety-three years, eighty-nine of them with all the marbles. You can't ask too much more from God than that, now can you?"

"No, you can't," I said, wondering, in fact, if you could. "You say his wife's home though?"

"Yes. Please, come in. But speak up when you talk to Mrs. Sherman. Her hearing is not too good. Eleanor?" she yelled up the stairs. "You have a visitor."

From atop the stairs Mrs. Sherman coughed loudly. "Fuck visitors."

The nurse took one look at my expression and began to laugh. "Don't mind her!" she said. "Old people, they get that way. The closer they get to the end, the more honest they be. My last employer, every morning when I come walking in, she say to me, 'Olivia, you are so fat!'" She laughed even harder now, her eyes crinkling with delight. "I take no offense. I am fat! So what? Eleanor, she don't like visitors because the only visitor she ever get is her son, and when he come for a visit, they yell at each other. Go on. She don't bite."

I walked up the stairs and turned left toward the sound of the TV, which was tuned, loudly, to the local news. "Coming up after the break," the announcer was saying, "A kitchen fire in a Rockville eatery leaves three dead and scores injured. We'll have the latest on this tragic story. Plus . . ." The wail of a siren gave way to a cat's meow. "Is your litter box safe?"

Mrs. Sherman lay in bed, surrounded by bottles of pills and lipstick-stained tumblers. The shades were drawn, the windows shut tightly against the cold, the air heavy with manufactured humidity.

"My litter box? What about Iraq, you fucking assholes? What's happening in Iraq?" Then she noticed me and pulled up her blanket. "Who are you?"

I'd done my share of hospital volunteer work, so I was not unfamiliar with the final stages of life, but something about the scene before me now—the damp room, the stench of Pine-Sol and soiled sheets, the husk of a woman hurling insults at her TV—made me pray for a better end to my own. "Hi, Mrs. Sherman. My name's Elizabeth Burns. I'm so sorry to—"

"Speak up. I can't hear you."

I raised my voice. "I said my name's Elizabeth Burns. I'm sorry to drop by like this unannounced, but I'm looking into the suicide of a patient your husband treated in the early seventies."

"My husband's dead." Mrs. Sherman seemed to take some delight in this fact.

"Yes, I know that. Your nurse told me. But I was hoping maybe he'd have talked to you about one of his—"

"He talked to me about nothing," she said, turning her attention back to the TV. The news came on again, its ominous music echoing into the room.

I tried another tack. "Did your husband keep any records or notes of his sessions with Adele Cassidy?"

Mrs. Sherman took a sharp, shallow breath and snapped off the TV with the remote.

"You remember her?"

She pursed her lips together. "I saw her," she said.

"Who, Adele?"

"Of course Adele. Who else would I be talking about?" Now she laid her skeletal hands on mine and used them to pull herself up to a near-sitting position. "That poor woman. She was always crying, even before she went in. Saul met with his patients here, in an office we built onto the garage—Olivia lives there now—and I used to go in there to dust after breakfast, right around the time of her appointment. She wouldn't read the magazines like everyone else. She'd just sit there, crying.

A lot of them cried afterwards—that was normal, that you could understand—but it was the before part that worried me. I said to Saul, 'Be careful with this one. Don't give her those pills, it'll make her worse.' 'Who's the doctor, here?' he'd say. 'You think you're the doctor?' I *tried* those pills. I knew what they did."

"Pills? What pills?"

"How do I know what pills? The ones they gave us back then. Little yellow ones. I forget what they're called."

"Valium?"

"Yes. That's right. Valium. To treat hysteria, they called it. Idiots. Treating depression with a barbiturate."

Mick Jagger began to croon in my head—*They just helped you on your way through your busy dying day . . .* —followed by the image of April's mother, lumbering into our classroom with her disheveled hair and eyes half closed.

"It's those pills that killed her," said Mrs. Sherman, as if reading my thoughts. "I'd bet my life on it." She looked down at her spotted hands, with their gnarled joints and raised veins and yellowed hue, and examined them like an archeologist studying a found object, something odd and incomprehensible apart from herself. "*Oy gevalt.* Could you help me with that, please?" she asked, pointing to the foot of the bed, and as I was leaning over reconnecting her catheter tube, feeling my esophagus starting to convulse from the fetid stench of fresh urine, she whispered, "They're in the garage."

"I'm sorry?"

"I don't know how big the files are, but they're in there," she said. "Notes. Transcripts of his sessions. Everything. My husband, the anal-compulsive. Taped all of his sessions, just like Nixon. Take the file, what do I care? I was going to throw them all out when Saul died, but I didn't. I couldn't. People's lives are in there. Not mine, of course. I was never allowed to see a shrink. Saul didn't believe in them, he said."

"But he was a shrink."

"What's that?" She cupped her left ear with her hand.

"But he was a shrink!" I shouted.

"Life's full of irony, *bubelah*. Haven't you learned that by now?" She reached for her book and opened it up to a ribbon-marked page. "Now go. And tell Olivia I'm still waiting for my teeth." She shook a bony finger at me. "A woman can't *think* without her teeth."

CHAPTER 12

THE WESTERN SKY was turning a deep purple by the time I tossed Adele Cassidy's file into the backseat of the Taurus. I'd wanted to sit down and read through it right there where I'd found it, in a dusty corner of the Shermans' garage, but I had one more stop I needed to make, one more place I wanted to see.

I plugged the intersection of Route 28 and Route 107 into the rental car's GPS system. The strip malls and domino-clustered houses of Potomac gave way to the dull thrum of outbound traffic on I-270, hypnotic and dense. I imagined myself a headlit cell, floating out from the aorta toward what? a foot? until an exit became a two-lane highway, clogged with Lexus sedans and Chevy Caravans, and a computer-generated voice announced, "You have arrived."

I pulled the car over to the shoulder and stepped out into the frigid air. To my right and to my left stood newly constructed McMansions, each one boxy, gargantuan, like weight lifters pumped up on steroids. I took out my video camera and, after a pan across the landscape, trained it on the windows of the house nearest me. I zoomed in on the bedroom, where a teenage girl communed with her computer, staring blankly ahead and IMing; now a swish pan to the kitchen, where, seemingly miles away from her daughter, a woman stirred a pot, expressionless; meanwhile, in the double-height plateglass window of the living room, crisscrossed by fake mullions, a boy squatted alone on the floor clutching a joystick. A joystick? Refugee camps I'd visited in Somalia had more joy in them than that house, yet there it was (I zoomed out until the whole house was in the frame): The American Dream.

I turned off the camera, stamped my feet, and blew into my gloved palms to stay warm. Somehow, the fact that the forest into which Adele Cassidy had driven her children on the last night of their lives had been razed and replaced by these giant, cheerless mushrooms of atomization seemed oddly appropriate, as if the soil upon which they—the trees, the girls—had been felled had become tainted by the woodcutter's axe for all eternity. On the other hand, I had no hope of seeing the forest for the trees if the trees had all been chopped down.

The sky had now blackened completely. I stepped back into the car, squinted my eyes, and tried to imagine a dark wood, the path leading into it, tree trunks and branches, moss and autumn leaves illuminated by the conical beams of Adele's headlights. I knew I wouldn't find the "clearing of dense underbrush" mentioned in the *Post*—thirty-five years of photosynthesis would have rendered it impenetrable—but I hadn't counted on the impenetrability of its absence.

I flipped the radio on to hear the top of the news—"*A van loaded with explosives drove into a crowded schoolyard in Baghdad today, killing thirty . . .*"—and snapped it off.

The previous weekend, Mark and I had taken the girls to an antiwar demonstration in Union Square. As we pushed our way through the crowds, Tess had suddenly said, from her perch atop my shoulders, "Mommy, who invented wars?"

"Well . . ." I'd shot Mark a help-me glance, which he answered with a smile and a feeble you're-on-your-own shrug of his shoulders. "That's a complicated question, sweetheart." I ran through some possible answers in my head: *It's part of our nature, this hatred for the other; No one really invented it, it just happens; Have I ever told you about testosterone?* Then I hit on the perfect answer for her six-year-old psyche: I'd remind her what we learned about mice when she had a brief flirtation with a cageful. She'd already picked out her favorite Beatles names, but then the mouse expert at Petco told her that male mice don't usually make the best pets. For one, their urine has a pungent odor. For another, they tend to be very aggressive and will often bite their young owners. But it was the third reason that had Tess running back to the gerbil display: if two male mice, raised separately, are placed together in the same cage, they will tear each other to shreds until one of them is dead. "You see . . ." I said, getting ready to launch into my lecture on mice and men.

But Tess had already grown impatient. "Well, whoever it is," she said, dismissively, her mittened hands gripping the side of my head, "I'm going to kill him."

The memory of this exchange suddenly made me laugh, sitting there in that rental car, on the shoulder of the last road down which Adele Cassidy had ever driven. With all of its invisible frustrations and sacrifices, motherhood was also a remarkable mosaic-in-progress, with such moments, like handmade tiles, painstakingly inlaid: up close, just a jumble of colors, haphazardly placed in no particular order; from ten feet back, so beautiful you could cry.

Maybe Adele had just forgotten to step back. Or maybe she simply couldn't.

I remembered her file in the backseat. I checked my watch. 6:07 PM. Three more hours until the last shuttle back to New York. If I left now, the girls would already be asleep by the time I got back anyway.

I drove to the nearest Starbucks, ordered a coffee, and plunked myself down in an empty chair. I held the file in my hands for a minute or so, half kid with a candy bar, trying to prolong the ecstasy, half cuckold with an envelope of photos, trying to prolong the moment of truth. Then I opened it. The pages, dated only from September 1972 until mid-October of that same year, were typewritten and yellowed around the edges. Had paper printed when I was a child had time to yellow? Somehow this fact seemed shocking.

I began to read.

Patient: Adele Cassidy, 39
Date of first treatment: Tuesday, September 5, 1972
Referring physician: Dr. Leonard Barlow
Date of birth: 2/14/33
Marital status: married, with two young daughters
Previous psychiatric treatment: none
General health: Obese, mild hypertension

Note: Patient called on 8/30/72, citing desire for treatment, which she expressed thus: "Dr. Barlow thinks I'm depressed. He thinks I need to speak to you." We agreed to meet the following week, after her kids were back in school, as well as to record sessions for research purposes, when I explained I was writing a paper on midlife-onset female depression. Patient showed up on time.

I flipped past the opening nervous exchanges concerning the weather and the origins of a paperweight on Dr. Sherman's desk until the real discussion began.

DR. SHERMAN: So, Mrs. Cassidy. Why don't you tell me why you are here.

MRS. CASSIDY: Dr. Barlow told me to come. He thinks I'm depressed.

DR. SHERMAN: What about you? Do you think you're depressed?

MRS. CASSIDY: I don't know.

DR. SHERMAN: Well let's talk about what you're feeling, and then we can decide whether it's depression or not. Does that sound okay?

MRS. CASSIDY: Okay.

DR. SHERMAN: So how have you been feeling lately? Try to describe it in words.

MRS. CASSIDY: It's kind of hard to describe in words.

DR. SHERMAN: Just do your best. This isn't a test. It's just a conversation.

MRS. CASSIDY: Okay, but, it's just . . . Something's not right. Something's off. I look around me, and I see everyone else living their lives—you know, going to work, putting gas in their cars, shopping for food, the normal stuff—and most of them seem happy. Well, not all happy, but you know, fine. Coping. I look at me, or rather inside me, and all I see is this . . . dark space. Blackness, I guess you could call it.

DR. SHERMAN: Can you describe what this blackness is like?

MRS. CASSIDY: What it's like?

DR. SHERMAN: Yes, describe it. For example, does it have weight, texture—

MRS. CASSIDY: I don't know. I guess you could say it's . . . sticky? Like tar. And other times it's just, well, nothing. Emptiness. It can be sunny and seventy-five degrees outside, and the girls can be giggling in the backyard, and all I can think is when is this all going to be over? These endless days. The sunny ones, especially. I mean, I know I should be happy. But . . . *[Long pause.]*

DR. SHERMAN: But?

MRS. CASSIDY: *[Patient does not answer.]*

DR. SHERMAN: Why don't you tell me a little bit about your family, Mrs. Cassidy. You're married?

MRS. CASSIDY: Yes.

DR. SHERMAN: To whom?

MRS. CASSIDY: My husband's name?

DR. SHERMAN: Yes, let's start with that. What's his name?

MRS. CASSIDY: Shep. Short for Shepherd.

DR. SHERMAN: And when did you meet?

MRS. CASSIDY: Oh, god, let's see. Twelve years ago? A little over twelve, actually. He was my patient. I'm . . . I mean I was a nurse, at Holy Cross. Shep came in for a hernia repair, and, well, my family always jokes that he walked in with a hernia and out with a bride. After the wedding, they joked that. None of them would come to the wedding, actually, either Shep's family or mine, because, you know, the whole religion thing. He's Catholic. I'm a Jew. Neither of us was really religious, but still, it mattered. To them, at least. So we eloped. Well not exactly eloped. My sister, Trudy, came to City Hall with us and stood up as a witness, and Shep's friend Marty came, and I wore a white dress, which wasn't really a wedding dress, but it was white, you know, like a wedding dress, with little white gloves, and we all went out to this bar on M Street afterwards to go dancing. Shep got so drunk, we had to wait until the next night to, you know. Be husband and wife. We must have gotten pregnant that same night. I had a miscarriage, though, right at the end of the first trimester, which, you know, I was a nurse, I knew it was no big deal, but Shep took it hard. Like he'd failed. He started going to church again, every Sunday. I kept telling him these things just happened, and there's no explanation, just nature's way of getting rid of babies that shouldn't be born, but he wouldn't listen. At one point he even talked about becoming a priest. But he didn't. Thank God. *[Patient sighs.]* So anyway I was a little down because of the miscarriage, but you know, pretty much fine after a month or two and actually kind of relieved to have a little more time before we . . . *[Patient stops talking. Several seconds elapse.]* I'm sorry. I got lost. What were we talking about?

DR. SHERMAN: We were talking about how you met your husband. Then the miscarriage. And before that the reasons you came here. The "blackness," as you called it.

MRS. CASSIDY: Right. The blackness. I guess it started when . . . actually I have to go back again. Okay, so, a few years after the miscarriage I got pregnant again. With Lily. She's eight now. April, my other one, she'll be six in October. And after Lily was born, and she was healthy and perfect and you know, just this perfect little baby—slept through the night at five weeks, hardly spit up at all, very easy to soothe and, well, just a perfect little baby—after she was born, I found it hard to get out of bed. Hard like there's lead on top of you. Like you're living on one of those planets, you know the small ones near the sun, where gravity pushes you down. Sometimes Lily would be crying in her bassinet, and I could hear her? I could hear her, and in my mind I knew I was supposed to go get her, but for some reason I couldn't. I'd just lie there in bed on my heavy planet, listening to her crying, wondering when her mother was going to come get her. And I guess, somewhere in the back of my mind, I couldn't believe I'd signed up for this. That I would be responsible for this little baby's life forever. Supposedly, when they brought Lily to me that first night in the hospital, when they woke me up to feed her, and I guess I'd been sleeping pretty deeply, probably in the middle of a dream or something, supposedly I turned to the nurse and said, "Oh, no, I'm sorry. You must be mistaken. She's not my baby," and went right back to sleep. Am I doing this right?

DR. SHERMAN: Why are you asking?

MRS. CASSIDY: Well, I just, I mean, I'm just sitting here talking, and you're just sitting there listening, and I don't know, I thought you were supposed to be helping me or something. Telling me what's wrong with me.

DR. SHERMAN: What do you think is wrong with you?

MRS. CASSIDY: Well, that's what I came here to find out. I just sit here and talk? What does that accomplish?

DR. SHERMAN: You'll see. Much can be learned from the way we tell our stories. Later on we might talk about your dreams, have you free associate, things like that. But right now let's just concentrate on your story. From your own mouth. Not Dr. Barlow's or your husband's—whom, by the way, I spoke to last night when he called, and I told him under no circumstances would I be reporting to him anything that might get discussed in here, so you should feel absolutely free to talk honestly. About him. About your feelings. About anything. So. You were talking about Lily. The night she was born. When the nurses brought her to you in the middle of the night.

MRS. CASSIDY: Right. Lily. Do you have children, Dr. Sherman?

DR. SHERMAN: Mrs. Cassidy, usually it's best if the patient knows as little as possible about the personal life of her psychiatrist. Trust me, it's better this way. What *is* relevant, however, is why did you want to know if I have children of my own?

MRS. CASSIDY: So you could understand me.

DR. SHERMAN: And you think if I don't have children of my own, I won't be able to relate to your story?

MRS. CASSIDY: Well, yes. I'm even a little bit worried that even if you do have children, the fact that you're not a woman will make it hard for you to understand.

DR. SHERMAN: I see. Well, Mrs. Cassidy, I think you can rest assured that I will relate to your story both regardless of my gender and regardless of whether or not I am a parent myself. So. You were talking about Lily.

MRS. CASSIDY: Well, we brought her home from the hospital, and I, well, I wasn't very good at it. I mean, my job was to take care of people, and here I was, unable to take care of my own child. I actually thought about going back to work, so I wouldn't feel like such a failure. Because work had never been a problem, right? And I had people there I could talk to. The only person I ended up talking to after Lily was born was my neighbor. Mavis. She had kids around the same time I did. But that's pretty much all we had in common. Her house always smelled like either nail polish or nail polish remover, and she was always sitting there with those pieces of cotton between her toes, putting polish on, taking polish off, putting it on, taking it off. Anyway, Shep kept asking me why I couldn't be more like Mavis. Why I couldn't just be content with taking care of Lily and making dinner and running errands. When I asked if I could go back to work, he said what would people think, a mother leaving her child in the hands of a stranger? It wasn't right. And then April was born. *[Patient pauses to choke back tears. Doesn't speak for a full four minutes.]*

DR. SHERMAN: And?

MRS. CASSIDY: And, I don't know. Things got worse. I got heavy. Fat, I mean, not heavy the way kids say it these days. I just, I couldn't help myself. From eating. All the time. I knew I shouldn't, I mean, I still know I shouldn't, but it's like this other person takes over. This really hungry person. Sometimes, when I'd take the girls to the Giant, and it was stressful when they were really little, you know? April was just a baby, flopping over in the kiddie seat, Lily would sprint off down the aisle if I so much as blinked, and I know—*I know*—people have four, five, six children, and they manage to get through the grocery store every week without a hitch, but I hated those trips to the grocery store. Hated them with a passion. So, kind of like a gift to myself, for getting through another week without losing my mind, I'd buy these big bags of Ruffles and Cheetos, and a gallon of mint chocolate chip and a couple of Baby Ruths and some Oreos and a box of Hostess cupcakes. These were not for the kids, mind you, but for me. To eat on the way home. And at first when I was eating I felt great. More than great. Like I was drunk or something. And at the same time, while I was feeling so great, I hated myself. I hated myself for eating all that food. It was a vicious cycle. Vicious circle?

DR. SHERMAN: Hmm. I think it's vicious . . . no. I believe either is correct.

MRS. CASSIDY: Anyway, it was vicious, in any case. Then five years ago, or maybe it was four? Yes, around four

years ago, because April had just turned two. Anyway, one
of my neighbors knocked on the door and said he could help.
With my weight, that is. I didn't really believe him, but he
and his wife were just splitting up, and he was looking to
start a new business as a dietitian, and, well, I just kind
of felt sorry for him. And I had nothing to lose, right? So
I said I'd be his guinea pig. His name was Lenny. Anyway,
Lenny came over every morning and helped me make these
blender meals and taught me how to exercise and just, I
don't know, he hung out with me. He made me laugh. I think
he thought that if he could just get me to lose fifty pounds,
everything would be okay in his own life. Like he could
conquer anything. He knew I was having a hard time, you
know, adjusting. And for awhile there, he was a godsend. I
was losing weight, feeling better about myself. I had someone to talk to. Even the kids liked having Lenny around. He
was fun. Unlike Shep, who can be, well . . . it's not that he's
a bad father. He doesn't do anything wrong, really. But he
doesn't try to do anything right, either. He sort of ignores
them. The children, that is. And I guess me, too. Yeah,
he's been ignoring me for awhile, too. He doesn't do it to be
mean, he just, well, he's a bit of a quiet man. Doesn't say
much, unless he gets angry, and then, well, he says a lot.
Anyway, things with Lenny were never intimate. At all. In
fact, there was really nothing like that whatsoever. There
couldn't be because he was, well, he didn't like women that
way.

DR. SHERMAN: He was a homosexual?

MRS. CASSIDY: Something like that.

DR. SHERMAN: Did you want to be intimate with this
homosexual man?

MRS. CASSIDY: No. Of course not! But Shep thought I did,

and that's what, well . . . He came home early one night and saw Lenny blending a meal in the kitchen. He went ballistic. Said I was a whore for inviting another man into our home when he wasn't around. At first I started laughing, right? because of Lenny and because it was kind of preposterous, you know, the whole idea of me being a whore?

DR. SHERMAN: Why is that?

MRS. CASSIDY: Because I barely, you know . . .

DR. SHERMAN: You barely what? Have sexual intercourse or enjoy it?

MRS. CASSIDY: Both.

DR. SHERMAN: And why do you think that is?

MRS. CASSIDY: I don't know. Maybe . . . It's embarrassing, I guess. All that extra flesh. I don't like to be without my clothes.

DR. SHERMAN: Plenty of larger than average people enjoy healthy sexual relations, Mrs. Cassidy. Can you be more specific?

MRS. CASSIDY: No. I don't think I can.

DR. SHERMAN: Alright. Let's get back to that night your husband called you a whore. What happened next?

MRS. CASSIDY: Lenny walked out. Then he left town. I think he moved to New York, to Greenwich Village or something like that. We lost touch, so I'm not sure. After he left, I started eating again. A lot. And, you know, I didn't have anyone to sit on my feet anymore while I was doing sit-ups, so . . .

DR. SHERMAN: I'm sorry, Adele, but let's go back a second. You said your husband—Shep is it?

MRS. CASSIDY: Yes.

DR. SHERMAN: You said Shep went "ballistic" before he called you a whore. Can you expound on that please?

MRS. CASSIDY: Ballistic. You know, crazy. Like I said, he's a quiet man, but when something ticks him off, he goes ballistic.

DR. SHERMAN: Yes, but what does that mean?

MRS. CASSIDY: It means ballistic. He starts yelling at first. Like that night, when he saw Lenny in the kitchen, first he said, "What the . . ." Can I curse in here?

DR. SHERMAN: Of course.

MRS. CASSIDY: I wasn't sure.

DR. SHERMAN: It's fine. Curse away.

MRS. CASSIDY: Okay. He said, "What the fuck is going on here?"

DR. SHERMAN: And then?

MRS. CASSIDY: Just, more yelling. Like when he was calling me . . . when he called me a whore.

DR. SHERMAN: And that was it? He said, "What the fuck is going on here?" and then, "Adele, you're a whore"?

MRS. CASSIDY: Well, no. Not exactly. It went on for, I don't know, ten minutes I guess?

DR. SHERMAN: And what happened during those ten minutes?

MRS. CASSIDY: *[Patient pauses.]* Well. *[Patient pauses again.]* I started laughing after he called me a whore—I guess it was nervous laughter, I couldn't help it, you know when you feel nervous, or when you hear that someone's died, and even though it's the wrong thing, you laugh?

DR. SHERMAN: Yes.

MRS. CASSIDY: Well, that's when he knocked over the blender. After I laughed. And all the fruit juice spilled all over the floor, and the blender—it was glass—it broke, into a thousand pieces, and then the girls walked in, and I was saying, "Don't come in here! Don't come in here! There's glass everywhere!" but of course that made them just want to come in more, and then Shep suddenly had Lenny by the throat, and he was shaking him, saying, you know, "You think you can just come in here and fuck my wife? Make her skinny so you can fuck her? Is that what you're doing?" and then suddenly Lenny was flat on the floor, covered in fruit juice and with cuts from the glass, and Shep was kneeled over him, punching him in the face, and April— the baby—April was screaming her head off and trying to get to Lenny, and Lily was standing in the corner of the kitchen crying, and I finally just screamed, "Get off him, Shep! There's nothing going on here. We were just blending!" which only infuriated him more, because I guess he took it the wrong way, so then he hits me in the face, and I'm holding onto my eye now, trying to get to the refrigerator to get some ice, and Lenny—I don't know how he did it—Lenny just pulls himself off the ground from under Shep, you know, like when they say a mother can lift a car off her baby? That kind of strength. And he goes running.

DR. SHERMAN: And?

MRS. CASSIDY: Nothing. I was just remembering something.

DR. SHERMAN: What?

MRS. CASSIDY: Nothing. It's stupid. Just a silly memory.

DR. SHERMAN: What kind of memory?

MRS. CASSIDY: Oh, I just. I broke a plate once. In the kitchen. When I was a little girl. It's nothing, really. Just the broken blender made me think of it.

DR. SHERMAN: Well, why don't you hold that thought, Mrs. Cassidy, because that's all the time we have for today. Let's meet again next week, same time.

Good for you, Adele, I thought to myself, taking a last sip of my coffee. You got right into the muck of it, right away. I wish I could have been so forthcoming. During my second session with Dr. Rivers, I spent most of the hour trying to pin her down on exactly how long my treatment would take while simultaneously denying that anything was really all that wrong. "But last week you said you felt lost," she reminded me. "This is not just about your episodes of fainting."

"But I feel fine today," I'd said. Then I made up some excuse about overexhaustion. It was so much easier to blame outside circumstances—fatigue, my husband, my responsibilities, my work—than to delve inside my own sticky tar pit, as Adele so aptly called it. The deep malaise, the nagging sense of a life wasted, the desire to find meaning: all of that, I was sure, was just a phase. Something I just needed to get through.

"What about your childhood friend?" Dr. Rivers finally said. "The one who died. Were you able to find out anything more about what happened?"

I told her about the police report I'd received in the mail after sending a FOIA request, about my plans to fly down to Potomac to shoot a couple of interviews, about my desire to get into the mind of her mother, to figure out the mystery of Adele Cassidy's final actions.

"And do you find the work meaningful?" the doctor asked.

And I said, "I guess so. Yeah. I do."

"And why is that?"

I paused to consider the question. "Because I care about the answers." And then our time was up.

I turned to the next page in Dr. Sherman's transcripts and read on.

Patient: Adele Cassidy

Date: Monday, September 11, 1972

Note: Patient arrives already crying. It takes a full ten minutes for her to begin speaking.

DR. SHERMAN: Would you like to tell me what's wrong?

MRS. CASSIDY: I'm a monster.

DR. SHERMAN: What do you mean?

MRS. CASSIDY: I mean I'm a monster. A monster of a mother. A monster of a wife. I'm just . . . a monster. Everyone would be better off without me. Everyone.

DR. SHERMAN: Why do you say that? Did anything specific happen, or is this just a general sense of melancholia?

MRS. CASSIDY: Melan-what?

DR. SHERMAN: Melancholia. Depression.

MRS. CASSIDY: Both then.

DR. SHERMAN: Both depression and something specific?

MRS. CASSIDY: Yes.

DR. SHERMAN: Okay, and what would that something specific be?

MRS. CASSIDY: *[Patient pauses before speaking, then bursts out crying again.]* I hit them.

DR. SHERMAN: Hit whom?

MRS. CASSIDY: The girls. *[Patient still crying.]*

DR. SHERMAN: You hit your daughters?

MRS. CASSIDY: Yes.

DR. SHERMAN: How did you hit them? Why?

MRS. CASSIDY: *[Patient can barely catch her breath now, she's hyperventilating and barely able to speak.]*

DR. SHERMAN: Had they done anything to deserve punishment?

MRS. CASSIDY: Yes. No. Not really.

DR. SHERMAN: So why did you hit them? What triggered your rage?

MRS. CASSIDY: I don't know. I just got angry. I got so angry. First I woke up, and I realized I'd made a mess of the sheets, because I got my, you know. So I was already in a bad mood to begin with, having to clean up the mess and strip the bed and remake it, when I'd just changed the sheets the day before. Anyway, after I cleaned up the mess, I went into the girls' room to wake them up. They're always late getting up. Last year they missed the bus all the time. And so this morning I said to them, I said, "Lily, April, you better get up and get in that shower and get out to that bus stop right now, because we're not starting off the year this way. I am not driving you to school if you miss the bus again." But they didn't get up. Lily just lay there in bed, snoring her head off, and April had this Super Ball I bought her in one of those bubblegum machines, and when she opened her eyes, she yanked it from underneath her pillow and was bouncing it against the wall, and SHE . . . KNOWS . . . SHE'S . . . NOT . . . SUPPOSED . . . TO . . . DO . . . THAT . . . She *knows* she's not supposed to do that. She knows . . . *[Once again, patient unable to speak. She sobs.]*

DR. SHERMAN: Is that when you started hitting them?

MRS. CASSIDY: No. First I filled up the cup we keep in the bathroom with cold water, and I threw it at Lily to wake her up.

DR. SHERMAN: Do you often throw water on your children in the morning?

MRS. CASSIDY: No. Just sometimes. If they won't wake up any other way. My mother used to do the same thing to me.

DR. SHERMAN: Did you like it when your mother threw water on you?

MRS. CASSIDY: No. But it worked.

DR. SHERMAN: And what happened after you threw the water on your daughter?

MRS. CASSIDY: She started screaming, saying she hates me. Then I started yelling.

DR. SHERMAN: What were you yelling?

MRS. CASSIDY: Oh, you know, the usual stuff. I said, "Don't you start the day sassing me like that, little Miss Thing. You get up and get yourself in that shower. And you!" That's when I pointed at April? I said, "You stop bouncing that ball against the wall or I will ream you so hard you won't know what hit you." Stuff like that. And I said, "I've told you a thousand times not to bounce that ball inside this house," but Lily just sat there, crying, saying, "I hate you, Mommy! I hate you!" and April just kept bouncing that Super Ball against the wall, like I wasn't even standing there, telling her to stop, and I just lost it. I completely lost it. First I grabbed Lily by the chin, and I said, "You will get up right now, young lady, do you hear me?" Then I hit her. I hit her on her arm and on her legs . . . like this and like this and like this, all over her body, until she ran into the bathroom. By then April had stopped bouncing the ball, and she was kind of cowering in the corner, but I turned around anyway and twisted her arm, the one that had been throwing the ball? I twisted it so hard *[Patient is crying hysterically now.]* . . . I twisted it so hard she started to scream. I could have broken it. She was screaming in pain. *[Patient still crying.]*

DR. SHERMAN: And where was your husband this whole time?

MRS. CASSIDY: He's in Detroit today. Maybe Chicago. I'm not sure. He's always on the road. Leaving me alone with his goddamned kids!

[Twenty-five minutes elapse, as patient tries to regain her composure.]

MRS. CASSIDY: I didn't mean to call them that. I love them. I really do. Oh, god, I'm a monster. *[Patient still crying.]*

DR. SHERMAN: Adele, while some of the actions you've told me about this morning require further discussion, you need to suspend judgment of yourself for the moment. You're not a monster. You're a woman in pain, who happens to be taking out her frustrations on her children, which, yes, is something we need to address. Look, unfortunately we're running out of time here today. Last week we left off, and you were going to tell me about the time you broke a plate, and we still didn't get to that, because you were too upset in here today to talk, but what I'm going to suggest is this: You need to gain control over your emotions. Quickly. The problem is that this will take time. Quite a lot of time. In the meantime, I'm going to prescribe a mild sedative. It'll take the edge off things for awhile, calm you down a bit while we sort through all these issues. You want me to call it in to Dart Drug or is a prescription okay?

MRS. CASSIDY: Prescription's fine. I have some errands I have to run before the girls come home.

DR. SHERMAN: Okay. I want you to take four of them a day, breakfast, lunch, dinner, and bedtime, for the next week, okay?

MRS. CASSIDY: Okay.

DR. SHERMAN: And next week we'll discuss maybe getting your daughters in here for a session or two.

MRS. CASSIDY: No. They don't need to come in.

DR. SHERMAN: I said we can discuss it. Not that we'll definitely do it.

MRS. CASSIDY: Okay. *[Patient pauses.]* Dr. Sherman, can I ask you a question?

DR. SHERMAN: Sure. But we only have a few minutes left, so—

MRS. CASSIDY: It's a quick question. Um, well, I seem to become more, well, I don't know what to call it other than "crazy," right around, you know, that time of the month. Almost like a Dr Jekyll / Mr Hyde thing. Like my body gets possessed or something. Does that make any sense to you?

DR. SHERMAN: No, not really. The hormonal fluctuations associated with menses are not significant enough to cause any substantial changes in mental functioning or personality. That's mostly a myth.

MRS. CASSIDY: A myth.

DR. SHERMAN: Yes, a myth.

MRS. CASSIDY: Oh. Okay. I was just wondering. And, but, so what about when babies are born? Because I've been thinking a lot about what I said last week, about how after Lily was born, how I felt back then, and I remembered that sometimes I'd be looking down at Lily in her crib? When she was sleeping? And I'd have these very vivid images of her being sucked into the earth. Or burned alive. Or, when April was born? After April was born, I used to think that if I kissed her cheek, her skin would boil up, like my saliva was hydrochloric acid or something, and then her whole face would disintegrate. Or I'd picture myself stabbing her to death. Over and over again. It got so bad I actually hid the kitchen knives on a really high shelf in case, well, just in case.

DR. SHERMAN: Sounds to me like someone's been watching too many horror films.

MRS. CASSIDY: No. That's not it at all.

DR. SHERMAN: Well, you probably just have a very vivid imagination. It's nothing to worry about.

MRS. CASSIDY: I don't have a vivid imagination, Dr. Sherman. I really don't. In school I couldn't draw a picture or write a story to save my life. No, these, I don't know what to call them—visions?—these visions just happened after the girls were born. And they lasted a long time. With April more than a year.

DR. SHERMAN: Again, I don't think it's anything to worry about. Now, we have to end our session today. We're already three minutes over—

MRS. CASSIDY: Are you sure? *[Patient starts crying again.]* Are you sure there's nothing to worry about?

DR. SHERMAN: Yes, I'm sure. Look, yes, there are hormonal changes associated with the birth of a child, but nothing that would induce any sort of, well, psychosis. It just doesn't happen.

MRS. CASSIDY: Oh. I see.

DR. SHERMAN: Are you going to be okay driving, Mrs. Cassidy? Would you like a tissue?

MRS. CASSIDY: Yes, please. Thank you. Sorry.

DR. SHERMAN: No sorrys. That's what I'm here for. To help. I'll see you next week. Take those pills. They'll do you a world of good, I promise.

MRS. CASSIDY: Yeah, okay. See you next week.

Amazing, I thought, that postpartum psychosis, or even its more mild manifestation, postpartum depression, were so ill-understood. How little credence was given to the effects of hormonal fluctuations in women back then. I'd been shocked to learn, when I was doing research on the Andrea Yates trial, that the diagnosis of postpartum depression hadn't even been added to the American Psychiatric Association's Diagnostic and Statistical Manual until 1994. 1994! Just five years before the birth of my own daughter.

No wonder my mother claimed she didn't have postpartum depression after Josh was born. It was 1972: the same year Adele Cassidy was being told that her visions of stabbing her daughter were simply the result of having watched too many horror movies. Postpartum depression, back then, simply didn't exist.

I turned the page in the folder and read on.

Patient: Adele Cassidy
Date: Monday, September 18, 1972

Note: Patient did not show up for her normally scheduled 11:00 AM appointment this morning. I called her at 11:30. She picked up the phone, but her speech was slurred. Patient apologized for missing the session and said I should not take it personally as she kept forgetting things the whole week: a haircut appointment, lunch with her sister, a carpool home from April's Brownie meeting. I asked how many pills she was taking a day, and she said eight. I reminded her that the prescription I gave her was only for four pills a day, but she said that she assumed since she was so large, she'd need to take twice as much. I explained that I'd taken her weight into consideration when I wrote the prescription, and that she should cut back to four a day. Patient promised to rectify the dosage and to meet the following Monday. She then asked if she had to pay for the missed session, and when I said she did, she said, "That's not very nice," and hung up the phone.

Patient: Adele Cassidy

Date: Monday, September 25, 1972

Note: Patient showed up at her session fifteen minutes late, looking mildly disheveled. She wore a housedress with a pair of rubber flip-flops, her hair appeared greasy and uncombed, her skin was sallow. When she sat down in her chair, she stared past me, at the window behind my head, and remained silent. After several minutes spent this way, I spoke first.

DR. SHERMAN: How are you feeling today, Adele?

MRS. CASSIDY: How does it look like I'm feeling?

DR. SHERMAN: I sense some hostility in that answer. Why?

MRS. CASSIDY: You're the doctor. You tell me.

DR. SHERMAN: I think actually it would be more helpful if you told me what you are feeling, since they are your feelings.

MRS. CASSIDY: I'm feeling fine today. No problems at all. Can I go now?

DR. SHERMAN: You're free to go whenever you please, but we do have quite a few minutes left, if you'd like to fill them.

MRS. CASSIDY: With what? More stories? What will that accomplish? It's been a whole month now, and I feel worse than I did when I first began. I can barely get out of bed in the morning. I walk around my house like a zombie. My daughters hate me. My husband won't touch me. Not that I even want him to touch me, but still. I don't see how telling stories in here is going to get me any better.

DR. SHERMAN: Adele, I can understand your trepidation.

Starting therapy can be a scary process. But I can promise you, after years of experience, that spending time talking in this room will help you. Provide you with some clarity. Stories are how we make sense of our lives. To tell a story is to own it: to own the narrative thread, to own a piece of our past. And when we own a story, when we put it in a tidy box and store it on a high shelf, it becomes manageable, so that whatever negative effects it's been having on us are, in theory, lessened.

MRS. CASSIDY: In theory.

DR. SHERMAN: Yes, in theory. And in practice, too. I've seen patients of mine who've been through tremendous traumas, upheavals, tragedies—even war—get on with their lives. People who've lived through far worse than you.

MRS. CASSIDY: Worse than me? You want to play that game? Fine. Here's one you can write down on that little yellow pad of yours: I found my mother. In a bathtub. Of her own blood. Wrists slit. Happy now?

DR. SHERMAN: Well, I wouldn't say that makes me happy. But I do think we're finally getting somewhere. Was this a recent occurrence or did it happen in the past?

MRS. CASSIDY: It happened when I was seven. But what do you mean, we're finally getting somewhere. Where exactly are we getting?

DR. SHERMAN: To your truth.

MRS. CASSIDY: My *truth*? What the hell is truth anyway?

DR. SHERMAN: Those are two separate questions. *The* truth we'll leave to the philosophers. *Your* truth is whatever is at your core. Your essence. That which makes you you. This is the first I'm hearing of your mother's . . . was she dead when you found her in the tub?

MRS. CASSIDY: No. She was still alive.

DR. SHERMAN: So it was a suicide attempt?

MRS. CASSIDY: Yes.

DR. SHERMAN: Okay, so, as I was saying, this is the first I'm hearing of your mother's attempted suicide, but I'm going to bet it has formed you in profound ways. Let's talk about it, shall we?

MRS. CASSIDY: No. I don't feel like it right now.

DR. SHERMAN: Okay, fine, but I must tell you Mrs. Cassidy, it's in your interest to cooperate with me in here. This should not be a combative relationship. If you don't want to talk about it, that's fine, but for me to do my job I need to know as much about you as possible. And the fact that your mother tried to commit suicide, and that you happened to mention it today, is relevant to your mental health.

MRS. CASSIDY: What's there to say? I walked into the apartment, she was sitting in a pool of blood, her wrists were slit, she survived. End of story. But like you said, it's not a war. So no big deal.

DR. SHERMAN: And you were seven when this happened?

MRS. CASSIDY: Yes. Or, wait. No, actually I was eight. Almost nine. Anyway, it was sometime after Pearl Harbor. I remember that, because somehow the two got connected in my head. It felt like one day we were sitting around the radio, listening to reports of the attack, the next day my mother tried to kill herself. Late December of '41. I must have been in third grade. My mother had been corresponding with her cousin Leah. Leah—she and my mother had grown up practically as sisters when they were little—Leah was trying to get out of Warsaw, to come live with us. She needed Mom to sign some papers. They'd been writing letters back and forth for a couple of years by then, trying to figure out a way to get Leah to come live with us, and that day, the day I found my mother in the tub, she'd just received a stack of letters she'd sent to Leah, returned and unopened.

DR. SHERMAN: And so Leah was . . . ?

MRS. CASSIDY: Yes. Or at least that's what we assumed, since we never heard from her again.

DR. SHERMAN: And your mother made her suicide attempt that same day?

MRS. CASSIDY: I think so.

DR. SHERMAN: And do you think the two were related?

MRS. CASSIDY: Sort of. It was kind of more complicated than that. She never liked Leah. She always said Leah drove her crazy when they were growing up. That even Leah's father had said she was ugly and stupid, that no man would ever marry her. And I think she was really unhappy with the idea of her cousin coming to live with us. She kept saying to my father, "What are we going to do with her when she gets here, huh? Put her in the kitchen? Or should we make Adele move her bed into the living room?" And my father would say, "How should I know? She's your cousin. You figure it out." I think it was more the story she told whenever people asked about the scars on her wrists. People would ask her about them—you know, they were quite large, and kind of dramatic-looking—and she'd say something like, "What? These? Oh, yes, well, it was terrible. It was the day I found out my dear cousin Leah had been sent to Auschwitz . . ."

DR. SHERMAN: So Leah was sent to Auschwitz?

MRS. CASSIDY: I don't know. We never found out. We just know Leah never wrote again.

DR. SHERMAN: So why did your mother say that her cousin had been sent to Auschwitz?

MRS. CASSIDY: Well . . . It . . . People could relate to

Auschwitz. It was a word that meant something to them. If she told them what really happened, that she'd been stalling with her cousin's paperwork because she didn't like her and then one day a stack of unopened letters came back, and then Leah never wrote again, and she didn't know what happened to her, it's, well, it's a different kind of story.

DR. SHERMAN: I see. Would you say that your mother suffered from depression before the letters from her cousin came back unopened?

MRS. CASSIDY: Depression? I guess. I know she was never very happy. She always had a little scowl on her face, these little lines at the corners of her mouth that turned down. But I guess I never figured she was so depressed she'd try to, you know . . .

DR. SHERMAN: How could you? You were a child.

MRS. CASSIDY: I suppose.

DR. SHERMAN: And how did you feel when you found her in the bathroom?

MRS. CASSIDY: I don't know. I was eight. It was a long time ago.

DR. SHERMAN: Give it a go. Put yourself back in your eight-year-old mind. How did you feel when you walked into that room?

MRS. CASSIDY: Scared, I guess. Because of all of the blood.

DR. SHERMAN: And?

MRS. CASSIDY: I'm sorry?

DR. SHERMAN: Were you feeling any other feelings when you saw her in that tub?

MRS. CASSIDY: Yes, but a stupid one.

DR. SHERMAN: No feelings are stupid.

MRS. CASSIDY: Okay. Well. I was . . . worried.

DR. SHERMAN: Worried about what?

MRS. CASSIDY: About who was going to put my hair in a ponytail. I used to wear it that way every day. To keep it out of my eyes.

DR. SHERMAN: That's a perfectly and developmentally normal reaction of an eight-year-old. At that age range, you would be worried about such things. You were too young to care for yourself.

MRS. CASSIDY: No. It runs deeper than that. Deeper than, you know, ponytails.

DR. SHERMAN: Go on.

MRS. CASSIDY: Okay. Well, when my mother brushed my hair?

DR. SHERMAN: Yes.

MRS. CASSIDY: When she sat on the floor of my bedroom in front of the mirror and brushed the hair up from my neck and back from my forehead so I could finally see? Even though she sometimes did it too hard, I didn't mind, because it was the only time when we were alone together. And quiet. Just the two of us.

DR. SHERMAN: And how did that make you feel?

MRS. CASSIDY: It made me feel . . . loved.

DR. SHERMAN: Didn't you feel loved at other times in the day? What about bedtime?

MRS. CASSIDY: She never put me to bed. I always put myself to bed.

DR. SHERMAN: After school?

MRS. CASSIDY: She didn't usually talk to me after school. She had headaches. Migraines. She'd leave me a snack on the kitchen table so she could stay in bed listening to the radio. You know, with her migraines.

DR. SHERMAN: And so when you found her in the tub . . .

MRS. CASSIDY: When I found her in the tub . . . When I found her in the tub, I felt angry.

DR. SHERMAN: Angry at whom, Adele?

MRS. CASSIDY: *[Patient pauses.]* At my mother. For doing that.

DR. SHERMAN: For doing what?

MRS. CASSIDY: *[Patient starts to cry.]* For not loving me enough to want to stay.

DR. SHERMAN: Good. That's good, Adele. Now I want you to hold that thought until next week, because we're out of time for today. I'd like to see you next week, at our normally scheduled hour, with your daughters. Can you take them out of school early?

MRS. CASSIDY: Sure, but—

DR. SHERMAN: Excellent. And please try to be on time this time next week. I'd like to use the entire hour we—

MRS. CASSIDY: Can't you just push back the next patient? I fell asleep. Those pills you gave me, they make me so tired. That's why I was late. It wasn't my fault.

DR. SHERMAN: No, Mrs. Cassidy, I can't push back my next patient. It wouldn't be fair.

MRS. CASSIDY: So, what, so I just pour out my heart to you, tell you about my most private and horrible moments, and you say, "We're out of time"!

DR. SHERMAN: I'm afraid that's how things work sometimes, yes. But give me a call at the beginning of next week, and we can talk about the dosage on your—

MRS. CASSIDY: Fine. *[Patient slams the door to the office behind her.]*

A dramatic exit. One with which I found myself empathizing. Of course I had the advantage of hindsight, of knowing what lay in store for Adele Cassidy one month later, but even so, I couldn't help thinking that if she were my patient, I might have made my next patient wait. Even if only for five minutes. Enough time to allow the epiphany to sink in. Enough time for Adele to "own" her story and put it in a tidy box and store it on a high shelf, as Dr. Sherman himself had suggested, where it would remain, part of her conquered narrative forever.

"My *truth*?" she'd said to him. "What the hell is truth anyway?"

Two separate questions, yes, but not wholly unrelated. For truth, no matter the modifier, is always intrinsically modified.

Adele's sister had said Adele was five years old and worried about braids when she found her mother in the bathtub and that she killed herself because of the patriarchy. Mavis Traub said Adele was having an affair with Lenny Morton, a gay man, and that she was depressed because she was fat. Mrs. Sherman said her husband, the psychiatrist, didn't believe in psychiatry. My mother said it was Mavis Traub having the affair and that Adele Cassidy was murdered by her husband. If she even existed at all. Dr. Sherman said hormonal fluctuations in women would not account for abnormal behavior. Miss Martin said April and Lily would not be coming back to school, ever. The kids on the bus said that April had been devoured by the Loch Ness monster or drowned in the JCC pool or fed gas.

How was I to ever know whether Adele was a cold-blooded, calculating murderer, a housewife at the end of her rope, or some other creature altogether? Even with the transcripts, the interviews I'd shot and planned still to shoot, how was I ever going to find out what happened in that station wagon, three decades earlier, somewhere near the very spot I was now sitting, drinking a small coffee everyone in the world seemed content to call tall? Because that's what I needed to know: what happened in that car.

Amazing, I thought, how the lie of omission told to a little girl—April and her sister, Lily, will not be coming back to school . . . but we'll always hold them in our hearts—could be held responsible for the obsessions of a grown woman. Was that *my* truth? Or simply *a* truth?

At least in a war, I thought, truth is, more often than not, verifiable. Person X was shot on Date Y in the Town of Z. A deadly battle was fought on Bridge A, near City B. The morgue of City Q became inundated today with R number of corpses, of which S number were children. Leader G proclaimed that Leader H was a scoundrel and a menace; Leader H called for the execution of Leader G.

The danger in covering a war was not in losing one's head getting the story wrong; it was in keeping your head down low enough and long enough to get it right.

My cell phone rang, blinking, "HOME."

"Mommy?" said Daisy, a strange muffled whimper hovering in the background. When had she learned my cell phone number by heart? I pictured Irma lying prostrate on the ground, felled by a container of LEGOs.

"Yes, sweetheart. What's going on? Is Irma okay? I hear someone crying."

"That's Tess. Irma's fine."

"Why is your sister crying?"

"Uh, well, don't get mad. She didn't want me to call you, because she thought you'd get mad."

"I won't get mad. Just tell me why's she crying."

"She's crying . . ."—I heard her whisper to Tess, *It's okay, she won't get mad!* I pictured poster paint spilled onto the girls' carpet, a gerbil set loose into the apartment—"about the cupcakes."

I gasped. The cupcakes. Shit. The girls' school had recently switched birthday protocol from cupcakes on the actual birthday itself to cupcakes on the second Friday of the month of the child's birth, or maybe it was the third, I could never keep it straight, which meant the teachers didn't have to deal with sugar-fueled children thirty days out of the year—granted, an intelligent plan—but also one that meant that only the most vigilant parents could ever remember when to bake. "Oh, Daisy, where's your sister right now? Can I talk to her?"

"She's here on your bed. Waiting for you to come home. But she says it's almost bedtime, and it's too late to bake, and now she won't have any treats to bring in for her birthday. Irma told her she could do it, but she screamed no." *It's okay,* I heard her reassure Tess once again. *She's not mad.*

"Oh, Daise. I'm such an idiot. Sweetie, please, put Tess on the phone." I threw the rest of the transcripts into my bag and my plans to sit and read quietly away. I was already halfway out the door by the time Tess got on the phone.

"Mommy? Is that you?" Tess was sniffling, her voice cracking on the last word.

"Yes, pumpkin, it's me."

"Mommy, you forgot—"

"No, Tessie, I didn't forget. I'm coming home right now to bake those cupcakes, and then I'll wake you up early in the morning and we can frost them together before school, okay?" I threw the car in reverse, nearly hitting a pedestrian. "Sorry," I mouthed, holding my hand to my chest. The woman flipped me the bird.

"Okay. Did you get the sprinkles?"

"Sprinkles?"

The driver in front of me slowed down to wait for another car to exit a parking space, and I nearly slammed into him, too. *Keep calm,* I thought to myself. *No point in committing manslaughter over baked goods.*

"Remember? I said I wanted to make them with purple sprinkles? And you said you'd buy them at the store?"

I had no memory of this exchange. Lately this had been happening to me more and more. The girls would be talking to me while I was doing some other activity, and I'd be standing there say, soaping a dish, staring straight back at them, nodding my head as if in rapt attention, but the noise of the water running and the sound of the phone ringing and the din of NPR would blend in with their words, and my mind would wander off to the medical forms I was supposed to have dropped off at the pediatrician's office; to my email inbox crammed full of messages—from other mothers seeking playdates, from a friend of a friend from college hoping to "pick my brain" about a career in TV journalism, from my production assistant from *That's Hot!* who needed to be called back *that night* before our piece on cellulite reduction creams aired—and before I knew it I was agreeing to honor some promise I'd never even mentally deciphered. Purple sprinkles? I'd never even seen such a thing. Red, blue, yellow, and green, sure. But purple?

"Of course I remember, Tessie. And I'm going to stop off at the store . . ." (which store?) ". . . on my way home to get them, okay?"

"With cream cheese frosting, like you promised?"

"Yes, of course, cream cheese frosting. Just like I promised." No. I'm not a mother. I just play one on TV. "Tessie, remind me. What color bottoms were we going to make? Chocolate?"

"No, vanilla. Remember? I told you Vanessa's allergic to chocolate? So everyone has to bring in vanilla?"

"Of course. Vanilla it is. Okay, sweetie, you go to bed now, and before you know it we'll be frosting those cupcakes."

As I sped along the Potomac River to the airport, trying to remember which grocery stores in my neighborhood stayed open late, and of those, which would be most likely to have purple sprinkles and confectioner's sugar for the icing, snow had started to flutter from the sky, first gently, like tiny pieces of confetti in front of my headlights, then more like the second coming of the ice age, in great fluffy, cotton bushelfuls.

All flights out of Reagan National were cancelled. I called Mark at work to tell him I wouldn't be home, that he would have to bake cupcakes and make sure to find purple sprinkles and vanilla bottoms and cream cheese frosting, and he grumbled something about how his data had been massacred by some insidious virus designed by a seventeen-year-old from a tiny town outside Stuttgart, to whom Mark referred, more than once during our conversation, as "that Nazi fuck," before he realized, upon closer examination — or maybe it was just the way I kept saying, "But, but, but . . ." — that I was perhaps more shaken up than him, because I hadn't just lost five months of my work. Oh, no! I was losing something much more valuable: my mind.

"I'll go to Hot 'n Crusty tomorrow and pick up some cupcakes on the way to school," he said. "Don't sweat it."

"Don't sweat it? Will they have vanilla bottoms? And purple sprinkles? *WILL THEY HAVE CREAM CHEESE FROSTING?*"

"No, Lizzie-bean, I can't promise that they will. But they'll have a candle, and her classmates will sing 'Happy Birthday,' and she'll be fine."

"What about Vanessa? Huh? *She can't eat chocolate!*"

"So we'll buy a corn muffin for Vanessa, okay? Calm down. You're blowing this way out of proportion."

"How do you know Vanessa is not allergic to corn, too? Huh? *HOW DO YOU KNOW?*"

"I don't. Now I'm going to hang up the phone, Lizard, okay? And when I hang up the phone, you're going to magically turn back into the woman I married, okay?"

"Don't hang up on me, Mark!"

"I'm hanging up now."

"Mark!"

LATER THAT NIGHT, as I lay in my childhood bed, wearing a pair of flannel pajamas left over from high school, which I found lovingly folded at the foot of my bed by the same hands which had once force-fed me a hot dog ("*Life's full of irony, bubelah. Haven't you learned that by now?*"), I read the final pages of Dr. Sherman's transcripts.

Patient: Adele Cassidy
Date: Monday, October 2, 1972

Note: Patient walked in five minutes late with her two daughters, Lily and April, still wearing the same house-dress and rubber flip-flops and looking even more disheveled than the previous week. The girls, however, were wearing clean clothes and looked relatively well-groomed and well-cared for. The younger one was clutching a rag doll.

DR. SHERMAN: Well, hello, girls. I've heard so much about you. You must be Lily.

LILY: Uh huh.

MRS. CASSIDY: Lily, answer politely, please.

LILY: Yes, Dr. Sherman.

DR. SHERMAN: That's okay, Lily. We're not going to be formal in here. And you must be April. How old are you, dear, six?

APRIL: No. Five and three quarters. My birthday's on Friday.

DR. SHERMAN: Well, happy almost birthday then! What a big girl you are. And who's that little friend in your hands? Does she have a name, your doll?

APRIL: She's not a doll. She's a rag person. And you don't have to speak to me like a baby.

MRS. CASSIDY: April!

APRIL: Well, he doesn't.

DR. SHERMAN: That's okay, Adele. Let her say what she wants. I'm sorry, April. I should not speak to you like a baby, you're right.

APRIL: Can we go now? I don't want to be here.

DR. SHERMAN: Why is that?

APRIL: Because . . . because I'm missing school. A film-strip. On mammals. We're studying them.

DR. SHERMAN: Really? And what are you learning about mammals?

APRIL: That they're just like us. Or, well, sort of like us. They care for their young. Which means they don't just leave them out, you know, in the rain or something, because then the other animals, bigger ones, might eat them. And the mommies all have breasts. I mean milk. They all give their babies milk from their mammaly glands, and the babies grow in the mommy's tummy, just like I did.

DR. SHERMAN: That's a very grown-up thing to know about. Mammary glands and babies growing in tummies.

APRIL: And you know what else? I remember being in my mommy's tummy.

DR. SHERMAN: You do?

APRIL: Yes.

DR. SHERMAN: What was it like?

APRIL: Oh, it was really nice. It was really warm, and there was a lot of light and lots of toys for me to play with, and I swam around all day long. Sometimes my mom would pop her head inside and tickle me, and we'd laugh so much together. Just the two of us, laughing our heads off and splashing in the water. Remember, Mommy? Remember when I was in your tummy and we used to laugh together? Remember?

MRS. CASSIDY: Sure, sweetheart. I remember. *[Patient begins to cry.]*

DR. SHERMAN: It sounds very interesting. But April, aside from missing your mammal filmstrip, which I completely understand—I wouldn't want to miss a filmstrip on mammals either—is there another reason you don't want to be here?

APRIL: I don't want to be here also . . . I don't want to be here also because, because there's nothing wrong with my mommy. She doesn't need a doctor. *[The girl starts to cry.]* She just needs to take a bath and get some peace and quiet, and everything will be fine. She's a good mommy. She makes our beds and gives us food and reads us books at night when she's not too tired. Like *Little House on the Prairie.* Please, if you just tell her to take a bath and get some rest, that's all she needs. And maybe she should stop taking those pills, because they make her tired. And she forgets to take her bath. And she forgets to brush her teeth and read to us. And so she should just stop taking those stupid pills and then she'll take a bath and brush her teeth and we won't have to come here and everything will be fine.

LILY: April!

DR. SHERMAN: Lily, what's wrong with what your sister is saying?

LILY: Mom doesn't have to take a bath if she doesn't want to. She works hard. And she has a lot, a lot of responsibilities. And Daddy never helps. And he makes her do things she doesn't want to do.

DR. SHERMAN: Like what? What things does your father make your mother do that she doesn't want to be doing?

LILY: Like . . . like . . . like putting garlic in his roast beef. She doesn't like garlic. She says it makes her feel sick. But he yells at her if there's no garlic. And ironing his underwear. She says underwear doesn't need to be ironed. You wear it *under* your clothes, so who cares what it looks like?

DR. SHERMAN: And if your mother doesn't iron his underwear, what does he do?

MRS. CASSIDY: Is this really necessary, Dr. Sherman? All this . . . talking . . . with my children . . . is it really necessary? I already told you what happens when my husband gets mad.

DR. SHERMAN: What happens when he gets mad at her, Lily?

LILY: He . . . he . . . Mom, can I say? Mom?

DR. SHERMAN: You do not have to ask your mother for approval for what you can and cannot say. We speak the truth in here. That's what this room is for.

LILY: Mom?

DR. SHERMAN: What, Lily? What does he do?

LILY: He . . . Mom?

DR. SHERMAN: Lily, speak to me.

LILY: Mom?

DR. SHERMAN: What does he do, Lily?

LILY: He hurts her. *[The girl starts to cry.]* Last year he kicked her in the shin. She had to use crutches.

MRS. CASSIDY: That's not true, and you know it, Lily Ann!

DR. SHERMAN: What's not true, Adele? That your husband hurts you or that you were on crutches after he kicked you?

APRIL: Lily's lying. My daddy is a good daddy, and my mommy is a good mommy, and she had crutches because she tripped on the stairs, and I want to go back to school now and see my mammal filmstrip and eat grapes with my friend Lizzie, because she has grapes in her lunch today.

MRS. CASSIDY: I didn't know you like grapes.

APRIL: I switched.

MRS. CASSIDY: Are you happy now, Dr. Sherman?

DR. SHERMAN: I'm going to assume that is a rhetorical question, Mrs. Cassidy.

APRIL: What's a rhetorical?

LILY: Shut up, April! Stop being so stupid.

MRS. CASSIDY: Come on girls, it's time to go. Say good-bye to the doctor.

DR. SHERMAN: We have twenty more minutes left, Mrs. Cassidy.

MRS. CASSIDY: Not on my watch. Come on girls. Say good-bye, and let's go.

LILY: Good-bye, Dr. Sherman.

DR. SHERMAN: Good-bye, Lily.

APRIL: Good-bye, Dr. Sherman.

DR. SHERMAN: Good-bye, April. Good-bye, Mrs. Cassidy. Will I see you next week, at our usual time?

MRS. CASSIDY: I don't know. Let's go girls. Let's get you back to school.

That was the day April "mistook" her mother for her mother's friend, because of the dust from the filmstrip, and I remembered the grapes I brought in, how I'd promised to share them with April, the odd way she looked when she walked into the cafeteria several minutes after the start of lunch. She was still wearing her windbreaker from outside, and her eyes had pink rims around them, and she was clutching an old rag doll with black *x*'s sewn horizontally across her chin for a mouth, which, I couldn't help but notice as she dropped the doll into the trash can next to me, looked as taut and unnatural as April's.

I turned to the final page in the transcript folder, which, unlike the preceding pages, was not typed. Rather, it was handwritten, on lined paper.

**Eleanor, please type ASAP!

Patient: Adele Cassidy
Date: Monday, October 9, 1972

Note: Patient did not show up for her normally scheduled session again. I called her house a half an hour after the appointed time, and she hung up the phone. I called her back immediately, and she said she didn't want to see me anymore, that I should stop calling her, and that she couldn't think straight on the pills so she'd stopped taking them. She blamed the pills for forgetting her daughter's birthday and claimed that since she'd stopped taking them she felt more lucid, more clear about what had to happen in her life for her depression to lift. When I asked her what that thing was, she said she was thinking of making a "big change." I asked if she meant going back to her job or hiring help, but she surprised me and said she was going to leave her husband. I urged her to come in and talk with me about this first, before taking any drastic measures, but she said, very firmly, that she no longer wanted to speak with me, that she would send in the check for the missing session when she got where she was going, but that I should take her off my schedule once and for all. Then she hung up the phone.

Patient: Adele Cassidy
Date: Tuesday, October 24, 1972

Two policemen arrived at my house this afternoon, while I was meeting with another patient. They waited until my session was finished and then walked into my office bearing a check, written out to me, in Adele's handwriting. The police then asked me questions about the patient's treatment, but I had to demur, to their visible frustration, to the laws of doctor-patient confidentiality.

Patient allegedly killed herself and her daughters by means of carbon monoxide poisoning late Sunday night, in the woods near Gaithersburg. According to the police, a suicide note had been found. I asked the police officers if I could take a look at the note. They said no. After they left, I tore up the check.

Attached with a staple to this handwritten page was the same *Washington Post* clips I'd found at the New York Public Library the day after my fall: "Maryland Mother, Children, Found Dead"; "Maryland Mother, Children's Deaths Ruled Suicide, Murder."

I closed the file and switched off the lamp above my head, suddenly remembering the day April came in to school, and her name was on the chalkboard, with a "Happy Birthday" preceding it, an exclamation mark to its right, and there was Miss Martin, at the morning meeting, asking her whether she preferred to hand out her treats during snack or after lunch, to which April had replied, with an overly cheerful smile, "After lunch," hoping, I now understood, to buy herself some more time, her mother a few more hours to do the impossible: wake up, get dressed, bake cupcakes.

CHAPTER 13

ASTRID WAS HUNCHED over clearing the last shovelfuls of snow from the steps of our building when the taxi dropped me off the next day. "Hey, you made it!" she said, leaning on the shovel and brushing a strand of gray hair, which had become loose in her exertions, behind her ear. She was always complaining that she had no time to dye it, no money to plump up the deepening lines striating her forehead, but I think she found a certain sense of pride in letting time's scythe mark her. "We were afraid you'd be snowed in for longer."

"You were, were you?" The taxi driver dumped my lights and camera equipment on a patch of thick ice on the sidewalk and drove off, which made lifting the heavy metal boxes without slipping quite tricky.

"Yes, Mark told me your flight got . . ." Astrid leaned the shovel against the banister and came down to help me. "Here, give me that one." She pointed to the largest of the three boxes.

"Thanks," I said. And we started up the stairs.

I'd first befriended Astrid a few weeks after Mark and I moved in, when she knocked on our door late one night, the color drained from her face, her hand wrapped in thick layers of bloody gauze, to ask if I could come down to her apartment and watch her boys until her husband could get home to relieve me. She'd been chopping tomatoes for a lasagna. The knife had slipped. "Of course, of course!" I'd said at the time. "What time do you expect him home?"

"I'm not sure," she said. She hadn't been able to reach him at his office. This was normal, she explained. When Jim was caught up in his work, nothing could rouse him. Except, as it turned out, one of his clients. And his partner's secretary. And a mother in their sons' preschool.

I went downstairs a lot after she became wise to these after-hour meetings. And when the divorce became finalized, I forced her to go out, even if only to take herself to a movie while Mark and I watched TV in her apartment. This was before my husband and I had children of our own, back when we did things like sitting on a couch together, sharing a bottle of wine.

"Mark called me last night," she now said, her demeanor turning serious, concerned. "He said he had too much work. He couldn't get home. I got upstairs around seven, so you probably owe Irma an extra hour or two."

"Oh, Astrid. I'm so sorry. Did he come home really late?" I was suddenly furious with him for not trying, the one night I was stuck in another state, to get home at a reasonable hour.

"No, I think he walked in around eleven, but Lizzie, you know how I feel about this so let me put it bluntly: it's not me you should be worried about." Astrid—because it took her six years of being deceived to figure out her husband was a liar—became convinced that everyone's spouse was having an affair, whether they knew it or not. I tried explaining to her, on several occasions, that I was 99 percent certain Mark's entanglements were with his data, not a woman, but Astrid said either way, abandonment was abandonment. Something had to give.

"Oh shit," I said, looking at my watch when we'd reached my landing. "What time do you have?"

"2:45," said Astrid.

"I gotta run," I said, quickly thanking Astrid for her help and shoving the equipment in the front door before skipping down the stairs two by two while mentally cursing the American school system for still clinging to the illusion that children were required to get home in time to till the fields. Fifteen minutes later, I was standing in the girls' schoolyard with all the other mothers and nannies and the lone father clutching his *Times* as a shield, all of us bouncing up and down on the balls of our feet to stay warm. "Did you hear about Finn Slater?" one mother said to another. "He fell off the jungle gym at the Diana Ross Playground and broke his arm."

"Oh my God," said the other. "I'm telling my kids to stay off of that thing."

A couple of nannies huddled off in the corner nearby, quietly discussing their friend's dismissal over a box of store-bought pasta. "She tell her employer, 'But I have no time to make the homemade pasta every day.' But does she listen? No!"

The two mothers in front of me stood face to face, the tips of their styluses poised and ready to plunder. "Monday, the nineteenth?"

"No, Chandra has oboe on Mondays. Tuesday the twenty-seventh?"

"No, Sidney's going home with Kira that day. I guess we're looking at March then."

"Fine, March. Wednesday the seventh?"

"She has skating. What about a Saturday morning?"

Tess finally emerged, her face barely visible between her scarf and hat. "Yoo hoo!" I called out. "Over here!" but she kept walking right past me, refusing to take my hand or even look in my direction, her rubber boots clomping through the sidewalk slush in a petulant blur of yellow.

"Hey, wait up, peanut!" I said, scurrying after her. "How were the cupcakes?"

The animals clipped via key chains to her backpack hopped up and down, a chorus of indignant furies, as she pushed her way through the sea of primary-colored knapsacks, and I tossed out the mea culpas. "I'm sorry, Tessie," I kept saying, nearly running to keep up with her. "The airports were all closed; I tried getting home; I wanted to bake them, I did, I really did." But she refused to turn around until the inevitable end of the block, where she knew she could go no further without at least acknowledging my role as her escort across the street, if not through life. "They were good," she finally said, her little chin quivering. "Not as good as the ones you bake, but good." Then she buried her face in my stomach and began to cry.

Tess had arrived in the world dark like me, with chestnut eyes and a somber intensity that sometimes threatened to swallow her. The summer she turned three, I'd taken her on a walk down the beach in Hilton Head, and we'd happened upon an enormous sea turtle, his shell cracked, his head dense with flies. "We have to help him," she'd said, her voice mature and matter-of-fact, her tiny hands attempting to push the inert creature back into the surf. The turtle was already dead, I told her. It was too late to try to save him. Tess threw herself on the stinking carcass and started to weep. "No he's not!" she wailed. "We have to save him!" And I helped her push the rotting remains back into the ocean, a short-term dodge from the issue of mortality which came back to bite me one month later, when I found her leaning over my father's casket clutching a handful of goldfish crackers, shouting, "Wake up, Grandpa! It's time for snack."

"Come on, kiddo," I now said, crouching down, hugging her to me, wiping her cheeks with my thumbs. "How 'bout we go get some hot chocolate at Cafe Lalo?"

She took a few deep breaths and composed herself. "With whipped cream?"

"Definitely."

She slipped her mittened hand in mine and squeezed it tight, a gesture whose emotional pull is never diminished. *This is all there is,* I thought to myself, self-consciously, *This is why we live.*

"Mommy?"

"Yes?"

"What's a dick and a bush?"

The warm, sentimental goo that had spread from my chest to my limbs froze midstream. "Tessie! Who taught you those words?"

"One of the fifth graders," she said. "He told a joke. It went, 'Why are we doomed?' and the answer is, 'Because our country is being run by a dick and a bush.' But I don't get it. What does that mean?"

"Oh, sweetie. They're just talking about *Dick* Cheney, the vice president, and George *Bush*, the president."

"So why is that funny?"

"Because . . ." I sighed. We were just entering the cafe, waiting to be seated. I leaned over and whispered in her ear. "Because they're bad words for private parts, too, which people sometimes use as insults. Don't repeat that joke to your friends or teachers, okay? It's not nice."

Tess covered her mouth so that all I could see were her big brown eyes bugged out in amusement and shame. "I'm sorry."

"It's not your fault. You heard a joke. When I was your age, we used to have this little joke we did on paper about President Nixon."

"Who's he?" she asked.

I signaled to the hostess that we wanted to be seated. "He was a Dick, too."

Over hot chocolate, she proposed her newest solution to ending the war—"They could just play chess!"—and fretted over the fate of baby Knut, the German polar bear cub whose mother had abandoned him. "He'll be fine," I said. "He's got a wonderful zookeeper taking care of him."

"Mom. He's a *man*," she said. Then she shook her head in exasperation at my ignorance.

"What? Men can take care of babies," I said, but Tess had already moved on to the story of her friend Asher, who got his head stuck in his sister's dollhouse, when my cell phone went off.

"I can meet you tomorrow morning," said Lenny Morton, in lieu of hello. "Will that work?" He was sorry about the delay in returning my call. He was in a mild state of shock. He hadn't thought about Adele Cassidy for more than, god, what was it now, thirty-five years? "A whole lifetime ago," he said. In the intervening decades, or so I'd learned with a bit of research, he'd built a small empire for himself, Morton's Gyms, with branches in Chelsea, Tribeca, the West Village, and East Hampton, catering to a largely gay, affluent clientele. And though he was not willing to sit for an on-camera interview—his PR rep for Morton's Gyms was adamant on this point—he was more than happy to tell me everything he remembered if it would help. We made a plan to meet for breakfast the next morning.

"Who was that?" Tess asked, when I hung up the phone.

"A man I'm going to talk to tomorrow when you're in school,"

I said, wanting to get back to the story of Asher's head in the dollhouse.

Tess was building little teepees out of sugar packets. She paused for a moment, seemingly focused on the structural exigencies of engineering. "Are you and Daddy going to get a divorce?"

"Tessie," I took her hands in mine. "What's with you today? Why would you ask that?"

Now she finally looked me in the eye. "Remember the night you came in to sleep with me? And you told me you had a bad dream about monsters?" Her chin began to quiver for the second time that day. "You didn't really have a bad dream, did you?"

"Of course I . . ." I picked up the fallen sugar packets and helped her build the tepee back up again. Clearly, whatever toxins were passing between Mark and me were now seeping into her.

One of my first epiphanies with Dr. Rivers, in fact, was how deeply, as a child, I'd inhaled from the noxious fumes of matrimonial limbo myself, watching my mother seethe and my father play dumb, while they simultaneously passed judgment on all the couples in the neighborhood who were suddenly, like a plague, getting divorced. "Destroying those poor children's psyches," my father would say, shaking his head, standing up from the table without clearing a dish. "It's just not right." I told Dr. Rivers that I'd always wondered whether my psyche might have been happier had my parents actually admitted defeat; that it might have been a relief, at least in a certain sense, to have shuttled between two relatively peaceful homes in lieu of being trapped between warring factions in one.

"It might well have been," said the doctor. "But let's concentrate on what actually *was*."

I decided to change tacks with my daughter, to stop under-estimating her powers of perception. She was six, yes. But I'd been six when April had died, and I could remember what that felt like, to be lied to. "You're right, Tess," I said. "I didn't really have a bad dream. I just didn't want you to worry, okay? So I kind of . . . fibbed. To protect you. Which was wrong. And I'm sorry. Come here." I motioned with my arms for her to join me on my side of the table. She slid off her chair, ducked under the table, and bored her little body into mine. "Look. Most mom-mies and daddies, at some point in their relationship, will fight with one another. Okay? This is normal. It doesn't mean that Daddy and I are going to get a divorce." I tried to make this last part sound as convincing as possible. "Do you understand?"

She nodded her head into my chest. I could feel her rib cage vibrating, her lungs sucking in short, tiny gulps of air.

"You sure you understand?"

Tess nodded again.

CHAPTER 14

LENNY MORTON MET me the following morning at Caffe Dante, a sun-streaked, clattering spot below his apartment. With his winter tan, full head of dark hair, and biceps ballooning beneath his cashmere sweater, he looked to be a lot closer to forty than to the sixty-odd years I knew he'd traversed. After the requisite pleasantries and introductions and the ordering of tea and scones, I casually asked him if he'd ever had sex with Adele Cassidy. Regardless of her sister's scoffing at such a notion or the articles identifying Lenny as a gay entrepreneur, there'd been something about Adele's denial to her shrink which had struck me as false.

Lenny blushed. "Boy," he said, "you go right for the jugular, don't you?" Now he smiled and bobbed his head back and forth, his fingers tented in a diamond in front of his mouth.

"So you *did* have sex with her?"

"Not exactly." He stared me in the eye, sussing me out. I remained silent, giving him the space he seemed to need to establish trust. "Do you really need to know?"

"No," I said. "But I would *like* to know. I understand it's uncomfortable, though, so—"

"No, it's okay. I get it." Lenny started bobbing back and forth again. Then he took a deep breath, puffed up his cheeks, and blew out the air slowly. "Okay. Full disclosure. We did have, well, it wasn't sex," he said, wrinkling up his nose, "but it was, I guess you could say a moment that was 'sexual in nature.'" (*Bingo*, I thought.) Lenny looked off into the distance and clenched his mouth. "But I couldn't, you know . . . I mean, I still didn't understand that what I was feeling back then wasn't just run of the mill sexual indifference to my ex-wife, or to women in general. That it ran much deeper. Or rather I did understand it but didn't want to admit it to myself. Classic case of closeting, no question about it. Happens all the time, especially back then." He paused again, and bit his lip, and searched once more for the right words. "Anyway, I'm not sure of the exact dates, but one day, after she'd lost all the weight—it was like sixty pounds or something, I mean she really lost a hell of a lot of weight—Adele says to me, she says, 'Lenny, I have to know something. You've been so nice, helping me get in shape, being my friend,' you know, stuff like that, and I have no idea where she's going with this, but I say, 'Well, you've been very nice to me, too, Adele.' She was a good person, really. I know it's hard to believe that, considering . . ." His voice trailed off. "She was depressed, of course, definitely. Could have used a good dose of Prozac, had it existed back then, as well as a more, shall we say, *empathic* husband, if you know what I mean. But you know, at her core, she was good. Kind. And so she says, 'Lenny, I have a hunch about you. I'd like to do a little experiment.' 'What kind of experiment?' I say.

"That's when, all of a sudden, right there in the kitchen, with her girls in the other room watching *Sesame Street* or whatever the hell they were watching, she starts unbuttoning her dress. Just like that. No warning at all. Or if there was a warning, I sure didn't see it coming. She gets all the way down to the last button, lets it drop to the floor, and now she's just standing there in her bra and underwear. 'What are you doing?' I say. I didn't know what else to say. It was just such a shocking thing for her to do. So then she shushes me and unhooks her bra, and now her breasts are staring at me in the face. They're huge, I mean just these massive mounds of flesh, with these gigantic nipples. 'Look at me,' she says. '*Look at me,* Lenny. I did this all for you. I starved myself for you. Can't you even look at me?' But I couldn't. I just kept staring at the floor. But also feeling guilty, right? I don't want her to feel bad about herself, or unattractive, or whatever, because God knows I know better than anyone about her issues of self-esteem, you know, distorted body image, food addiction, the whole nine yards. But I'm stuck. I can't move. I can't speak. I can't do anything, really, except mumble something inane like, 'You look great, Adele. All that work's really paid off.' So then, after about a minute or so of just standing there in her underwear, waiting for me to make a move, she sighs, puts her clothes back on and — this is the craziest thing, I still can't believe she did it — she goes over to the kitchen sink, opens the door of the cabinet underneath it, and pulls out, from one of those plastic cleaning buckets where she stashed it, a copy of *Playgirl* she'd bought specifically for me at some drugstore out in Olney, so no one she knew would see her buying it. She opens it up to the centerfold. Dylan Duke, his name was. I can't believe I still remember that name. 'What about him?' she says. 'How does *he* make you feel?' Well, I know how he makes me feel. I've known it probably since the summer I turned twelve, when I went skinny dipping with my best friend, Ben. So now Adele's standing behind me. She's standing behind me, and I'm between her and the kitchen table, and Dylan Duke is spread out in front of me, just sitting there buck naked on the plastic tablecloth, and Adele reaches from behind and starts, you know, touching me. And she says, 'Now, pretend I'm him. Look at the photo. Pretend I'm him.' And I'm laughing nervously, saying, 'What are you talking about?' trying to deny everything, right, to myself, to her, all the while staring at Dylan Duke and growing stiffer by the minute. But I'm also on the verge of tears, now, too, so I say something like, 'Adele, I think we should stop this, I don't want you to do that,' and she says, 'Of course, of course, I understand. Why don't you go into the bathroom and be by yourself for a little while,' and so I go into the bathroom and sit on the toilet seat, bawling, for like half an hour.

"I finally wash my face and walk back out, and Adele's standing there, chopping shallots for dinner, and she says, 'I had to make sure. I needed to know if you were . . .' Now *she* starts to cry, but she blames it on the shallots.

"'A faggot,' I said. Right out loud. For the first time in my life. Adele just, well, and I know this sounds totally asinine and new-agey, but what the hell: she helped me to speak a simple truth about myself. And I guess I just couldn't believe, when you called yesterday, that the same woman who could do such a thing for me, the most significant thing anyone's ever done for me in my life, would do what she did to herself and to her chil . . ." He fiddled with the salt shaker. "And then, well, it also made perfect sense." Turning his attention now to his tea bag, he ripped it open and dunked it three times into his steaming cup before coiling the string around a teaspoon to squeeze out the excess liquid.

"Why?"

"Because . . ." He paused for a moment, resting his chin on

his palm. "Because as hard as she fought to change her outward appearance, inside she was still a mess. A compassionate
mess, no doubt—which is why I'm sure she convinced herself,
however misguided, that she had to take her daughters with
her—but a big fat mess nevertheless."

"Was Adele in love with you?" I asked.

"Was she in love with me?" He took a sip of his tea and
sighed. "No. Or maybe yes. Yeah, I think she might have been.
In her own way, right? She never came out and said so, at least
blatantly, but yes, I think she was. At the time—or at least
before that particular morning, I would have said no way, absolutely not, we're just friends." He smiled wearily. "Of course
I would have also insisted back then that I was straight. And at
peace with my choices. And the apple of my father's eye." He
shook his head. "Anyway, I think what it came down to, really,
was that I listened to her. I listened to her, and I didn't interrupt. I actually enjoyed her company. A lot. I was in a pretty sad
state myself back then, you know, newly divorced, sexually confused, totally adrift, and in some ways it was avoidance, I know,
focusing all of my energy on trying to fix someone else, but it
was also helpful, if only to make me realize that no problem
is insurmountable. But Adele's husband, he sensed something
wasn't right. That's why . . . what was his name again? Jesus, I
can't believe I can't remember his—"

"Shep."

"Shep. Right. Of course. The man bashes my head into his
kitchen floor, and I can't remember his name, but Dylan Duke,
Stiffyboy, *his* name I remember. Anyway, that's why *Shepherd*—
talk about a fairy name, sheesh!—attacked me one day. He
knew she had feelings for me that went beyond the platonic.
And I guess he supposed—wrongly, of course—that I had
those same kind of feelings for her."

I left Lenny at the cafe and was about to descend into the subway when my cell phone began to vibrate in my front pocket. I glanced down at the caller ID, an unusually long string of numbers beginning with 39, international code for Italy. My pulse quickened. My fingertips grew warm. "*Mon Eliza!*" said the voice, deep and throaty, tinged with a smoker's rasp. In the background blared a distinctly American-style siren.

"Renzo," I said. "Where are you?"

CHAPTER 15

I SAW HIS GAUNT figure leaning up against the plate glass window of B&H Photo, blowing smoke rings from a thin cigar, held between forefinger and thumb, each perfect circle stretching into an oval before disintegrating into the frigid air. "What take you so long?" he said, shivering. The words were spoken calmly, without reproach, but he wasn't smiling.

"That's a joke, right? I got here as fast as I could." Barely fifteen minutes had passed between Renzo's call and the three short stops on the C train to Thirty-fourth Street.

His face melted, his trademark tabula rasa replaced by a sly grin. "Yes, of course, it was joke." His once boyish eyes had spawned deep crows feet along their edges, tiny switch brooms stretching all the way to his temples, while the eyes themselves had grown wetter, calmer, more amused, making his face seem both harder and softer than the frayed mental snapshot I'd been carrying around for so many years. "But also not. I mean what take you so long, in bigger sense." He stubbed out the remainder of his cigar on the side of the building and placed it in his breast pocket for future use.

"What's that supposed to mean?"

He ushered me into the store and took his place in line behind the other customers awaiting their turn to hand over their knapsacks to the Hasid manning the bag check. "It means, well, *come si dice . . .*" He stared up at the green baskets chugging along the ceiling-mounted tracks. "I keep wondering, all these years, when it is you will come back to life." His eyes met mine.

"To life?" I held my palms out in front of my breathing, conscious self. "Uh, in case you haven't noticed, Renzo, I'm not dead."

"I know that. I mean this life. Real life." He gestured toward the photographers hustling in and around the store, the two in front of us discussing the relative merits of the various Mac computers for transmitting pictures, the two behind us trading stories of auto-focus lenses clogged with sand. The atmosphere felt almost festive, the air humming with invisible balloons. "Bernie tell me you go with me to Baghdad, no? This is good. This is what I am talking about."

I nearly laughed. "Renzo, first of all, I told Bernie I'd think about it. Not that I'd definitely come. Second of all, you may be surprised to hear this . . ." — I dropped to a sotto voce — ". . . but not everyone would define 'real life' as choosing to work in constant proximity to death."

"Yes, but they would be wrong," he whispered, loudly, back. "Just one ticket is fine," said Renzo, grabbing my backpack off my shoulder and handing it to the Hasid along with his own. As if we hadn't just spent the past decade apart, living our separate lives. Carrying separate backpacks.

"Maybe," I said. "But most people are just happier, I guess, not thinking about it all the time. Or seeing it up close. All the time." Now I addressed the security guard. "Actually, make that two tickets, please."

"But what else is there?" said Renzo.

The man handed us two claim tags. "Thank you," said Renzo, but before he could stick both of the laminated numbers into his back pocket, I grabbed mine.

"Besides death?" I said.

"Yes."

"Oh, come on, Renzo. *Life,* for one."

"Semantics." He waved his hand dismissively and made his way past the flat screen TVs and iPod displays toward the back of the store, in the direction of the camera equipment.

"Look," I said, nearly running to keep up with him, "can we switch topics? You're pissing me off already, and I just got here."

"Okay, okay," he said, his face breaking into another mischievous grin. He loved to provoke, both in pictures and in life. I'd forgotten how simultaneously frustrating—and exhilarating— that could be.

Once, when we were in Rome, I'd invited him out for drinks with an old roommate of mine from college, passing through Italy on her way to Namibia to work for the Peace Corps. By the end of the evening, he had Maggie in tears, after he rolled his eyes at her claims of being motivated purely by selflessness. "Any halfway intelligent fifteen-year-old can tell you there are no selfless acts in life," he finally snapped.

"You're just so totally wrong," Maggie replied.

To which Renzo replied, after lighting a cigarette, and taking a seemingly endless puff on it, "Think what you want. Tell everyone you know you're doing this job to save people. But I tell you that in fact you have as much if not more to gain from digging all those sewers than the people who will be shitting in them. You think Mother Teresa's selfless? I meet her. I take many pictures of her. Two minutes before the shoot, she is yelling at one of her staff, calling her stupid, and shooing away the children around her, like little fleas. Then the camera comes out of my bag and, poof, she make her face of pity and put her hands on the head of a young, how you say, leper. I sell this picture many times. Everybody want this picture for their magazine and their *journal* and their *film documentaire*. But it is a lie. Just a convenient lie."

"But every picture's a lie," I'd said, trying to steer the conversation in a different direction. "As Susan Sontag wrote—"

"I know what she write," Renzo said, cutting me off. He stared at Maggie—who wound up parlaying her experience building primitive latrines in Namibia into a job in emerging markets at Bear Stearns—accusatorily. "I read that book. And many others. But some lies are more truthful than others."

"Okay, I'm sorry," he now said, leading us into another line to wait for one of the many green-vested equipment salesmen behind the counter. "Let's start again. Hello, Elizabeth. How are you?" He pronounced the words exaggeratedly, like a student of English learning the first dialogue in the textbook.

"I. Am. Fine. Thank you. Very. Much. And. You?"

"I am very well, thank you." He smiled. Then he leaned over to kiss me, gently, on the cheek. "It is good to see you."

My skin tingled at the point of contact. "It's good to see you, too," I said. "I'm glad you called." Then, noticing the sign at the front of the line, I said, "I think we're in the wrong line. That says medium and large format cameras. You want digital, don't you?"

"No. I want to buy a Linhof."

"A Linhof?" I knew the kind of vivid panoramas such large

format cameras were capable of producing. Thomas Struth had taken his into museums, forests, parking lots, and urban streetscapes and had produced some of the more arresting images of the mundane I'd ever seen. But why Renzo would want one to cover Iraq, especially if *Newsworld,* as I'd heard, had gone completely digital, was a mystery. "What for?"

"My Deardorf is too heavy."

"Too heavy for what?"

"I am tired of journalism," he said. "I want to make art. So, for this I need a lighter camera."

Now I was totally confused. "So wait, you're *not* going back to Iraq? But Bernie said —"

"No, of course I'm going back to Iraq. Where else would I go?" He shook his head at the absurdity of the thought. Of his missing a war. "It is just that I refuse to shoot the sentimental bullshit anymore. No more close-ups of the crying widows and the bleeding soldiers and the little child with the shrapnel stuck into the skin on his face in the hospital bed. We have seen these pictures too many times, in too many places. They have become meaningless. I am much more interested in the translation of this experience into something else, in the, how do you say in English this word, *recul?*"

"Stepping back."

"Yes. Stepping back."

"I don't understand."

"Like Matthew Brady, only color and further back. You know Matthew Brady?" Of course I did — Matthew Brady was the first real combat photographer, lugging his heavy glass plates and camera equipment through the bog of the American Civil War. "Anyway, I will show you. During lunch. I have some pictures I take with the Deardorf back in the apartment I borrow. It is just around the corner. I cook you lunch, yes? I make fish soup last night when I get in from Rome. We heat it up. You like fish soup still, no?" One night when we were in Tel Aviv, while I was busy filing a story, Renzo had gone out to the local fishmonger's to gather the ingredients to make his mother's famous *zuppa di pesce*. At the time he'd claimed it was the only dish he knew how to cook, but over the years we'd traveled together, I'd seen him create unbelievable concoctions out of the barest bones. He once took a packet of dried pea soup, mixed it with water, powdered milk, and half an onion he'd rescued from the trash, and made us two bowlfuls of green penne that rivaled anything I'd eaten in a three-star restaurant.

"Of course," I said, "I love your fish soup," recalling, with shocking clarity, the slow way he'd undressed me after we'd eaten it.

A man in his mid-twenties, lithe and leathered, strode up next to us. His sun-bleached hair brushed the top of his jacket, which was covered with a dozen pockets, one of which held an iPod whose earphones he was now removing, revealing the tinny bass of a rap song. On his shoulder hung a large digital Canon, along with a well-worn Domke camera bag. "What the . . . ?" He slapped Renzo's back and nodded his head up and down in recognition. "Renzo fucking D'Aubigny! How the hell are you? I didn't know you were in town! Dude, you should have called! I was out drinking with Anton last night. We closed the place down."

"I just got here," said Renzo, politely. "So I do not call anyone yet but my old friend here, Elizabeth. Elizabeth, this is Phipps. I share once with him a house in Tikrit."

Phipps nodded perfunctorily at me before turning his attention back to Renzo. "Dude, we fucking owned that story." He held up his hand as if to slap Renzo a high five, but Renzo looked at him blankly. "So when are you heading back, in time for the anniversary?"

"I'm not sure," said Renzo.

"You'll stay at the al Hamra again?"

"I do not know yet." Both lies: Bernie had told me that Renzo had booked two rooms at the al Hamra beginning one week before the anniversary of the war.

"Well, if you do stay there, I call first dibs on your extra bed. Anton, that little fuck, he got an assignment from *Time* while he was here, can you believe it? God knows which editor he had to ball to get one, but he got one. He leaves the day after tomorrow."

"This is fortunate for him." Renzo was trying to smile but visibly cringing. He kept looking over his shoulder to see how close we were getting to the front of the line.

"I might have an assignment from *Der Spiegel*," said Phipps, "but I won't know until next week." He was reminding me more and more of a young Labrador retriever: panting, salivating, wagging his big, hairy tail in a too-tight space and knocking everything down. "Hey, you want to join us for dinner tonight? We're all meeting up—Anton, me, Jonesie, Blake—at that place I took you last year, remember it was—"

"Next," the man at the camera counter shouted.

"Sorry," said Renzo, "but it is our turn. I see you soon in Baghdad, yes, *inshallah*."

"*In*-fucking-*shallah*," said Phipps, "Be cool, my man, be cool."

"You be cool, too," said Renzo, speaking the words robotically. He leaned over to me as we walked to the counter and whispered, "You see? This is why I need you to come with me. All of the young ones these days, they think they are Rambo. *Ça m'ennui*."

"Can I help you?" The man in the yarmulke said as he put away a Hasselblad.

"Yes, please," said Renzo. "I would like to purchase a Linhof."

WE LEFT B&H a little less than an hour later, carting the new camera and two hundred rolls of film and an ultralight tripod. "Where are you staying?" I asked Renzo, as we made our way down Ninth Avenue, and he explained that his friend Simon, a Reuters photographer who'd been holed up in Baghdad since the start of the war, had told him he could stay in his apartment on West Twenty-ninth Street whenever he pleased. The owner of the deli downstairs kept an extra set of keys for any of Simon's colleagues passing through. All Renzo had to do was to say the secret password—"f-stop"—and ask for them.

I could already picture the apartment: A single room, facing a brick wall. A futon on a bare floor. A halogen lamp. Photography books stacked in one corner, a battered file cabinet in another. A stack of framed sixteen-by-twenty-inch exhibition photos pushed up against one wall, to be dealt with at some nebulous but never-to-be-reached point in the future. A makeshift kitchen area, furnished with a hot plate, a waist-high refrigerator covered in fake wood-grain, a toaster oven, a set of mismatched plates. A bathroom taken over by an enlarger and several half-used bottles of chemicals, an empty toilet-paper holder. A table with a lightbox. A sagging couch either rescued from the sidewalk or pushed home on a dolly from the Salvation Army. A metal desk stacked with unopened mail, a giant iMac, a half dozen LaCie hard drives, an aerosol can of Dust-Off. And somewhere on the floor an Afghan rug, carted home like a bison over Simon's shoulder after his last trip to Kabul.

"So, here we are," said Renzo, jiggling his keys into the various ancient-looking locks to get them to unlatch, and I saw that

I was right about nearly everything except the color of the squat refrigerator (it was olive green.) "It is not the Chez Raton," Renzo continued, invoking the French argot for Sheraton—"Chez Raton": *at the rat's house,* literally—a double whammy of an insult, both to Americans, for building such hotels, and to North African immigrants, for being the rats infesting them. "But it is *confortable.*"

No, I thought. *It is not comfortable. It is dust-covered and lonely, and it is exactly how I would have wound up living, minus the photo equipment, had I stayed on this path.* My apartment wasn't much larger—and with four of us occupying it, it could feel much smaller—but it was filled with color and light, with children's drawings and soft places to sleep. On the other hand, what it had recently lacked in warmth could have filled a room—was now filling, in fact, this cavernous space—from the moment Renzo had shut the door behind us: a molecular charge, ricocheting off our skin, of tension and possibility.

While Renzo heated up the soup, I found a sponge under the sink and got to work wiping down what I could. Then I ran the bowls and spoons under some hot water with soap, scrubbed the grit out of two mugs, filled them with tap water and ice, and unearthed a couple of dish towels for napkins. The kitchen area, if one could even call it that, was an afterthought of a nook, which meant Renzo and I kept bumping into one another, and each time this happened, a dull ache of need, of which I'd been previously oblivious, grew more acute.

We sat down to eat. The card table which served as the dining area was set back into the darkest corner of the room, so Renzo brought over one of the clamp-on lamps, clipping it to the back of his metal chair and bouncing it off the wall behind him so we could see our food. "I forgot the wine," he said, returning with a bottle of Chianti he'd bought duty free at the airport. He uncorked it with his Swiss Army knife, took a nice, big swig, and handed it off to me to do the same. And thus the bottle passed back and forth between us, along with the various narratives of our lives, while the briny broth warmed my tongue and filled my stomach. I stared at the dusty cone of light behind my ex-lover's head, then at the angles of Renzo's face, made more linear by the bounced shafts, then at his long, delicate fingers curled around a fifty-cent spoon. The whole scene felt at once both familiar and foreign. Familiar, because we'd spent many long nights thus, eating in borrowed rooms, often with just a flashlight wedged between us for illumination; foreign because it had been almost a decade since our last real discussion, on the floor of an abandoned house near Djakovica, on the darkest night of my life.

CHAPTER 16

IT WAS EARLY 1999, my last trip to the Balkans, my last story with Renzo. Mark and I were already married by then, and I was already carrying a small cellular entity that would become, a few months later, our daughter Daisy. "Don't go," Mark had said, the morning of my flight, but I'd wanted to prove to him—to myself—that having a child would change nothing about our lives. "Don't be silly," I'd replied. "I'll be fine."

Renzo and I were driving along the outskirts of Djakovica, a Kosovar Albanian enclave where, according to British and American intelligence, the Serbians had set up a rape camp. This was after the NATO air strikes, and I was trying to ascertain the veracity of these reports, which some were claiming to have been politically timed to deflect attention away from civilian casualties.

A light rain was falling, Renzo was at the wheel, and I was navigating with various maps of the region, whose borders, though drawn less than a year earlier, were already out of date. "I think we have to turn left up here," I said, sending us up a steep, wooded hill. But it seemed to veer away from the town, rather than toward it.

"Are you sure?" said Renzo. He pulled the car over next to a patch of evergreens and flipped on his hazard lights.

"I thought this was the right way . . ." I said, trying to talk and think quickly over the metronomic slap of the wipers. Though I was uncertain about the existence of the particular rape camp in question, both Renzo and I were well aware of what the Serbs were capable of doing to the contents of an idling car. Back in Bosnia a few years earlier, an Italian journalist we knew had been murdered, along with two of his colleagues, by a band of thugs known as the Fish-Head Gang, who terrorized motorists along the route between Gornji Vakuf and Vitez. Others had had their cars, their equipment, even their shoes stolen off their feet.

Renzo was still studying the map, his hand resting on the clutch, when they suddenly appeared: eight heavily armed Serbs, in ragged uniforms with three-day-old stubble and Kalashnikovs slung over their shoulders.

"Oh fuck," I said, my heart shooting up into my larynx.

"*Calmati,*" said Renzo.

Three of them, reeking of alcohol and stale sweat, held guns to our heads, forced us into the backseat, and drove us, rifles now dug into our ribs, a couple of miles north to an abandoned house in the woods, where we were joined by the others, who'd followed behind in a sputtering Yugo. Shouting wildly, arguing, it seemed, over what to do with us, they wound up pushing us into the house and tying Renzo, with the scraps of an old sheet, to a chair. Me they shoved into a corner, guarded by the short one, his gut hanging out over his pants. Their apparent leader, a redwood of a man with matted blond hair, took the butt of his rifle and banged it into Renzo's forehead, slashing a bloody gash between his eyes that would leave a permanent scar and deprive him, over the course of the next hour, of liters and liters of blood, which poured in stripes down his nose and cheeks. "Stop it!" I screamed, which made the men laugh.

Seeing the butt of the rifle poised for a second strike and judging my overweight warden to be slow and weak, I slipped out from behind him and ran over to try to protect Renzo, only to be tackled halfway by two of the larger men, who threw me on the floor and dug their knees into my spine. I breathed in the dust, tasted the particles of mica on my tongue.

"You!" the redwood shouted to Renzo. "American scum! Spy!" He struck him again, this time in the ribs, then kicked him, repeatedly, in the gut.

"He's not American," I kept repeating. "Or a spy. Please let us go."

The leader shouted something to the men, which I only understood in context, once I felt myself being flipped over onto my back, my arms pinned behind me by one man, my belt unbuckled, roughly, by another.

"No!" I shouted.

"No!" Renzo said, "Stop that!" but by then another man — he was dark, with a face ravaged by the deep craters of childhood acne — was already straddled above me, his pants pulled down to his knees.

"Please!" I now begged. "Don't do that!"

Renzo was cursing in both French and Italian, trying to stand up with the chair still attached to his body. He made it three steps closer to me before falling over onto his side.

The leader, whose men I heard addressing him as Vasa, stared down at Renzo, a stranded turtle, then at me and the kneeling crater-face, who was now reaching to pull down his stained underwear. Meanwhile, the rest of the men lit cigarettes, standing around us like an audience outside the theater, waiting for the second act to begin.

"Please," Renzo repeated. "I beg you. I am the spy, okay? Not her. No spy."

"Please . . ." I was crying now. "Please don't."

Vasa smiled tentatively: behind his eyes, a new plan. He whispered in the ear of the crater-face, which caused the latter to pull up his pants and step aside. Then Vasa knelt down over Renzo and untied him. That's when I allowed myself to believe we'd make it out okay, or at least without further incident. The men had our car, our equipment, our clothes, all of our cash. Surely they could now let us go. But just as I was mentally trying to figure out how that would happen—we'd have to walk into town and hitch a ride or, because of the darkening hour, find a nearby house in which to hide for the night—Vasa pulled Renzo to his feet.

"Okay. You do it."

Renzo stared back at him, confused. "Do what?"

"You . . ." He poked his finger into Renzo's blood-stained chest. "Do sex . . ." He made two fists and pumped his elbows back, his hips forward. "To her!" He pointed down on the floor at me.

"Are you crazy?"

"No," I begged. "Please."

Vasa hit Renzo again with the butt of his rifle. "You do sex. To her! Now! Like American film. XXX." Then he grabbed him by the hair and dragged him to where I lay, still immobilized. "You!" he shouted again, spit flying. He pushed Renzo to his knees and kicked him in the back. "Do sex!" As Renzo fell over, grabbing his back in pain, Vasa started laughing, which made his minions crack up as well. Then, taking a sudden dislike to the cacophony of voices, he removed a small revolver from his pocket and shot it into the roof right above us. The room became silent. So silent you could hear my syncopated gasps, the floor creaking, the tiny bits of plaster fluttering down from the ceiling.

"Renzo," I said to him, the tears flowing freely now, "*Fai quel che ti dicono di fare. Non preoccuparti per me. Cerchiamo solo di uscire di qui.*" Just do what they say. I'll be okay. Let's just get through this.

"*No!*" Renzo snapped. "*E'inumano!*" It's inhuman.

Vasa held the revolver to Renzo's head. "You. Do. Sex! To her!" he said once again. He cocked the trigger to make his point clearer. "Or . . ." he made a show of unbuckling his belt ". . . I do it."

"Renzo, please!" I said now in English, my voice frantic, pleading. "Just do what he says." My hands, still held tight by the man behind me, were starting to lose feeling from the wrist up. "We'll be okay. I promise . . ." I said, trying to convince myself.

Renzo closed his eyes and breathed deeply. Then he turned to face his captor. "If I do this to her, you *NOT* do it, yes?" His face was emotionless, stone. "We make deal, yes? No one but me, yes? Deal?"

Vasa smirked. "Deal." He motioned with his eyes for the man holding my arms behind me to release his grip. Then, gun still in hand, he yanked off Renzo's jeans, revealing a penis that hung down as flaccid as the ear of a basset hound, the sight of which caused Vasa to laugh. With his right hand he pointed the gun at Renzo's crotch and started to yell, his face growing bright pink with the effort. "Do sex now! Like American film. XXX. Now!"

"Okay, okay!" Renzo said. "Stop yelling. I can't just do, like that!"

So Vasa grabbed Renzo's penis in one hand, the back of my head in the other, and shoved the two parts of us together. "Make hard!" he said.

The gun was now pointing at my skull. I did as I was told, my mouth moving up and down along Renzo's still-jowly flesh, which caved and folded in on itself each time it reached the back of my throat. "Renzo, please," I said, coming up for air and crying. "Just fake it. Pretend if you have to."

"I cannot pretend!" said Renzo. "This is insane . . ." His entire body, except for the one part that needed to be, had turned tense and stiff.

"Of course it's insane. Let's just get through this." I'd been to a live sex show in Bangkok once, the couple stationed on a raised translucent platform above us, the woman's rear squashed flat into a bifurcated heart, the man's sweat falling in tiny splats onto the scratched Lucite, like rain against a windshield. From either this sight or from the *tom ka gai* I'd slurped down earlier—it was impossible to say—I'd spent the rest of the night retching.

I lowered my voice to an intimate whisper. "Imagine we're actors, on a stage. Or all alone, like we used to be. Remember that? Focus on that. Please . . ." If Renzo were unable to perform his duties, how many members of our watchful audience—laughing, pointing, flicking their ashes onto Renzo's naked backside—would relieve him of them?

"Okay," he said, the blood on his face now close enough to drip onto mine. And with his lips held together between his teeth, he climbed on top of me and simulated the act as best he could, moving his hips, squeezing his gluteal muscles, even making soft moans to avert the attention away from the protuberance hanging lifeless between his legs.

"No no *no!*" Vasa yelled, enraged by the performance. "You fuck her. Like man! Like man. Watch!" He pulled Renzo off of me and literally threw him into the wall, screaming something in Serbo-Croatian before spitting into his face.

"Don't touch her!" Renzo said, on the verge of tears, his hands held over his groin in shame. "We had a deal!"

"Yes, and you break it," said Vasa, as if scolding a child, first wagging his forefinger in disapproval, then making the same deflating motion with it as before.

"No. Please!" I screamed. "Please!"

"*Elle est pleine!*" screeched Renzo, in a last-ditch effort for leniency. "*Vous comprenez? Enceinte!*" He mimed the orb of a pregnant belly with his hands. As if uttering this fact in the authoritarian tongue of his father could actually sway these men one way or the other.

Afterwards, while Vasa, then the crater-face, took their turns demonstrating, with my newly ripe body, their versions of fucking like a man, while I wailed and kicked and felt myself transmogrifying down the Mohs' scale first to gypsum, then to quartz, then into a solid slab of industrial-grade diamond, four of the others took Renzo outside, into the cold night air, where they made him lean with his head against the side of the house and began to douse him, continually, with a garden hose.

The next morning, making our way on foot back into town, Renzo and I made a pact: we would keep the incident between us. For him, the humiliation was too great, the memory of his ineptitude too painful. "They would have done it anyway," I kept assuring him. "Stop beating yourself up."

For me, as usual, it just felt easier to try to erase it.

CHAPTER 17

"Wow," I SAID, finishing up the last spoonful of my soup, "that was excellent. Where'd you buy the fish?" *Do you ever think about that night? That awful night, when both of us pretended to sleep, you with your teeth chattering, forehead bleeding, me getting up every ten minutes to try to clean myself off?*

"Just down Ninth Avenue. Chelsea Market it is called? Simon beam for me this address into my Treo." Renzo downed the water in his mug and filled it up halfway with wine. Then he did the same to mine.

"Hey!" I said, laughing, "I was still drinking that." *And yet Daisy came out fine in the end. More than fine: my happy child, the spitting image of her father.*

"Drink the wine. It is better for you," he said.

"Better for me or better for you?" I said. The words reverberated in the air, a gauntlet's echo. Though I hadn't meant to throw it down.

"Better for both of us," he answered, and from his tone and the ensuing silence and the way he'd leaned his body forward and was staring at my face, unblinkingly, I could tell he'd met me there, in no-man's-land, awaiting further command: the tiniest gesture, the slightest of openings.

"Renzo, listen, actually I shouldn't, I mean I've never . . ." I couldn't even say the words: *I've never cheated on my husband.*

"Shhh." Renzo placed his index finger on my lips. "No need to speak about any of this." And like that the moment was over, both of us safely back behind each of our fences. He pushed his chair away from the table and grabbed the bowls to clear them.

We cleaned up the dishes together, falling back reflexively into our old formations: me at the sink, Renzo clearing and wiping and sweeping. And as we stood there with the water running, the broom swishing, the rhythm and choreography of our two-step ingrained, Renzo rattled on about the plans he'd made: the driver and armed bodyguards he'd hired for us; the amount of cash we would need to pay them daily; the contacts we should call, once we'd arrived; the satellite phones we would need to procure from Bernie's assistant. "Let's not talk about a 'we' yet," I said. "I told Bernie I'd decide by this Friday, but I haven't even had the chance to discuss it yet with Mark. Theoretically, I'd like to go, but . . ."

"Don't worry," said Renzo. "The war is not going away anytime soon. You still have time."

And even when it does go away, I thought, *it won't, really.* All that blood, all those bodies: they never lie dormant. What kind of revenge would this one exact? Another building? A whole city? An entire planet, going up in flames? *Did you know I still dream about those men who raped me, sometimes snipping off their penises with a pair of garden shears, sometimes simply ripping their heads from their necks with my bare hands?* Revenge! It's built into our RAM just as surely as hunger. "Hey, can I see those photos you were telling me about?"

Renzo dried his hands on a dish towel and planted a kiss on my forehead. "Of course, *mon Eliza*."

"Hey." I crossed my arms over my chest. "I'm not *your* Eliza anymore. Nor will I be, okay? Let's get that straight."

He laughed. "How is—*comment il s'appelle*—Mark?" Then he walked over to his suitcase to retrieve the photos.

Aside from when he's unwittingly recreating that very scene of torture? "He's fine. Everything's good." *I still haven't told him, you know. It's been eight years, and I still don't have the words for it.* "How's that girlfriend of yours?" I wondered if he'd told her, if he'd been braver than me. Or would that moment stay between us forever, binding us to one another just as surely as the *ketubah* in my closet. Bernie had told me that Renzo had recently moved in with a woman named Paloma, a young gallery owner who'd exhibited his most recent show in Rome. If true, it would have been the first time, since leaving his parents' home, he'd ever shared his living quarters with another living creature. Pets included.

"Pregnant," he said, with no more or less sentiment than if he'd said *good*. "Due in a month." He held a large portfolio in his hands which he carried over to the couch. "Come, sit." He patted the space next to him.

"Pregnant?" I walked over to the couch and sat down. "Bernie didn't tell me *that*. Renzo, that's so . . . so optimistic of you. But wait. If she's due in a month, what are you doing going to Iraq?"

"What I always do. She know that. The real question is what are *you* doing going to Iraq?"

"What am *I* doing?" I could feel the blood rising up the back of my neck, stopping just north of the scalp line. "For Christ's sake, Renzo, you're the one who told Bernie to give me the assignment!"

"Yes, this is true." His face broke into a smile. "But I do not think you will actually take it."

"Stop smiling. It's not funny. This is my life we're talking about. If you didn't think I would come, then why the hell did you even—"

"Why not? I will not work with Carl. Jonesie's too old. The young ones, these days, well, you see that *gosse* at B&H. They are foolish. They take too much risks. At worst, you say no. At best, you come. Nothing to lose by asking, *non*?" He pulled out a cigarette and lit it.

"We can smoke in here?"

"What do you think?" Again, a smile crept over his face. "This may be the Fascist Republic of America, *mi amore,* but here we are in the international no-fly zone of chez Simon." He blew out a puff of smoke, aiming it toward the crack in the window to his right. "So? You still have not answered. Why is it you are thinking of going with me? Last time we speak, after the first baby, you say your career is finish. What makes the change?"

"What makes the change? First of all, I never said my career is finished. I said my career *covering war* was finished. And second of all, god, your English has really gone down the toilet since we were together. It's not 'What makes the change?' but 'What made you change your—'" I looked at my watch. 1:05 PM. Irma would be picking up the girls from school that afternoon; I had another four hours before I had to take Daisy to her piano lesson; my editing could wait. "—mind. Pass me one of those."

"I thought you quit."

"I did." And as I sucked on the cigarette, filling my throat, then my lungs with the ammonium-tinged heat, I told him about producing segments on nail polish to cover the rent, about the feelings of shame at pouring so much time and effort into fluff. I missed the excitement of my old job, I said, but not the physical danger; I just hadn't been able to figure out a way to have one without the other. On a more positive note, I said, there was April's story, the documentary I was working on, but A) I hadn't been able to secure funding aside from that one day of shooting, and B) I realized that what I really wanted to know about the story was unknowable. Then I turned to the broken fragments of my inner life: the bouts of depression; the fainting episodes; my crumbling marriage.

"But before, just ten minutes ago, you say everything is fine." He stubbed out his cigarette and pulled the half-used cigar out of his breast pocket.

"Well what was I supposed to say? My work sucks, my husband's into S&M, and I can't seem to stay vertical? No one wants to hear that. So I say I'm fine, he's fine, we're all fucking fine!"

"I see," said Renzo, looking suddenly deflated. "I understand now. You want to go to Iraq to escape all this problems."

"No!" I said. I was now smoking my second cigarette and contemplating a third. "I want to go . . ." I sucked in the smoke, let it burn my throat. ". . . because it's a great assignment. Because I should get back out there. Because it's important."

"And this mother who kill herself and your little friend, she is not so important?"

"Of course she is. It's just that . . . I don't know."

"Yes you do. Elizabeth, be honest with yourself. You are thinking about going back to war because war, unlike the rest of your life, you understand. Everything is simple there, on the surface: I hate you, you hate me, if I don't kill you, you will kill me. *Basta.* End of story. In civilian life all this gets hidden, pushed down under the earth, but it has to come out somewhere, right? So you have the maniacs in their Mercedes. The teacher who gives the bad marks even to the good student. The *functionnaire* who tells you with big smile you forgot this form or that, and you must return to the back of the queue. You even have the old woman in my building who secretly presses all the buttons on the lift before getting off. I see her do it one day, I know. Or more extreme, you have these boys who come to school with AK-47s to shoot the students; the teenager outside his shitty HLM, throwing Molotov cocktails at the *gendarme;* or, as you have discovered, you have the mother who hate her husband and take the children into the woods and never to come home again."

"What the . . . what are you talking about?"

"I am talking about motivation. *Your* motivation. Me, at least I am honest with myself. I am attracted to war, like a lover. Before to see for myself this 'banality of evil' and stand at the doorstep of history and all that other blah blah blah. Now, to make of it art. You? I think it has become too hard for you to try to figure out the rules of regular life, so you want to go back to something you understand."

"You're so wrong."

"Oh, yes? Do not get me wrong. I am happy you want to go. I would like this very much, your presence there. But I do think you are lying to yourself."

"Well, you're wrong. I'm not lying to myself. I want to go because the story is important. Because truth matters."

"What do you mean, this truth?" Renzo looked as if he were about to laugh again.

"I mean the opposite of a lie. What's so funny?"

"You are hoping to find truth in Iraq?" Now he was, in fact, laughing. "You . . . want to find truth . . ." He wiped his eyes and tried to keep a straight face. ". . . *in Iraq?*"

"No!" It was hard making myself heard over his convulsions. "I want to *report* the truth in Iraq. To write about something that matters. For Christ's sake, Renzo, just what *is* so funny?"

Renzo waited until he composed himself before speaking. "Elizabeth, please. You think that reporting on a war is reporting the truth? You know as well as I that the only truth you will find over there in the desert is that man is beast. So what? You already know that. The truth? I am surprised you are so naive after all this time. We do not report the truth. We report only what we see. Who was that philosopher? I think he was one of yours. I read him only in French. *'Il n'y a pas d'histoire, que de biography.'* Or something like that."

"There is no history, only biography."

"Yes. Something like that. The transcendentalist, what is his name?"

"Thoreau?"

"No."

"Emerson?"

"*Si*, Emerson! I believe. He is a smart man. Listen to what he has to say. You want to make something true? Come on, Elizabeth. You know what to do. Put aside your footage, all those interviews you do. Who cares? They do not matter. These people you talk to about the mother of April, they do not know her. They may think they do, but they do not. But you, *figure-toi*, if you look deep inside your own self, you can write her story anyway. Or the story of anyone like her. Make it up if you have to! It does not have to be true to be true, *capice*? I read a statistic: over one million people every year do the suicide. One million! This is more dead in the world than everyone who die from murder and war combined. So what if you do not have yet all the facts of the story, *tous les détails*? You think you need facts to write truth? You think that making a documentary is truth?

This is bullshit, *mon Eliza,* and you know it. You say this yourself, when we go together to see *À Bout de Souffle,* remember?
That Godard think all good documentary has in it the fiction,
and all fiction has in it the—"

"Documentary. You remember that?"

"I remember a lot, *mon Eliza.* Especially these words, because I think of them all the time in my own work, but also
the woman who teached them to me. This was a woman who
knew what she wanted. Who was not afraid to take risk. What
happened to that woman?"

She was raped, I thought. But it suddenly felt like an excuse.
I was stronger than that, and I knew it. "She had children," I
said. "She made a bargain to stay alive."

"So write about this!" said Renzo, nearly shouting now.
"Write the story of one mother who do not make it, who was
pushed—how you say?—over the ledge." His face was now less
than a foot away from mine.

"Edge," I said.

"What is difference?"

"One leads to the other."

"Ah. So I walk on the ledge, but I try not to fall off the edge,
this is correct?"

"Yes." I was breathing hard. Neither of us spoke for a moment, caught, as we were, once again, on the lip of our own
precipice.

"*Bueno,*" he finally said, pulling his face back a foot. "So,
you, you are on your ledge. Dancing, working, shooting your
little *reportage* on the nail polish, whatever it is you do to fill
the hours. But I am sure you feel close enough to that edge
every day, *si?* Maybe you even peek over it from time to time?
Everybody do this. So. Why you not go over this edge, but this
friend of yours mother, she go? What is the difference between

you and that woman? There is your truth. Right there, between the ledge and the edge. Go find it."

"You seem to know a lot of facts about suicide," I said.

"Because I am interested in this topic."

"Why?"

Renzo looked out the window and stared at the brick wall.

My voice grew sterner. "Why?"

"Putain . . ." He sighed. "Because, okay. My mother, she kill herself. And her father before her. Because everyone I know who do this job I do has a little bit of this wish inside. You, including."

"Bullshit," I said. "That's just not true."

"Oh no?"

"No. I mean yes, it's not true. And I had no idea your mother killed herself. Why didn't you ever tell me that?"

"You never ask."

This was not fair, but I let it drop. I had asked, several times, about his upbringing, but Renzo was always an expert at deflection. The one conversation he'd ever allowed started over drinks one night in Warsaw, on the eve of Walesa's election, when I heard him speaking fluent French to the journalist from *Libération* sitting behind him. "So what are you, then?" I'd said. "French or Italian?"

"Both," he'd answered. Before he and his father moved to Paris, he'd spent his early childhood in a farmhouse in Sicily, in the shadow of Mount Etna, whose moods, he'd claimed, smiling slyly, were nearly always in sync with his mother's. She was a painter, he said with some pride, who modeled herself after Frida Kahlo. Greta Garbo had even purchased one of her paintings, during the heyday of Taormina. "Is your mother still living there?" I'd asked.

"No," he'd said, shaking his head. Then he'd quickly changed the subject back to Solidarity.

"So what made her do it?" I now asked.

"*Mon Eliza!* I always tell everyone you are intelligent woman, but sometimes you say stupid thing. You think you can point to one moment and say, 'This is why'? She was depressed. She suffered. As long as I knew her. End of the story. It was actually a relief when she died."

"A relief? That's an odd thing to say about your mother's death."

"Oh, you think so?"

"Yes, I think so."

"That is your right. You do not live with her. I do. And it is my right to say it was a relief. For her especially, but for me also and for my father. You know, everybody always say that suicide is act of the coward. And yes, perhaps it is. Morally, at least. But it is also, *il faut dire,* the act of courageous. A 'clumsy experiment,' like Mr. Schopenhauer say, because the answer come from the destruction of the question, but courageous, too.

"Think about it this way. We do not judge someone who do something crazy to end his physical pain. A soldier who cut through his own leg to release it from under the rubble. A person who must eat the raw flesh of the dead in order to survive. Heroes, we call them. We put them on the TV and say look at this! Incredible! He eat his brother's dead wife! He saws the knife through his own bone! But when a person do something crazy to relieve mental pain we judge. We say bad person. Evil, cowardly person. Maybe a little sympathy for the suffering, yes, but we say, I never do that. I am better than that. But maybe somewhere deep inside we want to do that same thing. To end it. To find peace. To be or not to be, right? That is *always* the question. But we are afraid of that feeling. That wish for the dark. So we pretend it is not there. So who is the coward? The man who figure out a way to end his pain or the man who sits there *comme un imbecile* and endures it?

"You want to know why my mother kill herself? Because she had a piece of rope and she could. *Basta.*"

We didn't speak for what seemed like several minutes. "May I see your photos now?" I said. I felt a sudden, overwhelming urge to flee that dusty room, my cobwebbed past, Renzo's crystal clear lenses, but I knew that to have done so without at least a cursory glance at his work at that point would have been rude.

"Yes, okay." Renzo opened his portfolio so that it lay half on my lap, half on his, to the first picture, a single house in an open field, tiny in the frame, going up in flames. Everything about the image, except the house itself—the late-afternoon light, the slight blurring of the foreground grasses, suggesting a gentle, spring breeze, the fluffy cumulus clouds punctuating a perfect blue sky, the sun-dappled leaves of the scattered trees, the carefully considered physical arrangement of objects in the frame—all harkened back to classical landscape painting. And yet without the burning house, the composition would have seemed, at least to the modern eye, bland. With it, the image was nothing short of masterful.

"Wow," I said. "That's gorgeous. Where was it taken?"

"Djakovica," he said. "The day you left." His voice struck a surprising note of umbrage. Somehow, in all the years that had passed since our break-up, I'd never once considered how it had affected him. *I* was the one who'd been told I wasn't loved. I—or at least I'd always assumed—was the injured party. "I like it better when it's enlarged, actually," he said. "These are just work prints—"

"Stop," I said. "It's lovely. Let me see the next one."

He turned the page to reveal a picture taken in the mountains of Afghanistan, with snowy peaks in the far distance, a group of mujahedin walking single file along a steep ridge—their figures tiny, insignificant in the frame. Then I looked more carefully and noticed the two dead bodies, their mid-ground placement in the composition more of an afterthought, accidental. "Renzo, these are . . . these are really amazing. I've never seen anything like them."

And for the first time since I've known him he blushed. "Thank you," he said. "I am pleased with it, I think. But it is just the beginning. *Juste un petit gout.*"

I flipped to the next page. Then the next. First a funeral on a hillside overlooking what looked like Jerusalem, shot from a polite distance, the bodies gathered around the gravesite like ants around a crumb of bread. Then a young mother, cradling her dead son, but again tiny in the frame, like a cigarette butt, or a crushed soda can, just one of the many abandoned elements littering a nondescript sidewalk, somewhere on earth, probably Baghdad, but it didn't matter where. And that, I realized, was the point of the whole exercise: destruction, anger, grief, all that detritus of humankind didn't need a dateline, didn't need to be locked forever in time and space. Hatred has never warranted a sell-by date. It simply is. And will always be.

I tried to approach the work with a cold and critical eye, but as each page was turned, each landscape devoured, I found myself transported, emotionally at one with the man who made it. Renzo could clearly sense this, or perhaps he'd guessed even before he showed me the photos what my reaction to them would be, as our knees began pushing against one another, the pressure between them mounting in a way that had become impossible to toss off as innocent. Then it was our shoulders, our elbows, the backs of our hands. "I really like what you did here," I said, barely able to form a coherent sentence, pointing to a puff of smoke, presumably left over from a bomb, but floating, like a postscript, in midair. "If I had to choose one, I think this might—"

But before I could finish, Renzo pushed the portfolio to the floor, took my face in his hands and began to kiss me, roughly. Without the slightest resistance, without any remorse, I climbed into his lap and let his hands wander. Now he was unbuttoning my blouse, one frustrating impediment at a time, until the only barrier left was an easily unhooked bra, which he tossed, without ceremony, behind the couch. I pulled off his shirt and buried my face in his neck, breathing in his once-familiar scent, running my cheek along the taut sinew of his shoulder.

Renzo stood and carried me over to the futon on the floor and laid me down, yanking off my jeans in one swift motion. I'd like to say I had a small tinge of regret at that point, lying there, naked, before a man not my husband. I'd like to say I felt guilt-stricken, or paralyzed. But in fact, nearly the exact opposite was true. As I lay there under Renzo's gaze, I felt ecstatically alive, the years slipping away, one by one, like icicles under the sun, until there was no more Tess, no more Daisy, no more Mark, no more me. I was just a body, pulsing with need; just a vessel, begging to be filled.

"*Laisse-moi gouter,*" he whispered, and he bent down between my legs. I closed my eyes and ran my hands through his fine hair, my thumbs over his ears. "Wait, wait . . ." I now said, scooting away, wanting to prolong the moment.

He flipped me over onto my stomach and, with tiny flicks of his tongue, ran his mouth up my spine until I could stand it no longer. I turned to face him. "*Vas y,*" I said. And I led him inside. Our bodies moved together as they had a hundred times before, the languid rhythms and syntax of our past couplings rushing back.

He stared into my eyes now, his expression uncharacteristically vulnerable. "Do you know . . . how often . . . I think about this?" he said. "Do you know . . . how much . . . I missed this?"

"Then you're an idiot," I said, tears now welling in my eyes. And after his body shivered, after his arms clung to me as if he'd tumble to his death otherwise, after he lifted me out of my own body and into the only version of heaven I know, I reminded him of our conversation about love.

For a long time afterwards neither of us spoke. I was halfway to sleep when Renzo, still clutching me, finally chipped through the wall of silence. "I actually said that? I said love is a 'mythical construct'?" He clucked his tongue and shook his head in disbelief.

I turned around to face him, propping myself up on an elbow. "Yes, you did." The brick outside the window was growing darker. Soon it would be time to go. "Right after you told me that the story I wrote about those lovers who died on the bridge—what're their names?—was sentimental—"

"Admira and Bosko."

I stared at him in confusion. "You remember the names of the dead lovers, but not what you said about love?"

"Names stay the same. Opinions change."

"Oh, give me a break. A half hour ago you were reciting, nearly word for word, Godard's opinions on docu—"

"This was theory. Not opinion."

"You have an answer for everything, don't you?"

"Not everything."

"Fine. What about my name? How does that fit into your little theory about flux?"

"Flux? What is this word 'flux'?" He cupped his hand under my breast, circled his thumb around its rising center.

"That's flux," I said, glancing down at my hardening nipple. "It means change. Instability."

"Oh. Life."

"Not exactly."

"Yes, exactly. That Greek man say this, remember? About never putting the foot in the same river twice."

"What are you, a one-man quote repository?"

Renzo laughed. They were precious, his laughs: infrequent enough to be surprising even to him. I suddenly wished I could box this one up and store it with my emergency supplies, between the jugs of water and the batteries.

"Heraclitus," I said.

"Yes. You see? His name stay the same. You remember it. But this is true what you say about your name. It, too: flux. You surprise me that you change it." Now he was kissing the other nipple, feeling it stiffen between his lips.

"I surprised myself." I turned my back to him again, pulled the covers over my body.

"Why you do that? I always wonder."

"Because I'm not a Greek man," I said. When I got married, they wrote in the paper, *The bride, who will be keeping her name* . . . Mark was called simply, *The groom,* without caveat. Even stasis becomes a political statement when you're a woman. Now I lay on my back, staring up at the ceiling. "After Daisy was born, I . . . I just decided to change it one day. To have the same name as my kids." I yawned even wider, feeling suddenly incapacitated by exhaustion.

"*Ah, oui. Toujours le sentimentaliste.* In this you do not flux."
He planted a light kiss on my forehead. "But I interrupt you
before. The lovers on the bridge. What did I say about your
story?"

I looked him in the eye, biting my lip to keep from crying,
before turning away to stare at the ceiling. "You called it 'sentimental bullshit.'"

"Oof," said Renzo. "What an asshole. No wonder you leave
him." He nuzzled his nose in my neck, placed his right thigh
over mine. "It is funny, the way life turns out, no?" Now he was
kissing my cheek. The curl of my ear.

"No. It's not funny, Renzo." Tears began to form again at the
corners of my eyes. "It's not funny at all."

"Oh, *mon Eliza.* You cannot have one without the other. The
comedy without the tragedy. You should know this by now."

CHAPTER 18

I ARRIVED AT the front door of my apartment at a hair past 5:00 PM and found Irma and the girls sitting on the landing, their backs against the wall, the contents of my daughters' backpacks—Daisy's homework, a leftover banana from Tess's lunchbox, several scarves and hats and a pencil or two—spread out before them.

"What's going on?" I said, breathless from climbing the stairs, brushing off the snowflakes dusting my coat. I'd showered, dressed, and bolted from Renzo's to catch the subway home, after waking up in his arms, disoriented. By the time I got off at Eighty-sixth and Central Park West, it was already 4:55 PM, and a new snowstorm had begun.

"I forgot my keys in Jersey City," said Irma, looking ashamed. "I realized it when I was on the PATH train, and I thought about going back home to get them, but yesterday you said you'd be working from home today, so I thought—"

"But why didn't you call? I would have—"

"She did call," said Daisy, placing her math homework back in her purple folder. Her tone had an accusatory edge to it. "Lots of times. Where were you?"

I pulled my cell phone out of the front pocket of my jeans and saw "6 missed calls" emblazoned like a wagging finger across its screen. Of course. I'd switched the phone to silent during my interview with Lenny Morton. Then Renzo had rung. Then we'd had soup. For several hours. When the guilt finally came, it announced itself suddenly, flooding my veins with dark sludge. "Oh, sweetie, I'm so sorry. I was, uh . . . interviewing this guy for a story."

"What guy?" said Daisy.

"What story?" said Tess. "Why is your hair wet?"

Daisy stared down at the striped Swatch we'd given her for her seventh birthday. "I'm going to be late for piano," she said, ever the stickler for arriving both at school and to her various activities with extra minutes to spare.

"No you're not," I said. "We've got plenty of time."

"I'm so sorry," said Irma, shaking her head and still looking sheepish.

"No, Irma. It's my fault. You're right. I told you I'd be here working. I'm the one who should be apologizing. And my hair is wet, peanut"—I was now addressing Tess—"because it's snowing outside."

"But you were wearing a hat," she said, cocking her head to the side in confusion.

"Come on girls," said Irma, sensing my anguish, "let's get you inside." I recalled a conversation between two nannies outside the girls' school about having to clean one of their employer's adulterous sheets. I wondered what kinds of suspicions and judgments I'd now triggered in Irma's mind. It was so much easier maintaining the illusion that she never thought about the way we conducted our lives.

TWO DAYS EARLIER, I'd brought up the possibility of my going to Iraq; I'd asked Irma if she thought the Gilmores, the other family for whom she worked, would possibly agree to allow Sam, their two-year-old son, to accompany her back and forth to my daughters' school for pickup on the Mondays and Fridays that I would be gone.

Irma was sitting cross-legged on the living room floor, carefully loading the pieces of the girls' Operation game back into the cartoon body, setting off a loud buzz with every slip of the tweezers. "Doctor, will he live?" I'd said, knowing Irma, whose early knowledge of American life was gleaned from soap operas, would find this funny, but Irma simply dropped in the Adam's apple, then the broken heart, remaining stone-faced and silent.

"Iraq? Why would you want to go there?" she said.

Coming from Irma, the question caught me off guard; she was not in the habit of asking why. Her queries were normally of the when/where/how variety, as in "When is the makeup piano lesson?" or "Where is the birthday party?" or "How do you expect me to pick up one from piano and the other from a birthday party at the same time?"

"What do you mean, why?" I said. "It's an important story. I got an assignment. I'm thinking very seriously about going." I could hear my voice tinged with the anxious conviction of a teenager. *I was invited. All my friends will be there.*

"And the girls?" She laid the tweezers down astride the slot for the spare ribs, setting off the buzzer once again. "Oh for goodness sake." Then, quite uncharacteristically, she ripped the instrument from its cord.

"Irma!" I laughed. "Oh my god! I've been wanting to do that for—"

"What about the girls?" she repeated, staring down in mild shock at the frayed edge of the wire, as if suddenly realizing the depths of her power.

And I told her that the girls would be fine. Irma said she

didn't think so. I said I thought she was wrong. She said she thought she was right. And thus we continued, back and forth, lobbing the ball gently, politely, until I finally asked her *why* she didn't think the girls would be fine. That's when Irma raised her eyebrows so far into her forehead that I suddenly became defensive and muttered, "People who live in glass houses . . ." before instantly regretting it.

Irma had three children, several years older than mine and living with her mother thousands of miles away in Mambajao. Most of what she earned paid for their school tuitions, clothing, food, and her mother's rent, while the rest covered her daily filet-o-fish, her Christmas visits back home, and a windowless room located a good thirty-minute walk from the nearest PATH train. I'd learned of her domestic arrangement when she first came to our apartment for her interview, back when Daisy was still joined to me at the hip, back when I was still naive to the rudiments of late twenty-first century American childcare. Unaware that this was the trade-off for many women in her field, I idiotically teared up and asked how it felt to be so far away from her children. Irma smiled politely and said, "They live with my mother. They are in good hands." Then she promptly changed the subject back to Daisy's nap and bowel schedules.

"Glass houses? What does this mean?" she was now demanding. As I sheepishly explained the origin of the phrase, she tightened her eyes into little knots. "I may be far from my children, yes, and believe me every day I know what I am missing, but I'm not holding a gun to my head while I'm gone."

"Irma, I . . ." I was now sitting on the bench inside our front door, watching Daisy search for her piano books, wanting to explain myself but finding it hard to formulate a thought, let alone voice it. I was struck by an unfamiliar scent. Of course.

The bar of soap in the apartment had been Dial. Our family used Dove. I realized, with another sinking feeling, I'd have to shower all over again. And then, with yet another one, that maybe Mark wouldn't even notice.

"Why don't you stay here with the little one today," said Irma, again seeming to sense my inner noise. "I'll take Daisy to her piano lesson."

"That's a great idea. Thanks, Irma," I said, suddenly wishing I could pay her twice her salary.

I threw myself into a guilt-induced state of maternal over-drive, playing six games of pick-up sticks with Tess and listening in rapt attention as she jumped from her surprise upon learning that Dr. Seuss was a man to her concerns about global warming to the plots of the last three episodes of SpongeBob SquarePants. But all the while, as I watched her mouth move, I couldn't stop replaying the afternoon with Renzo, which ran like an endless loop on the movie screen behind my eyes. My clothing began to feel restrictive. I needed to be free of them. And, I suddenly realized, of my daughter.

"How'd you like to watch SpongeBob *right now?*" I asked Tess.

She looked at me as if I were insane. "What about homework?"

"You can finish it later."

Her eyes widened even further. "But we're not allowed to watch TV before dinner. That's the rule," she said.

"Well," I said, picking up her birdlike body and plopping it on the couch, "That's the great thing about rules. Sometimes they're meant to be broken."

"*Really?*"

I flipped on the cable box. "Really," I said. I told her I'd be right back, that I was just going to take a quick shower.

"But you never take showers at night," she said.

"Didn't I tell you? Today is opposite day!"

"Opposite day? . . ." Tess was saying, scrunching up her nose, but she was already sucked in by the TV, and I was already half-way to my bedroom, throwing off my clothing onto the floor piece by piece, turning on the shower nozzle as hot as I could stand it. I scrubbed my body with the family brand of soap, vigorously rubbing my arms, my legs, my torso with Dove, trying to erase every last trace of Renzo and his Dial. Now I ran the bar between my legs, half mortified, half stunned by the swell of delicate skin there, still sensitive from the afternoon. I placed the soap back in its holder and returned to the same spot, my knees growing weak until it was all I could do just to lie on my back, the water hitting my chest like rain on a windshield, the cold porcelain tub growing warmer beneath me, until I was shuddering, crying out once more.

Of course Adele disrobed for Lenny Morton that day in her kitchen, it suddenly struck me, as I lay there under the warm water, drowning in shame. It was the only logical way for her to go on living. To prove to herself that she was, in fact, alive.

CHAPTER 19

"DO YOU DREAM about having intercourse with him every night?" asked Dr. Rivers.

I'd just owned up to what had happened between Renzo and me, after explaining how I'd spent the rest of the week in an agitated state, trying to decide whether or not to take the assignment in Iraq while madly screening and transcribing my footage of Mavis and Trudy; tracking down various manufacturers of Kevlar vests while simultaneously rereading through Dr. Sherman's sessions with Adele; struggling to find the right moment to discuss the idea of couples' therapy with Mark while dreaming nightly of Renzo, who'd emailed me upon his return to Rome:

To: lizardbs@yahoo.com
From: renzo@renzophoto.it
Re:

Mon Eliza,
It was lovely to seeing you the other day. Too lovely, perhaps, and I will keep these souvenirs of our rendezvous in a safe

place, as I hope you will, too. I am assuming you will not to join me in Iraq, but perhaps I am wrong. It seems to me that you have other things to which you must attend. I do not want to be of interference. I myself have complications. A baby who will to come very soon, as I explain, but other things as well. But not to worry. I will call to Bernie, and I will tell him I make this change of mind. (Jonesie is old horse, but he can still pull the wagon.) But I will also be pleased for your company if you decide to do the voyage. Please continue your other reportage. It is interesting to pursue, I think so, this mother in the woods with her children, so write it and perhaps I will get a chance to read it one day. Bisous, Renzo.

"Nearly every night," I said.

Dr. Rivers looked at me, hard. "What do you think this man represents?"

"Oh, I don't know. All the normal cliché things, I suppose. Freedom. Love. The path not taken. I've been ashamed to even admit it to you, much less to myself."

The night I received Renzo's email, I'd finally called Mark at his office to broach the subject of Bernie's assignment, which, in my state of heightened agitation, I was suddenly leaning toward taking. At the sound of the word *Iraq*, Mark actually picked up the receiver without my having to ask him to get off speakerphone. "Iraq!" he'd yelled. "Elizabeth, have you lost your fucking mind? Do you remember what you were like when you came home from that last trip to Kosovo? You didn't get out of bed for three weeks. Three weeks! And what about the girls, huh? Have you thought about them?"

"I was pregnant with Daisy," I said. "I was tired. As for the girls, I have two words for you: Christiane Amanpour. She's been in and out of there, and she has a son."

Which he'd countered with, "Well I have three words for him: *years of therapy.*"

I hung up the phone and peeked in on my daughters asleep in their room, feeling that familiar ache, like a cavity, in the center of my chest. Tess was lying on her back, her mouth half open, her cheek nuzzling the blanket in which she'd been swaddled as an infant. Daisy was smiling, even in sleep; there were times at night when I'd actually hear her giggling, out loud, middream. Would that continue if I left? What about if I never came back?

I wandered into their room and sat down on the toy-cluttered floor, where I watched, by the light of Daisy's lava lamp, with a mixture of fascination and revulsion, Tess's gerbil John Lennon trying to traverse the length of the cage with nine babies attached to his underside.

The hairless, blind, pink-brown creatures had been deposited from John Lennon's uterus into the far left corner of the cage in the wee hours of the morning. The pups spent the next week alternating between squeaking and sleeping, with frequent visits to John Lennon's nipples in between. We'd spent the next weeks watching them. We watched them sleep upon our waking and wake upon the girls' arrival home from school. We watched hairs sprouting on backs and eyes opening up, first the left then the right, or sometimes the right then the left, depending on the pup, which frightened Tess at first until we Googled "gerbil babies" and discovered that a twenty-four-hour delay between eye openings was normal. We watched each one take its first tentative steps away from the warm pile. We watched John Lennon playing Sisyphus while trying to keep order in the cage, or at least a majority of the pups in the same general vicinity as the others, as he ferried them in his mouth, one pup at a time, from one end of the cage to the other and then back again.

But mostly we watched John Lennon nurse. Or rather, *I* watched John Lennon nurse. I watched him nurse in the morning, while helping the girls get ready for school. I watched him nurse during working hours, when I should have been either time-coding my footage or at least drumming up paid work to subsidize the whole endeavor. I watched him nurse an hour a day, two hours a day, three and sometimes four hours a day, watched the little bodies of John Lennon's offspring squirm, writhe, and wiggle under his still-swollen belly, while he sat there, patiently, and I sat there, transfixed, on the floor of my daughters' bedroom, squishing Daisy's water yo-yo ball in the palm of my hand, squeezing the liquid in it back and forth, back and forth, back and forth, until one morning its rubbery surface sprang a pinhole-sized leak, sending a fine stream of liquid in a great arc.

I watched that furry, fluffy, formerly male gerbil, whom I still wasn't able to connect with a female pronoun, even though clearly *he* was a *she,* nurse and nurse and nurse and nurse until my eyes were blurry and red, until I was interested in nothing else, until even Dr. Rivers, who was initially intrigued by her patient's identification with a lactating rodent, became alarmed. "What do you think this avoidance is all about?" she asked, and I shrugged it off, like an alcoholic dismissing the severity of her affliction. "It's not like I look in on him *that* often," I said. "You mean *her.*" "Huh?" "You said him. You meant *her.* The gerbil's a her." "I haven't been able to make that transition yet," I snapped.

John Lennon was struggling that night I received Renzo's email, the weight of the pups pulling him down as he hobbled along toward the exercise wheel. He'd never tried such a feat before, never tried to move from here to there while suckling the pups. Ringo Starr might have been running around the cage at top speed, hopping on and off the spinning wheel like a kid with ADD, but John Lennon was always sitting there perfectly still, perfectly quiet, patiently nursing.

And now, here he was, the mother of nine, trying to make his way across the cage. And as he struggled to take each step, I found myself rooting for him, willing him to make it to the wheel.

"Go!" I whispered. She—*she!*—was halfway across the length of the cage, when a few of the pups lost their grip and fell off, freeing her to move more quickly to her goal. Now she was less than an inch away from the wheel, with only five pups remaining on her teats. And then she took her snout and nudged it into the remaining suckling pups, until each and every one of them were, once and for all, unsuckled. Triumphant, she hopped up on the wheel and started to run, unencumbered and free.

"You did it!" I said.

I trudged, lead-footed, into the kitchen. I poured myself a small glass of wine and fumbled around in the back of the battery drawer until I found a pack of stale cigarettes and lit one. It tasted wretched. After a few puffs, I laid my head on the table and gave into the blackness, my chest convulsing up and down without restraint.

When I'd finally calmed down, I opened my laptop and composed my reply.

To: renzo@renzophoto.it
From: lizardbs@yahoo.com
Re: re:

Dear Renzo,
Yes, it was lovely. Too lovely, you're right. And there's no need to call Bernie. I'm going to call him tomorrow to turn down the assignment. But when you come back . . .

. . . *if you come back,* I thought to myself, erasing the last fragment. I paused for several minutes before composing the rest, knowing what I wanted to say, but petrified by the thought of actually typing the words.

> But if you ever make it back to the States, I would like to see you again. I'm not sure how that can happen, or if you even want that to happen, or if you have any plans to be back here anytime soon. I just wanted you to know that the possibility of spending another afternoon with you is something I could hold onto, even if it never comes to pass. Love, E.

I hit "Send" before I could convince myself not to. Then I erased both his message and my reply.

"So do you think you love him?" said Dr. Rivers. "Or do you think you love the idea of him?"

"I could answer that if I were rational right now," I said. "But I'm not feeling rational these days. In fact, some days I feel completely paralyzed." *Besides,* I thought, *Renzo never even bothered to write back.* Not that I expected him to do so, just that I still held out hope that one day he'd become the kind of man who would. "The other night Daisy walked into my bedroom when I thought she'd already gone to sleep, and she caught me crying into my pillow. Then she asked if maybe I was thinking about killing myself, like the woman in my documentary."

"And what did you tell her?"

"I told her of course not. Of course I would never kill myself. But . . ."

"But what?"

But, I wanted to say, *it felt a little bit like a lie.* "Nothing. I lost my train of thought."

After a long pause, during which neither of us spoke, Dr. Rivers asked how my editing was going.

"Okay," I said, perking up a little bit. "Not great, but okay." On the one hand, I told her, it was nice being able to edit the material right on my computer. Plus the footage I'd shot of Dr. Rivers's office—slow pans and zooms and rack-focus shots of her couch, the walls, her Eames chair, the rustling trees outside the window—wound up working really well under the dialogue between Adele and her psychiatrist, which I'd hired two actors to read. On the other hand, the two main interviews I'd shot so far didn't cut together well at all: the segues between Mavis and Trudy were jarring, ill-flowing. And frankly, each of their explanations as to why Adele killed herself and her children seemed predominantly influenced by their own biases and experiences. "I'm just not sure it'll hold together. Everyone's versions of what happened are different."

"Of course they are."

"I know, but it just means there's no central voice. No reliable guide through the footage. I mean, I can't be the guide, because I have no idea what happened. But if I let the characters tell the story themselves, *Rashomon*-style, they all, well, it's not that they *lie,* per se, it's just . . . I want it to be true."

"As in factual."

"No, as in true."

"I'm not sure I understand what you mean."

I'd taped my first-grade class photo up on the wall facing my desk, to remind myself of the task at hand: to find out why April Cassidy never made it into that photograph. But of course to answer that question, I had to try to imagine the mind-set of her mother, and it was there, in the realm of the imaginary, where I kept stumbling. Worse, the harder I worked at finding my way into those woods, the more times I sat in front of the footage and tried to splice it together into a cohesive whole, the further away from the "truth" of the story I felt. I didn't want to judge Adele, though I sometimes did, or to castigate her, though I couldn't help doing so, or to create a polemic attacking the crime, though the first introductory paragraphs of voice-over I'd written were just that. I wanted, more than anything, to understand her: to crawl under her flesh, to feel her heart beating in my chest, to see a world turned hopeless and dim through her own eyes.

"You want to empathize with her," said Dr. Rivers.

"Yes," I said. "Something like that."

She nodded her head. "I had a student once a few years ago, finishing up her psychoanalytic training. She was interested in the same thing. Filicidal mothers. A topic still widely under-researched and poorly understood, so I thought, great. Good for her. Why not? But the entire class turned on her, said it was impossible to empathize with such monsters."

"What did you say?"

"I said I thought such a reaction said more about us as doctors and human beings than it did about filicidal mothers. I don't want to discourage you even further, because obviously I think the issue deserves closer scrutiny, and I can sense your excitement at chipping away at it, but I'd be careful if I were you," she warned. "You're treading into waters most people either can't or won't go."

I'D ALSO MADE several attempts at writing a letter to Shep Cassidy, but I'd get to the second paragraph, read over what I'd written, and cringe. "Dear Mr. Cassidy," I wrote. "Thirty-five years ago you lost your family, and I lost my best friend." *No. Too purple.* Then this: "Dear Mr. Cassidy, I'm a journalist hoping to make a documentary about the death of your wife and children in 1972, and I would like to sit down with you, during the next few weeks, to shoot an interview." *No. Too clinical.* I'd never before had a crisis of conscience convincing the bereaved to talk, but this time the whole idea felt unseemly, wrong.

There's a famous story, passed down from journalist to journalist, about the TV reporter who one day showed up in a camp full of violated nuns during the first Congo War and called out, "Anyone here been raped and speak English?" It's a story which never fails to amuse both journalists and non-journalists alike, but its comedic power over the former lies not in its slapstick absurdity, but rather in its too-close-for-comfort, self-loathing familiarity: *Anyone here been raped and speak English? Anyone here lost his entire family and want to spew into my video camera?* I couldn't get past it.

Then one night, as I sorted through the pile of mail, I came across a letter with a return address, handwritten, which made me jump.

I tore it open. And read the following:

7865 Thorn Apple Way
Potomac, MD 20854
February 27, 2007

Miss Elizabeth Burns
151 West 85th Street, #2A
New York, NY 10024

Dear Miss (Mrs.?) Burns:

It has come to my attention, from my friend Mavis Traub, that you have been looking into the death of my wife and children, so you can put it on TV. Needful to say, I was upset at first by hearing about your show, and while I'm not going to ask you to cease and desist it, I will ask that you listen to what I have to say, human to human.

If you are, as you told Mavis, a friend of April's from elementary school, you must know that she left this world for the next thirty-five years ago. I'm surprised you remember my little girl, being close to her age, since she died so young, but I'm willing to suspend belief and say, okay, maybe she did know April, but does that give you the right to write about her? I'm not saying you don't have the right, only look deep into your own soul and ask if you do have the right. When that poor man Rusty Yates lost his five children in the bathtub, I kept thinking, well at least on top of everything else I didn't have to deal with Katie Couric. I even wrote him a letter, telling him how sorry I was for his tragedy and giving him my phone number in case he felt like talking to someone who could actually understand him instead of pretending to.

I've spent these past thirty-five years trying to understand what happened to my family, and I still haven't figured out why. I thought about selling the house and moving to North Carolina when it first happened, because my sister and her family live there, and my company has a branch office I could work out of, but over the years I came to understand that this house is my cross to bare. I need to live here and suffer through it because God is testing me. He's testing me like he tested Job, and he's asking me to look deep inside myself, deep into every corner of my house to figure out what went wrong here, so I can ask forgiveness for my sins.

Just so we're clear, this letter is off the record, and if, after you finish reading it, you still want to make your TV show about my family, well, I guess I can't stop you, but I will sue you if any word from this letter appears. But, because I'm trying to show you good faith, in the hopes that this good faith will sway you not to make your film, I will tell you the few things I do know, for your own curiosity's sake. For example, I've already figured out some things I could have done different. Father Joseph, he's my priest, has been helping me to see things more clearly. He made me realize that I have a bad temper, and this probably made my wife scared. But my father had a bad temper and his father before him, too, so I know I came to mine honestly. Father Joseph also taught me to realize that since Adele was of the Jewish persuasion, we probably shouldn't have gotten married in the first place, or I should have insisted, like I many times tried to, that she convert. If she had converted to Catholicism, she would have understood that killing herself and her children would make her go to hell, and she wouldn't have done it. I believe that with the fullness of my heart.

I also know that my relationship with Mrs. Traub was foolhardy and a sin. She told me she didn't tell you about it, since you were recording her with a video camera, but I have faced my inner demons and if I can confess to both God and Father Joseph my own guilt then I can confess to anyone that I tasted of that fruit, and I regret it. Deeply regret it. But I will also say this: a man can only take so much neglect inside his house before he starts looking outside of it. If Adele had kept to her end of

the bargain, if she'd tried to be a good wife, things
would not have gone where they went. And I believe
that to this day. Like Father Joseph says, a branch
can only bend so far before it breaks.

The thing is, too, I had no idea my wife had such
difficult problems in her psychology. When I met her,
she was my nurse at Holy Cross. I know you might
find that hard to believe, because of what happened,
but I tell you she had a way about her that was so
caring, any man would have melted. I fell in love
with her even as she was sticking my arm with a
needle. In fact, maybe because of the way she stuck
in the needle. Not like some nurses, who don't even
tell you they're about to do it, they just stick it in
when they think you're not looking, but gentle. Real
gentle. I got better fast just to be able to ask her out
on a date, and we were married soon after. A few
years later, the girls came along.

Adele was never the same after that. After the
girls, that is. It's like she became possessed or something, overnight. She stopped smiling. She stopped
caring about herself, you know, eating whole boxes
of cupcakes out of the box and forgetting to take a
bath and sleeping all day and whatnot. One day she
asked me to get rid of the knives, because she was
afraid she'd do something with them. I kept saying,
What Adele? What would you do with the knives, but
she just said, something bad and walked out of the
kitchen. I got rid of the knives, the big ones at least,
not the steak knives because we needed them for
steak, but by God one day I came home from work
and Adele had a scratch on her arm that looked

exactly like it was made with a steak knife, even though she said she cut it on a fence, and so I got rid of them, too.

But I didn't think to get rid of the vacuum hose. Father Joseph tells me I couldn't have known, that I can't blame myself, but sometimes I feel like if I'd just thought of getting rid of that hose, my family would still be with me today.

Look, I don't know you, so I can't possibly know your intentions, but even if you have the best intentions and even if you are the best journalist in the world, how do you think you'll be able to explain the story of my wife if I still don't have a clue why it happened and I was married to her? I ask you to please just take the time to think about that for awhile before going ahead with your documentary.

I'd also like to ask you to, just for a minute, try to put yourself in my shoes. How would you feel if I turned on a video camera and started asking your friends and neighbors all sorts of personal questions about you and your family so I could put it on TV for everyone to see? I know that's your job, and I'm glad there are still people out there digging up the dirt on the politicians and whatnot, and if you ask me they should be digging up a lot more dirt these days with what's going on in the news, but why should my life be microscoped just because I lost my family? People lose their families every day, for all sorts of reasons, and I think we should all be left alone to deal with our griefs in private. I'm not a celebrity. I've never run for office. I sell pipes for a living, and I won't even be selling them for much longer. I retire in three months, with a decent pension. Enough to keep me going for however many more years I've got left until I'm finally allowed to be reunited with my little girls up in heaven, if God will even let me in up there, which I have my doubts about even though Father Joseph assures me I'll make it. I'm an old man now. An old man with some big regrets who had a tragedy happen to him a long time ago and would like to keep it there, in the past, where it belongs. I go to church every Sunday, I give money to charity, I do all the things a decent man is supposed to do. Am I perfect? Of course not. I still drink too much on occasion, and I still have a bit of a temper, especially when an order gets screwed up at work. I curse, and I covet, and I take the name of the Lord in vain more often than I should, and once upon a time, when I wasn't paying close enough attention, my family disappeared. I'm not proud of my behavior back then, and I know I wasn't really listening to what Adele had to say, because I guess I just couldn't believe that a mother could worry about sticking knives into herself or her children, and I will go to my grave wondering how I could have done things different, but that does not mean I want a stranger to pick apart my family and what I did or didn't do looking for someone to blame. I'm betting you have things you'd like to keep hidden, too. Things you're not so proud of either, stuff you've said that you wished you didn't, moments you wish you could redo if clocks went backwards but they don't.

So please, for my sake, for the sake of my late wife and children, whom I loved more than life itself,

let sleeping dogs sleep. If you really want to honor
April's memory, if you really want to do her justice,
let her rest in peace.

Cordially yours,
Shepherd H. Cassidy

I folded the letter back up again and slipped it into its envelope, my heart pounding. *So,* I thought, that's that. One less
element with which to tell the story.

I thought about Mark: what would he write about us, about
me, if I were to meet the same fate as Adele, and he were composing a letter to a nosy journalist thirty-five years hence? Did
he even realize how miserable I was, playing house all alone?

Every night since Tess asked about our possible divorce, I'd
called him at work and asked him to please come home. "I have
something I need to talk to you about, and I don't want to do it
over the phone," I'd say. "Please, it's important."

To which he'd promise to leave within the hour, which would
invariably turn into two; by the time he'd finally walk in the
door, shouting, "Z! I'm home! You awake?" I would have already
fallen asleep, still propped up in bed with the lights on and a
book on my chest. How was I going to get him to commit to
trying to fix our broken marriage, I wondered, if I couldn't even
find the time to ask him to do so? The whole endeavor seemed
hopeless, absurd, like trying to make a documentary about a
thirty-five-year-old crime without the participation of the key
witness. I couldn't help wondering if Mark and I wouldn't have
more open lines of communication if we were officially separated,
instead of just separated by default. At least then we'd have to
actually spend time talking to one another, if only to discuss
who would get the kids and when.

"Adultery," Dr. Rivers had explained to me, after I kept obsessing over what had happened with Renzo, "is usually a symptom of unmet needs, not a sign, necessarily, that you should call it quits." She'd asked me, as an exercise, to list the things I presently loved or had once loved about Mark, and I was surprised to hear myself yammering on for nearly half of our session about his attributes: his calm in the face of adversity; his pitch-perfect sense of humor; his excellent fathering skills, when he was actually around; the fact that I was still very much physically attracted to him, despite everything going wrong in our bedroom. Then I recounted, thinking as I did about Renzo's nonchalance toward his own impending fatherhood, the day of Daisy's birth, how the entire east side, from Murray Hill to Fifty-ninth Street, had been gridlocked due to visiting dignitaries at the UN, and yet Mark had arrived in the delivery room, sweaty and panting, no more than a half hour after my call, having sprinted the thirty-four blocks between his office at CUNY and New York Hospital. "Seems to me those are things that are worth fighting for," Dr. Rivers had said. And I'd left her office that day determined to do so.

But it had been a week since that resolution, and I'd yet to make any headway.

Enough, I thought.

I picked up the phone. "Mark, please come home," I said. "I need to talk to you."

I could hear the usual tap-tap of his keyboard in the background, the hollow buzz of the speaker phone. "Sweetheart, I can't," he said. His voice had the tinny echo of a 1930s radio broadcast. "I'm having some real structural issues here with my data mining. The whole project is on the verge of collapse."

So is our marriage! I wanted to scream, but I was determined to make my case—quietly, and without tossing his speakerphone across the room — in person. "What time do you think you'll be leaving?"

"I'm not sure," he said. "I really gotta go."

When he hung up, I weighed my limited options. Then I called down to Astrid and asked her if she wouldn't mind coming up. "Sure," she said. "I'll be right there."

"Where are you going at this hour?" she asked, her left eyebrow raised into a question mark. She propped her slippered feet up on the old trunk we used for a coffee table and started flipping through the channels on the remote.

"To the SoHo Grand. I answered one of those ads on Craigslist?"

"No way!" she squealed. "A friend of mine from college did that. He wanted a woman for a threesome with his wife. Now the wife's living with the woman, and he has custody of the kids. Total mess. I'd be careful, if I were you."

"Astrid!" I hit her lightly on her head with Tess's homework folder, which I'd rescued from the floor. "I was joking." I shoved the folder in her backpack and spied a Ziploc bag filled with mold-encrusted apple wedges, the odor and sight of which made me heave. "Ugh. That's where the smell was coming from! I keep telling her to clean out her backpack, but she — "

"Never does. Give it up. She never will. Mine are taller than me, and they still leave their rotting shit around everywhere when they come home from college. So where *are* you going then?"

I tossed the moldy apple into an empty plastic bag and tied the handles tight. "Astrid," I said, trying to make my voice sound throaty and southern, like Dr. Martin Luther King Jr.'s, "I'm going to the mountain."

"Huh?"

"You know, if the mountain won't come to Mohammed, Mohammed must—"

"Go to the mountain. Got it. Good for you, Elizabeth. Give him my regards. Tell him I talked to Diego about fixing that flap of carpet on the stairs, but he said Weintraub won't pay for it." She bypassed several stations showing the latest suicide bombings in Baghdad and stopped on channel 34, the *E! True Hollywood Story* of some young actor born the year I graduated high school. "And if you get there and he's schtupping his partner's secretary in the kitchenette, don't tell me I didn't warn you. Can you believe this guy? Barely out of diapers, and he's fucking what's-her-name. You think she gets Botox?"

I glanced at the TV. The middle-aged actress in question was walking down one red carpet or another with her young sire, looking like a wax version of herself. "What do you think?"

"I think what's missing from my life is a teenage boy and a little botulism."

I smiled. Stole a peek at the kitchen clock. It was just after ten. "Look, if the girls wake up, which they shouldn't, just give them a glass of water—no juice, Daisy had two cavities last time we were at the dentist—and tell them I'll be back in an hour, okay?" I pointed out the open bottle of wine on the kitchen counter which, should she not drink it, would go to waste. Then I thanked her, profusely, for coming up at the last minute.

"Hey, what are friends for?" she said. She stood up and hugged me. "You deserve a break. Speaking of which, how's that thing you're working on?"

"Huh?"

"The thing thing. About your friend whose mother—"

"Oh that," I said, feeling the sting of Shep's letter afresh.

"Not so well. I got a letter today from the woman's husband asking me to cease and desist."

"Shit. I'm sorry about that. You seemed so excited about making it."

"Yeah, well. *C'est la vie,* right? Anyway, I should be back soon. Thanks again. Really." I wrapped a scarf around my neck and fished my hat out of the closet.

I took the B train down to Forty-second Street, trudging through the slush to the corner of Forty-fifth and Sixth, where Lortex had its main headquarters. The normally bustling streets of midtown were mostly empty, with only the random briefcase-toter turning up the lapels of his overcoat or hailing a taxi.

The guard at the desk asked to see my ID. "Go on up, Mrs. Steiger," he said, handing me a visitor's pass without calling up. Eight taunting bars of Muzak Manilow later (*"I can't laugh, and I can't sing, I'm finding it hard to do anything . . ."*), I reached the twenty-third floor and walked down the darkened corridor toward Mark's office, the only one illuminated from within. Through his glass wall, from afar, I could see him sitting on his ergonomically designed swivel chair, staring at his computer, glancing back and forth between the screen and something on his desk.

I slowed as I neared the glass. I could see the numbers on his computer screen, carefully organized into various rows and columns, stretching across the screen and down, as incomprehensible to me as the man who'd placed them there. On the floor surrounding his chair stood piles of paper, all with numbers, endless numbers, meant to reinvent our present notions of mortality.

I saw Mark scanning the screen with his eyes. Then I saw him grab a fresh printout to his right, a huge pile of pages attached one to the other with perforated edges and tiny holes running up and down each side. He lifted the top sheet and began scanning it somewhat frantically as the bottommost pages fell to the floor. He scanned with both fingers and eyes, searching page by page until the topmost layers began grazing the floor. Now his eyes fell back on the screen, then to the pages, then to the screen, where he opened a new window, stared at a different set of data. Now back to the pages. Now back to the screen. And then, his back muscles tensing, his fists clenched into balls, he screamed, "Fuck!" and threw the whole mess onto the floor.

He took a swig from a water bottle and threw the heels of his feet up on his desk. Bouncing one foot absentmindedly, he stared in the direction of the family photo I'd recently had framed for him. It was the four of us, standing in Sheep's Meadow the previous fall, the midtown skyline rising up out of the fiery-hued trees behind us, a family perfectly captured by a passing tourist. Daisy was beaming warmly at the camera, her hair aglow with yellow light. Tess, who'd become distracted by an ant below and was worried that one of us might step on him, stood half bent over, her forehead wrinkled with concern. I was kneeling next to Tess, midsentence ("The ant will be fine, sweetheart, I promise . . ."), while my face was in profile, staring up at Mark, who stood with his fingers gripping Daisy's shoulders, his eyes turned out of the frame, away from us.

Next to the photo sat a small Yahrtzeit candle, its flame casting a flickering shadow against the wall. Of course. I should have remembered. The anniversary of his mother's death. Then again, he could have reminded me. We could have lit a candle at home, with the girls, by the kitchen window. They were always asking him about his mother. Was she funny, smart, nice? "She was wonderful," was all he could muster. Even to me. In fact, over the years we'd been together, I'd only ever been able to extricate the tiniest nuggets of information: she was studying to be a clinical social worker, with an emphasis on counseling unwed mothers; she'd become fascinated with Jung's collective unconscious, and at the time of her death had been researching the archetype of the "goddess mother," who appeared nearly uniformly in people's dreams and mythologies, no matter their cultural, socioeconomic, or religious heritage; she had a raging sweet tooth, especially for licorice.

"But what was she *like?*" I'd ask, hoping for a more nuanced portrait.

"She was . . . wonderful," he'd say again. And then he'd change the subject. At first I thought it was because the memory of her was too painful. Then I realized it was simply too dim.

Every once in awhile a ray of detail would break through. One night, after Tess had been particularly moody at bedtime, Mark recalled the night a couple of weeks before his mother was killed, when she came into the communal children's room to kiss him good-night. "I'm too old for snuggling," he'd said out loud, so that the other children would hear. To which she'd responded, trying to validate his feelings like she'd been taught in her training, "You're right, Mark. You're almost thirteen. I can see why it would be difficult for you to be treated like a baby." From that night forward, his mother would wave good-night to him from the doorway, and though he'd been meaning to talk to her about this—maybe she could come in *every once in awhile* to give him a good-night kiss—by the time he felt ready to broach it, she was gone.

According to the few outside accounts I managed to scrape together, she was indeed "wonderful," or at least as close as humanly possible to the Jungian archetype of her studies. But so many blanks had been left unfilled by her early departure that expecting Mark to recite Kaddish and light a candle in front of his family was probably asking too much.

Suddenly feeling too spylike for comfort, I raised my hand to knock on the glass when I saw Mark turn to his computer and click open a new window. This one had no numbers. Or letters. Or columns or rows. It did, however, have breasts. And a vagina. And a length of rope attached to its wrists. Now another figure appeared, much like the first but with a disembodied hand touching its shoulders. Now a third, bound and gagged. Then a fourth. And a fifth. Now Mark began switching maniacally back and forth between his data and these images, the fingers of his right hand working the mouse (breasts, data, lips, data, thighs, data, mouth, data), the fingers of his left running back and forth across his scalp, until his shoulders were heaving and his head collapsed into a convulsing heap on his keyboard.

"Mark!" I said. I pounded my palm on the glass wall dividing us. "Mark!"

Mark swiveled around in his chair. "What the . . . ?" He wiped his eyes with the back of his sleeve and walked to the door to let me in. In our decade together, I'd only seen him cry twice, once each at the births of our daughters. He nearly cried one other time, during the N'ila service the year the towers fell, when all of the children, including our then two-year-old Daisy, were marching in their white clothes down the aisle of the darkened sanctuary, carrying flashlights in the shape of candles and singing a mangled version of *Hatikvah,* but he nipped that one in the bud. "How long have you been—"

"I wanted to talk to you."

"Why?"

"Mark, you're crying."

He stood there in the doorjamb, his arm leaning against it, blocking my entry. I could feel the support beams within me loosening, splintering.

"Can I come in?"

"Of course," he said, stepping aside.

We sat on the windowsill, staring out over the grids of light stretching in perfect vanishing point perspective toward New

Jersey. I could just make out a barge in the far distance, slicing its way through the ice floes on the Hudson, pushing its giant load upstream. Airplanes were conjured out of the dark, only to fade into the night just as brusquely. Mark pointed to the new building that would soon block his view, which he'd only noticed after overhearing a couple of tenants ten floors down lament the loss of their sunsets.

"What's that?" I said, trying to bring us back into the room. I gestured to the piles of printouts littering his floor.

"That," Mark said, "is a fucking mess." The whole concept behind his project was a fallacy, and Mark was only just beginning to realize to what degree. It was one thing to try to restructure the mathematical model of risk, to hyperindividualize the variables for each client seeking coverage, but to do so without accounting for chance was like building a brick wall without mortar. "I build it up to about this high," he said, marking with his hand a random spot in the air just above his head. "And then, boom! I plug in the catastrophic event and the whole thing falls to pieces."

"An earthquake hits," I said.

"For instance, yes."

I turned my gaze in the direction of the candle. "Or that."

"What?"

"The catastrophic event."

"Zab, I'm talking numbers here. Not people."

"But don't they represent people?"

"No. They represent statistical models of . . . Okay, people. To a certain extent. And to a certain extent not. But it's complicated. God, what was I thinking? I knew I'd have this problem the minute I took the job. I knew fundamentally the premise was flawed. Predict individual probable death to within an hour? Fucking joke. Some marketing executive's idea. *'Here at*

Lortex, we know exactly when you're going to die.'" He shook his head and slumped against the window. "You want a soda? They give them out free in the kitchen."

"How nice of them," I said, thinking that for the hours Mark put in every day, they should maybe be handing out free magnums of champagne. "Yes," I said. "Sure. A ginger ale."

Back from the kitchen, sodas in hand, he no longer wanted to talk about his work. So I told him about my own work and its less-than-stellar progress: the letter from Shep, the conflicting accounts, the lack of information about Adele Cassidy's final hours. I told him about two other stories I'd tried to pitch, after turning down the assignment in Iraq, one in rural China, on the effects of exporting so many girl babies abroad, the other in Bangalore, India, on the economic realities of outsourcing; about how the executive producer I'd contacted had said that recent budget cuts and lack of interest prohibited her from commissioning any segments outside the US. I told him of Tess's concern over Knut, the orphaned cub in Berlin, and about Daisy coming home from school upset over an assignment to write a report on one of the early explorers, a list of whom, she was miffed to learn, contained not a single female. I told him about Weinreb refusing to fix the flap of carpet on the stair, about the camp bills that were overdue, about how Astrid believed me when I told her I was going to the SoHo Grand on a Craigslist sex date.

For a moment we were silent, staring down at the white and red stripes of light vibrating up and down Sixth Avenue, and then Mark told me about some guy in his office who got a tattoo of the Starship Enterprise on his left butt cheek he wanted everyone to see.

"So what did he do, moon everybody?" I said.

"Better. He sent a digital image of it into everybody's inbox."

And as I started to laugh, as I felt myself being drawn once again into Mark's quirky orbit, I thought to myself, *Okay, now, I remember this. This marriage might actually be salvageable. But it might require more work than either of us is able to muster.*

"Light of my life?" I said.

Mark squeezed my hand in his and smiled. "Yes?"

"Why were you . . . why were you crying before?"

Mark stared at his feet, uncomfortably. "I wasn't crying, Z."

"Yes you were. I saw you."

"Look, I know where you're going with this, and I want to go there with you, I do, I really do, but can we talk about all of it tomorrow?" He put his arm around me and hugged me to him. "I promise we can talk through everything you want tomorrow. I just, I don't know." He stole a glance at the candle. "I can't deal with it tonight."

"Fine," I said. "But I'm going to hold you to that promise."

"We can grab dinner together tomorrow night, how about that?" he said. "I'll even find a sitter. And I promise—I promise!—I won't stand you up again."

"Oh, you better not. That would be a really bad mistake," I said.

"Bad mistake," he repeated.

Later that night, Mark spooned me to him and kissed the back of my neck and told me he loved me.

"I love you, too," I said. And I meant it right then, I really did.

But then I heard the familiar scrape, the metallic clang of the handcuffs sliding along the bottom of the bedside table drawer.

— CHAPTER 20 —

ASTRID ANSWERED THE DOOR, peeking out from behind her safety chain looking half asleep and annoyed, but when she saw my face her expression instantly softened. "Oh, sweetie, hold on a sec," she said, closing the door and unlatching the chain. "What happened?" She ushered me to the couch, her arm draped over my heaving shoulder. "Half an hour ago you two looked fine. Like a pair of newlyweds even."

"I . . ." I couldn't catch my breath, let alone speak. "He . . ."

"Shhh, shhh," she said. "Forget it. Don't talk. Can I make you some tea? Do you want something to eat?"

I shook my head no. The thought of food, of going through the motions of daily sustenance, made me dizzy with dread. I started mumbling incoherently again, the words and phrases surfacing one by one, without the ballast of language to hold them together: *What if? Can't. I tried. But.*

"Shhh, shhh," said Astrid again, rubbing my shoulder. "You don't have to make any decisions right now. Okay?"

She held me to her, tightly. Then she suddenly pulled away. "Wait," she said. "Hold on a sec. I have an idea." She fished around in a nearby drawer until she located a set of keys. "Here." She tossed them to me. "My cabin. Just go. Clear your head. Works for me every time."

Astrid had a small cabin in the middle of the Catskills near New Paltz, where she retreated nearly every weekend. It had been a gift to herself a couple of years after her husband, who'd never cared for the sight of trees, had left. We'd been invited as a family once, when the girls were toddlers, and Tess had drawn all over the kitchen wall with a red Sharpie. Astrid had shrugged it off with a smile, saying she'd been meaning to get a new paint job anyway. I remembered wondering at the time what kind of a man had left a woman like her: a woman who didn't care that her wall was ruined; a woman who toted huge casseroles of lasagna up the stairs after each of our girls were born; a woman who, every Halloween, treated the neighborhood kids to a haunted house leading from the stoop, which she covered in fake spider webs, all the way through her apartment; a woman who spoke several languages, ran six miles every other day, and was still, at fifty-three, as beautiful and astral as her starry name implied.

When Jim left her, with her two small children and a mountain of debt, she abandoned the dissertation she'd been working on and took a job as a communications director for an Italian bank. She didn't want anything else about her sons' lives to so suddenly and painfully change again: not their home, not their schools, not their precarious (she now realized) existence. Meanwhile, as the years had passed, she'd been secretly working away during stolen moments at the cabin in the Catskills, putting the finishing touches on the long-abandoned dissertation. Now Princeton University Press, she'd just heard, wanted to publish it as part of a ten-volume anthology they were compiling on *The Inferno*. *Pain and Pain's Outlet: A Dialectic,* she'd called hers, in reference to the trees in the Wood of the Suicides, who, because they'd thrown away their lives when they were mortals, were now forced to spend eternity rooted firmly in the earth, unable to speak unless pecked by Harpies. In the fall, she would finally apply for the teaching job she'd always wanted. It didn't matter where or how; she wanted to reclaim the life she'd put on hold.

"The Medeco unlocks the front door," she was now saying. "Sometimes it sticks, but if you just jiggle it a bit to the left, you'll be fine."

"Oh, Astrid, that's a nice offer, but I can't. We don't even own a car."

"Take mine. Keys are on the same chain."

"What about the girls? I can't just leave them here with Mark."

"Why not?" This last question was uttered harshly, with fading compassion, like a teacher grown suddenly frustrated by a promising student's lame excuses. "Lizzie, at some point, you just have to let go. Trust that things will be okay without you. Okay?"

"It's not that," I said, even though every time I left Mark alone with the kids when I had to travel for work, something always broke: a toy, a glass, a bone. Then there was the weekend I'd spent with my college roommates up in Vermont, when Tess had hidden herself in the hamper for several hours, emerging only after Mark had called the police.

"Then what is it?" said Astrid.

"It's . . ."

When I'd asked Tess why she hid herself in the hamper for so long, when everyone was worried sick, she'd shrugged as if the answer were obvious. "I needed to smell you," she'd said.

Astrid stared at me, awaiting my response.

"Nothing," I said. "You're right. I'll go."

I MADE MY WAY up the nearly desolate Palisades Parkway and onto Route 87, taking swigs from a cup of sludgelike coffee I'd bought, along with some groceries, at the Korean deli near where Astrid's Honda Civic had been parked. I stole a glance through the rearview mirror. The girls were folded over one another like rag dolls, all flaccid limbs and isosceles joints, Daisy's head lying limp on Tess's lap, Tess's arms splayed across Daisy's torso, her mouth ajar to the sky.

I'd snuck back into our apartment to gather some clothes, but when I kneeled by the side of the girls' beds to kiss them good-bye, I couldn't go through with it. What if I were gone for days, weeks? What if, having left, I never returned? In the back of my mind, I could already hear the cross-examination at the custody hearing: *And yet didn't you, on the night of March 2, 2007, abandon your children and flee to the Catskills?*

"Where are we going?" Tess had muttered, rubbing her eyes as the three of us stumbled out the door into the frigid night, down jackets tossed over our pajamas.

"On an adventure," I'd said. "A secret one."

Luckily the girls were too tired to ask for details. I had no idea where we were going. To Astrid's cabin in New Paltz, yes, but after that, what? We couldn't just stay there indefinitely, hiding out from reality. As a kid I'd been so good at chess, at sinking down in my seat until my eyes were level with the board, planning ahead several dozen moves to the moment when the path to the king would become clear. But the pawns this time felt too big, too heavy. I could barely see around them, let alone lift one.

I turned on the radio, hoping to drown out the static in my head. "Crocodile Rock" came on. *Good,* I thought. Then I remembered Leslie Lifshitz belting it out while standing on our family-room coffee table, gripping the baguette my mother had planned to fill with cold cuts for lunch. When Mom discovered the bread in Leslie's hand, she snapped. "You couldn't have used a goddamned flashlight!" she yelled. "And just look at these crumbs!" I pretended it had been my idea, turning our lunch into a microphone, the coffee table into a stage. But Leslie never came over again.

Even then I knew my mother was not like other mothers. That she was slightly damaged inside, like a cracked vase, whose thin veneer of grace would, if held up to the light, reveal a web of spindly fissures. But I always thought her brokenness could be contained in the presence of outsiders. In that I was much less savvy than April, who even at six sensed that attempting to project normalcy to the world would only end in disappointment. A mother was either busy fighting her inner diamonds or she was not.

A three-song Led Zeppelin medley struck next, thrusting me back to my first hit of marijuana, my first slow dance, those first gropings in the back of Joey Capistrani's Trans Am. Adolescence, we were taught in biology class, was the time when we would break free from our parents and form our own separate identities. "Severing the cord," our teacher had called it, but I didn't understand what he was talking about. I'd always stood apart from my mother, for as far back as I could remember.

I turned off the New Paltz exit and onto a small road, where I took a left at the church, just barely visible in the twilight, and flipped on the windshield wipers against yet another new flurrying of snow. "Coming up," said the DJ, "a blast from the past. But first, a real blast—of cold air, that is—from the present. We have a winter storm watch on for tonight, folks. Twelve to fourteen inches we're expecting by 8:00 AM tomorrow. That's twelve to fourteen inches, over the next few hours. So get out your shovels, throw another log onto the fire, and crank up

that stereo. Because we've got a little sunshine to warm you up.
Here's one-hit-wonder Terry Jacks with his 1974 smash single, a
cover of an old song by Jacques Brel . . ."

The lyrics began as I pulled into Astrid's drive, a dirt road
abutting the woods. *"Goodbye to you, my trusted friend . . ."* My
first forty-five: the song I'd listened to, endlessly, back in 1974.
Which would have been, I quickly calculated, two years after
April died. Hadn't it been her face I'd pictured every time I
heard it? Those damned pink erasers, they could never erase all
that well. Maybe I hadn't forgotten her completely, like I'd told
Dr. Rivers. The past was always leaking into the present, no
matter how tightly one plugged the dike.

Dr. Rivers had asked why I felt losing April had been such
a significant event. "You knew her for two months. Why the
strong association with her disappearance?" she said. "What else
was going on at the time?"

I'd sat there in that office, with its soothing eggshell walls and
book-crammed shelves, and thought. My baby brother Josh had
just been born. Nixon was running for reelection. Long-haired
students were marching downtown, carrying peace signs. My
mother had begun to retreat further into the sanctuary of her
bedroom. Slight chaos, sure, but nothing unreasonable. "Nothing," I'd said. "Nothing significant at all."

But later that week, I reconsidered my answer. What else had
been going on? Not nothing. Everything if you were six years
old. Josh was not only born, he was born to much more fanfare
than his older sisters. Nixon was not only running for reelection, he'd broken locks and laws and lied about it. The hip-
pies had been carrying photos of napalmed children along with
their peace signs, giving me nightmares for months afterwards.
And my mother was not only retreating into her bedroom, her
bathtub, anywhere on earth and in her head where we weren't,

she was also frequently becoming unhinged: losing her temper; hitting me with the kind of ferocity normally reserved for unruly inmates; digging her nails into the flesh of my arm until I bled.

April's murder, I realized, coincided not only with the fraying of the social fabric, whose ragged edges even I, at that young age, could feel chafing, but with the moment when each of my childhood fantasies—and thus my childhood itself—was torn asunder. In a single year, at age six, everything I'd been taught, everything I'd held to be true, was revealed to me as a lie: friends last forever; girls are equal to boys; adults tell the truth; soldiers don't target children; mothers nurture their young.

Some part of me even then must have known that those boys on the bus were right. That April's mother, whose responsibility it was to take care of her, like all the other mammal mothers we'd been studying, had done the exact opposite. Which would have only served to underscore another truth I'd been figuring out in my own home: that a mother could exist but not always mother. That the noun could hold true without the verb.

In the course of my research into April's story, I'd come across the work of Harry Harlow, who set out to prove that a mother's love was developmentally important to a child's welfare. This was in the late fifties, an era during which such an idea verged on blasphemy; when pediatricians and psychologists alike were telling new mothers not to hold their infants, not to pick them up when they cried, not to kiss them more than once a month and certainly never on the mouth. Harlow separated baby rhesus monkeys from their mothers and placed them in a cage with two inanimate surrogate mothers: one, made of wire mesh, who would dispense milk; the other, made of soft terrycloth rags, who had no milk. While the infants would go to the wire mother for material sustenance, they ended up spending only one hour a day, on average, with that mother, while an average of seventeen hours was spent seeking emotional sustenance—love—by cuddling with the soft rag mother. Once the babies had become attached to the rag mothers, Harlow added a twist: he retrofitted the dolls with blunt spikes, which would spring out and injure the baby monkeys quite violently whenever the dolls were hugged. Even so, the babies kept trying to hug the so-called "evil" mother, kept trying to get back into her good graces, shunning peers and even food in the vain attempt to win back her love. When the spikes were removed, Harlow claimed, the baby monkeys acted as if the evil mother had never existed. They forgot the spikes altogether.

But what if they didn't really forget? I now thought. What if every decision made from that moment on could be traced directly back to that early mistreatment? What if one day, half a lifetime later, one of those monkeys, now fully grown and a mother herself, happened to have seen a play or heard a song or witnessed a scene that suddenly triggered a memory of a friend whose mother had had so many spikes she wound up impaling both herself *and her babies* on them. Would that fully grown monkey, her memory thus jogged, suddenly recall, with searing clarity, her own mother's spikes? Would the remembered dissonance between spike and rag send her darting around her cage, banging her head against the bars? To fear the object of love; to love the object of fear: it was enough to drive a monkey crazy.

"I hate her," I'd finally announced to Dr. Rivers, remembering what it had felt like, year after year, to be pummeled for some minor infraction: a drop of pancake batter left behind on the kitchen table; a chair not pushed in; a wet towel found languishing on a floor. "I *hate* her!"

"Why, Lizzie? Tell me why." Dr. Rivers had put her notepad down.

"Because she hit me. Often."

"Okay, but take it one step further."

"Further? That's as far as I go."

"I don't believe that. Tell me why you're angry at her."

"Because . . ." I said, trying to form the feelings into words. Dr. Rivers stared at me, waiting for my thoughts to gel.

"Because . . ." I finally said, "Because she stole my childhood. And I can never get it back." I collapsed into a puddle of grief from all those years of mental solitude, of hiding the truth from everyone, even myself.

Dr. Rivers handed me a box of tissues and waited for me to compose myself. "But?" she finally said, waiting for me to fill in the blank.

"But what? That's it. That's all I've got." I blew my nose as further punctuation.

"There is a *but*, Lizzie. Think about it. Think hard. She 'stole your childhood,' yes, that's a perfectly acceptable way of phrasing it, but what *didn't* she do?"

I now leaned my head against the steering wheel of Astrid's Civic and began to weep again, feeling the absence of an arm around my shoulder not like an amputee remembering a lost limb, but rather like a person born without any appendages whatsoever.

"Mrs. Cassidy had one arm wrapped around each of her daughters. The two girls . . . were lying on pillows, their feet toward the tailgate. They were dressed in flannel pajamas." She held them while she killed them. She loved them, even as she was suffocating them. But she must have hated herself more.

Down I fell, further and further into the void, the vortex growing deeper. Narrower. Colder. Darker. Until there was only ice.

"Mommy, what's wrong? Where are we going?" said Daisy,

my wails having woken her and Tess, both of whom were looking around the car, disoriented.

I wiped my tears with the back of my wrist and feigned san-
ity. "Where do you want to go, pumpkin?" I said.

"Home," said Tess. Her voice was tinier than I'd ever heard it.

"Home?" I said, not knowing what that meant anymore.
"But look at the snow! Look at this place! This is Astrid's
cabin, remember Daisy? Tess, you were just a baby last time we
were here, but look: these are Astrid's woods! Her land! Isn't it
beautiful?"

The snow had started falling furiously now, blinding confetti
dropping straight from the sky as we stepped out of the car into
the elements.

"Yes," said Daisy, grabbing Tess's hand. Shivering. "It's pretty.
Can we go inside now?"

But I didn't want to go inside the cabin just yet. I wanted
to be out in the woods, wandering through the frigid air, feeling the snowflakes on my skin, the icy branches crunching underneath me, the black ink of darkness enveloping my body. I
wanted my shell to feel like my innards: damp, and blind, and
lost, and cold. "Fine, you can go inside. But I'm staying out
here."

"But you'll freeze," said Tess.

I had to restrain myself from telling her to shut up. I held my
face up to the falling snow, each flake a tiny prick of welcome
numbness. "No I won't. Look! I'm not cold at all!" I tossed off
my down jacket to prove the point, then the hat, the scarf, the
gloves, until I was wearing only my flannel pajama bottoms and
a cotton tank top. "See?" I said. "No problem. Come on, let's go
exploring. My mother never took me on adventures. Grab those
flashlights on the floor of the car. Let's all go!"

Tess studied me as if examining one of her found creatures. "You should put your jacket back on, Mommy," she said.

"I'm not cold," I said. I was growing frustrated, restless. "I don't *need* a jacket. Are you coming with me or not?" The question was rhetorical. Of course they would come with me. How unnatural it was to be a human child, to depend on another for so long, so completely. "See?" I said, leading them toward the woods. "Aren't you happy? Isn't this fun?" I shook a sapling for added emphasis and watched its snow scatter into the wind.

Daisy gripped her sister's hand. "Yes, Mom," she said, ever the obedient first child. "We're having fun."

"It's cold," Tess said, hugging herself.

Sighing, I gripped my flashlight between my thighs and rubbed my palms up and down Tess's bony shoulders to create friction. "Is that better, pumpkin?"

"Sort of," she said.

"Good," I said. "Come on, let's go dig up some worms. Do you like worms?"

The girls looked at one another.

"Well, do you?" I said.

"Yes, Mommy," said Daisy, shushing Tess, who was trying to whisper into her ear.

"It's snowing," said Tess.

"I know," I said. "Isn't it beautiful?" One hand on the flashlight, the other held up in front of my face for protection, I led our little threesome into the tangled woods, the space between trees growing narrower, such that even with my hand held up as a shield, stray branches strafed my cheeks, the inside of my wrist, my goose-pimpled shoulders, until one of them gouged an actual hole. I sat down on a felled log to assess the damage, the cold dampness of the wood seeping its way into my pajama bottoms. I started to shiver. "Shit," I said, shining the light on the inside of my wrist, which was now bleeding. I held the torn skin up to my mouth and sucked on it, comforted in some perverse way by the warm, metallic gush.

"Mommy," said Daisy. She was hopping up and down on the balls of her feet to stay warm. "Are you okay?"

"Of course I am," I said. "It's just a little blood." And as I sat there, half-naked on the frozen log, sucking on my blood, my body growing colder and wetter by the second, until I could hardly feel anything, inside or out, I realized how easy it would be for us to sit there, in that precise spot, keeping our bodies very still, the snow covering us until we disappeared. How easy it would be to fade away.

I thought of what Astrid had once explained to me, what she was trying to get at in her dissertation: how the act of suicide, which contains both pain and pain's outlet simultaneously, could be compared with . . . with what? I couldn't remember. She'd shown me the passage in the poem itself, a passage she'd memorized along with the rest of the canto, where the two poets meet Pier della Vigne, whose fall from political grace provoked his suicide. Dante both identifies with and feels so much compassion for della Vigne that it "chokes" his heart and renders him speechless. Pier, with Virgil's prodding, tells the poets that the soul of someone, like him, who has committed suicide falls into the woods, takes root, and becomes a tree who can only speak when pecked by Harpies.

I'd imagined myself a tree when she read it, stuck forever in Suicide Wood. How bad would that be, really? It hardly seemed like a real punishment. Much less harsh than some of the other sinners' fates, like having your face devoured by serpents, or carrying your own severed head around like a lantern, or picking scabs off the putrid body of a neighbor. "But don't you see?" Astrid had said. "They can only speak when the Harpies peck them. They can only communicate—release their pain—through the infliction of pain upon themselves."

"I see," I said, but only in the literal sense.

But now, sitting there with my shivering daughters, our bodies growing progressively more numb, her words finally sank in. Pain and pain's outlet. Simultaneously.

"So what if you do not have yet all the facts of the story," Renzo had said. "You think you need facts to write truth? You think that making a documentary is truth? This is bullshit, *mon Eliza,* and you know it . . . Write the story of one mother who do not make it, who was pushed—how you say?—over the ledge . . ."

"There is a *but* there, Lizzie," Dr. Rivers had said. "Think about it. Think hard."

But what? I'd wondered, walking out of her office, completely confused. Wasn't it enough to have finally spoken the words out loud, to have finally found release for the long-buried emotions?

"But . . ." I now whispered, sitting there on my log, and the revelation suddenly entered my body and shot straight up my spine, like the sliding weight to the bell after the anvil falls. "But . . ." And now I saw it, clearly. So clearly, I could hardly believe it had never occurred to me before. "But she didn't kill me," I said.

Sometimes I remember having simply imagined the words, my mother's face, not having spoken them out loud, though I know this can't be true, because the next several minutes of my life are seared, second by second, into my head: Tess, shivering, sniffling, her lips indigo, saying, "Who didn't kill you, Mommy? What are you talking about? Are you okay?"; Daisy, hugging her sister to her; me, staring at the blue of my daughters' lips, the red of my wrist, the white of the snow, seeing myself and the neglect I was capable of committing finally, wholly, through their petrified eyes.

"Oh my god," I said, leaping up from the log, suddenly horrified by my selfishness, my stupidity, how close I'd just pushed all three of us to the ledge, edge, catastrophic event, hell it didn't matter, did it? because it all led to the same place: numbness; eternal darkness; the end of all pain, but the end of life, too. I scooped a daughter into each arm, the *sorrys* tumbling out of my mouth as fast as they could form, and began to run out of the woods, Tess on my left hip, Daisy on my right, the weight of their bodies counterbalanced by adrenaline, my forward propulsion fueled by sheer fumes of will. "Hold on," I said. "Cover your faces with your hands!"

Tess looked bad, as if she were succumbing to hypothermia. "I'm . . . so . . . cold . . ." she said. Her body was becoming leaden.

I could see the outline of Astrid's cabin through the thicket of trunks. "We're almost there," I said. "Look, there's the cabin! Come on Tessie, just a few more minutes. Count backwards with me from one hundred. Come on! One hundred, ninety-nine, ninety-eight . . ." As Tess struggled to utter the numbers, I commanded Daisy to rub her sister's shoulders, while I blew tiny puffs of warm breath onto her neck.

"Wake up, Tess," said Daisy, holding her sister's hands in her own. Kissing them. And it nearly felled me just then, the magnitude of what I'd nearly thrown away. "Let's think of another game. And you don't have to carry me anymore. I can walk." She wiggled out of my arms, as she would pretty much do from then on, and advanced slightly ahead of us, clearing branches so I could use both arms to hold Tess.

"Okay, another game . . ." I said, trying to think. License plate ABCs? I Spy? God it was cold. I couldn't think.

"How about the love game?" said Daisy.

"Perfect," I said. "Go ahead, Daisy. You start." The love game was something Mark had initiated one night to ease Tess off to sleep, when nothing else had been working: a way of naming and appreciating the opposite of the dark—all the people she loved—to face her fear of it. He knew it would work because he used to play the same game himself when he was a kid. Until he ran out of names with which to play it.

"Daddy!" said Daisy. "Because he's funny. Your turn, Tess."

Tess looked slightly disoriented, lost. But then she finally muttered, through chattering teeth, "Mommy. Because she takes me out for hot chocolate."

"Oh, peanut," I said, squeezing her even more tightly to me. "Okay, my turn. Daisy, because she's the best big sister in the whole wide world."

"My turn!" said Tess, and Daisy didn't even argue that her turn had been skipped. "Grandma! Because she's the best grandma in the whole wide world."

We'd reached the open field now, between the forest and Astrid's cabin, and I had to bite my lip to keep the floodgates from opening anew. *How ironic,* I thought. As overwhelmed as my mother had been as a parent, she'd metamorphosed into a burnished gem of a grandparent: present, benevolent, brimming with love, both for my daughters and for me.

"That's cheating," said Daisy. "You can't use the same reason twice."

"That's okay, Daisy," I said. "Let her say it. It's true."

WHEN WE FINALLY reached the cabin, when we were finally inside, and I'd built a fire, and we'd settled in front of it, Tess laid her head on my lap, her eyes heavy with sleep. "Are we safe now?" she said. The fire crackled as the logs shifted.

"Yes," I said, "we're safe." I ran my palm over the top of her head, stroking her hair, then her sister's. After awhile, as the flames settled down, I carried them to bed.

I should have been exhausted, too. Instead I sat fidgeting in front of the fireplace, my head buzzing with embers. Renzo was right. April's story could not rely solely — if at all — on fact or third person accounts or anything reality-based or external. What it required was internal: an imagination for the unimaginable, an empathy for monsters, a tolerance for yanking off scabs. At six I'd had all three. Then somewhere along the way I'd lost them.

I threw another log onto the fire, pulled out my first-grade class photo from my purse, and stared at it, hard: the toothless smiles; the plaid dresses and blue Stride Rites; the dead girl's spot usurped by the living. It was spring when the class photo was finally taken. April's bones would have just begun to thaw.

I let my eyes drift toward the flames; then back to the photo; then back to the flames. This was an old habit from when I was young. I'd lie on my bed, after having been sent there, and hold up my thumb in front of my face, shifting focus back and forth between thumb and dresser; thumb and window; thumb and sky. It calmed me down, focused my thoughts. Then I'd pull out a pencil and start to write.

I need some paper, I thought. *Now.* I rummaged around in Astrid's drawers until I found some.

And then, pen in hand, I began the painful process of resurrection. I borrowed the opening image from my lunch with Renzo. I lifted a shard of glass I'd once found on the kitchen floor. I stole my darkest thoughts, the books off my children's shelves, my mother's moods, Daisy's drawing off our refrigera-

tor, a memory of a slice of pizza in College Park. I built a strip
mall where one had never existed, paved a road where I needed a
fork. It felt like cheating. Like pretending to be God. Like writing a poem to an unworthy recipient. But then, as it began to
sputter out, as I accounted as best I could considering the limitations of memory and circumstance, what was dropped there
and left on the page felt more and more like a distilled version
of truth. Not *the* truth, but my truth, however imperfect.

Herewith is the final version, slightly edited from the original.

CHAPTER 21

I.

ON THE MORNING she decided to kill herself, Adele Cassidy scrubbed the kitchen floor with a new sponge. The old one had been shredding at the edges and smelled of mildew and old milk, and to have used it now would have been no way to have left a floor. Even so, she made a point of burying the old one in the trash under a pile of coffee grounds. Shep would have enough to deal with in a day or two. It didn't seem fair to add the waste of a perfectly good sponge.

She pressed hard as she scrubbed, going over the same spot several times, wringing out the dirt in the bucket of soapy water after every square foot covered, making sure each of the four corners and especially the tiles around the trash can and under the lip of the cabinets were free of grime, stray hairs, dried food. She was amazed at how productive she could be when the time stretching before her suddenly had a limit, how she barely even registered the annoyance of wet knees. And she marveled at the irony of how, having finally made a choice to put a limit on the clock, she could almost enjoy the hours she had left. *Almost,* she reminded herself. Let's not get carried away.

At the nexus where sink met floor she found a small fragment of broken glass, the size of a baby's fingernail. She picked it up and held it in her palm, wondering which of the many recent accidents were to blame. The glass of orange juice April had dropped? The Coca-Cola bottle Lily had left too close to the edge of the counter? Or was it another piece of the blender Shep had smashed to the floor the day Lenny was over? The blender had been a wedding present, their only one, left on their doorstep a few weeks after they'd eloped, by friends with whom they no longer kept in touch. "Blend well!" the card had said. As if that were possible. She kept finding tiny shards of it for months afterwards, in the front hallway, under the kitchen table, once even wedged into the rough edge of her heel, which she had to dislodge with a pair of tweezers. She hadn't come across another stray piece for at least a year now. She took the mystery shard and scraped it against her thigh, drawing just the tiniest stream of blood. The sting felt good, like a test run.

I am nothing if not my mother's daughter, she thought, watching the blood trickle down her leg. She'd tried to fight it, to be the kind of mother hers had never been. And in some ways, she knew, she'd succeeded. She'd listened, as best as she could, to their endless chatter. She'd sat on tiny chairs for tea parties with Lily, helped April build the edges of her jigsaw puzzles. She'd read to them at night, all those tales of wicked mothers and orphaned children, giving shape—and thus release—to their darkest fantasies. Making her look, by comparison, not so bad. She'd even indulged their after-school baking whims, like those mothers on TV. Cupcakes, banana bread, brownies, chocolate chip cookies: she tried to keep a fresh supply of eggs, flour, and baking soda on hand. But during the past year, or maybe two, she found herself making excuses. I couldn't get to the store. I'm too tired. I can't today. Go ask your sister for help. No you can't use the oven by yourselves. Fine, I don't care, do whatever you want. Please, just leave me alone!

She felt like one of those goslings she'd seen on a recent nature show, who'd been tricked into following a wooden mother with wheels for legs and a click-clack patter when you pulled it, the kind Lily used to drag around the house. She had no blueprint for flying. No fumes of early nurture. Only a heart petrified for lack of succor and a pair of pine wings.

She tossed the shard in the trash atop the coffee grounds, but then changed her mind and buried it underneath with the old sponge. Everything reminded her of Lenny. She might as well bury the reminders she could, since the ones she couldn't were always in plain view: the front hallway where he first rang her doorbell; the living room where he would gently press the small of her back with his knee as she tried to touch her toes; the back-yard where, in warmer months, they'd lie on chaise longues with their faces toward the sun and discuss everything from the nu-tritional benefits of spinach to their shared disappointment with the hand life had dealt them. The kitchen table where they . . . no. She couldn't go there. It was too pathetic to even conjure, still made the back of her neck prickle up with warm shame. Even the sight of this yellow bucket, filled with soapy, gray wa-ter, could make her plunge into despair. It was where she'd hid the *Playgirl* she'd bought Lenny on a hunch, guessing correctly how it would affect him, and thus her, knowing it was one of the few hiding places in the house Shep would never happen upon. It was just her luck to fall in love with a man like Lenny. She couldn't even get adultery right.

The girls were still sleeping by the time she started unloading the dishwasher. She wanted them to stay in that state for just a little while longer, until everything could be cleaned and prepared, packed and put away, so she went about the task quietly, carefully, even if it meant pulling out one dish at a time and fishing the pieces of silverware out of the mesh basket like so many pick-up sticks. Normally, she'd make a racket unloading the dishes, not so much to let everyone else in the house know what she was doing, as Shep maintained, but to prove, to herself, she existed.

Outside, the sky was overcast but unthreatening, thank goodness, despite the weatherman's prediction otherwise. Shep had a weekly golf game on Saturday mornings, and she was counting on his absence to make her escape.

She'd called Trudy the night before, while Shep was out taking swigs from a bottle of scotch in the station wagon, even though he'd promised to quit. He was crouching low in the backseat, but not low enough. "I can see him from the second-floor window," she told her sister, watching him, through wobbling binoculars, down another shot. "He parked under a streetlight, five houses down." She tried to make herself feel something—anger, or guilt, or even pity for her husband's addiction—but all she could feel was numb, as if her body had been shot through with Novocain.

"Adele, what do you want me to say? You married a goy. That's what they do. They drink. They drink in cars. They drink in bars. God, I sound like what's-his-name, from Dr. Seuss. Just leave him if you're so unhappy."

She gazed through the binoculars once again, thinking *They drink here, they drink there, they drink everywhere . . .* "Sam I am. Leaving him." She was both stunned and not surprised to spot her neighbor Mavis walking down the street, glancing over her shoulder toward her own house, twice, as she made her way to the car, where she rapped on the window and then shut the door with the tiniest thud behind her. An odd sight made more peculiar by the fact that, aside from Halloween night and the week or so of Girl Scout cookie season, nobody in the neighborhood ever walked farther than the distance between their front door and the end of their driveway. In fact, most of the women in the neighborhood, including Adele, had perfected the art of driving up to the mailbox, on their way to or from some errand or carpool, so unless the paperboy's aim was really off, tossing *Posts* into yards and bushes, a person could go for weeks without ever seeing another soul on the street. How did Mavis explain it to Arnie? "Bye, honey, I'm going for a walk?"

"Wait, I'm confused," said Trudy. "You *are* leaving him? Who's Sam?"

"Yes, tomorrow." She watched her husband push Mavis down, hungrily, onto the wide seat, where they fell into a place she could no longer see. Shep was lucky the seats of the family station wagon—the *family station wagon,* for Christ's sake!— were made of vinyl. Leather would have stained. "I want to see you before I go," she said to her sister. She laid the binoculars down.

Most women, she knew, would be searching the house for a weapon by now, running outside and screaming obscenities. Or at least that's how they would have done it on a soap opera. Again she tried to make herself feel something: fury or jealousy or even grief over what had been lost. But what had been lost had been lost long ago, including her ability to care. "But you have to promise not to say a word to Shep if he calls looking for me. And I mean promise, okay? I need a few days to . . . to get settled in my new arrangement."

"Of course, of course," said Trudy. "I wouldn't say a word. What new arrangement?"

And then Adele did something she'd never done to her sister

before. "I found a nursing job in Frederick," she lied. "And a cheap apartment near the hospital, until we get our bearings."

"That's wonderful, Adele! Good for you!"

It didn't really feel like a lie. A former colleague had recently told her about two new openings on the maternity ward at Frederick Memorial, and she had entertained the notion of sending in her resume. A daily infusion of life's greatest miracle might be just the jolt her battery needed. Although she wondered if the constant exposure to all that happiness wouldn't eventually dull her reaction to it, the way the body habituates to morphine. And then there'd be the babies who wouldn't make it. Babies with Down's syndrome, without spinal columns. Babies born to parents who would beat them, or ignore them, or tell them they were worthless. There would be babies whose mothers would arrive home from the hospital filled with hope and good intentions only to wake up the next morning begging their husbands to hide the knives. Babies who would grow up into adults who'd spend every waking hour bent over dirty floors and unloading dishwashers and wondering why the fuck anything even mattered.

She'd checked out the real estate section of the *Washington Post* to see what the rent on a two-bedroom apartment in Frederick would run her. She would have had to figure out some sort of after-school care for the girls, or she could have given them each a house key to wear around her neck on a lanyard, like two of the kids in Lily's class had started wearing when their mothers, to the amazement of everyone but her, went back to work, but otherwise it would have been a perfectly reasonable remedy to a decaying marriage. Provided, of course, that's what the problem was.

Because gangrene, she knew, was only a symptom of the dying tissue, not the disease itself. Back when she was at Holy

Cross Hospital, she was constantly having to explain this distinction to her patients and their families. Some kid would come in blue with pneumonia, and the parents would insist, "He just has a really bad cough. We've been giving him syrup, but for some reason he's not getting any better."

"Because you're only treating the symptoms, not the disease," she'd say. Then she'd go on to explain that while giving the child Robitussin might temporarily alleviate some of his suffering, it would not combat the underlying infection of his lungs, which was the actual source of his illness. "Do you understand the difference?" she'd ask.

Sometimes they did. And sometimes they didn't. Depending upon their education. Actually, sometimes even the educated ones got confused. Or maybe they just couldn't process the fact that they'd ignored what was right in front of their faces for so long.

"Your leg is bleeding, Mommy." April walked into the kitchen, rubbing her eyes. It was still strange seeing her daughter without Raggedy Ann clutched to her chest. Like she'd lost her female markings. Or a limb. Adele recently asked where poor Raggedy had gone, and April answered, with the slightest blush of shame, "Somewhere better. Where they speak doll." The last time she'd seen the doll was during their ill-fated visit to Dr. Sherman's (god what a miserable day *that* was), but she was sure April had taken it into the car when they left, because she remembered seeing her crying into its smocking in the rearview mirror on the drive back to school afterwards. Maybe she left it in her classroom, in that cubby with her accident clothes. If she did, it would be found soon enough, once the cubby was cleaned out.

Oh god. She was actually going through with this, wasn't she? Her heart pounded inside her like a rebuke.

"You need a Band-Aid?" April was now shouting. How long
had her daughter been standing there?

"A Band-Aid?" Luckily she'd perfected the art of repetition:
when in doubt, just repeat the last two words of any question the
children asked. This had worked well until recently, when April
finally wised up to her tactics.

"Yes. A Band-Aid," said April. "Why don't you ever listen to
me?"

"Yes, yes. I'm listening to you. A Band-Aid." She looked down
at her bleeding leg. The words clicked in place. *Band aid:* aid
in the form of a band. "No, muffin." A Band-Aid. She nearly
laughed at the absurdity of a band of cloth ever offering her aid.
"I'm fine," she said. "It's just a nick."

She'd counted on Dr. Sherman to help her. But she might as
well have been a parakeet for as well as he understood her. Or
any woman. Not that she begrudged him this deficiency. How
could a person who'd never given birth, never worn a maxi pad,
never known the type of fluctuations in mood and temperament
she'd experienced since that afternoon of her thirteenth summer, when her mother slapped her across the face—how could
he ever understand what it meant to live, to think, to bleed in
a woman's body? She'd gone to the public library in Rockville
one morning to see if she could find any mention in the medical
literature regarding hormonal variations at the onset of menses,
but there was nothing. Not a single citation in the entire library.
The only books that came close to describing her particular form
of lunar-rhythmic torment were listed under fiction in the card
catalogue, in the drawer labeled *W–Z*: "Werewolves and other
transmogrifying creatures of fantasy." That these cyclical aber-
rations were ascribed to men and to fantasy was hardly surprising. Trudy, who studied these things, said it happened all the

time. She told Adele about the faculty Christmas party where she fumed to a male colleague, who'd claimed that the lack of childcare in America was not a "real" problem, *Nothing* is ever real unless it happens to a man.

Adele was starting to see her point. But when she called her family physician to ask for a new referral, the man laughed and said, "Stick with Dr. Sherman. He knows what he's doing."

Right, thought Adele. He knows what he's doing. Giving me those pills which made me forget my daughter's birthday. Suggesting that all I have to do is tell my story and everything will be better. Bringing my daughters into his office and making them feel worse than they already did beforehand. Where the fuck was that doll? It would have been helpful for her to have had it, today of all days. "April, sweetheart, go wake up your sister and get dressed." She was writing a check to Dr. Sherman, which she would slip into the envelope she'd left by the door, with Shep's name written across it. Inside the envelope was also a key to a safety deposit box, containing her wedding ring, the girls' birth certificates, the instructions she'd painstakingly written two days earlier explaining how she wanted the bodies to be buried. "You can skip your shower, honey. Just go quickly. I'm taking you both on a little adventure."

"An adventure?" April said. "Really? What kind of adventure?"

How long had it been since she'd taken the girls on a real outing? Aside from the yearly pilgrimage to Dewey Beach and the biannual visits to Montgomery Mall to buy clothes, all she could remember was a trip to the pumpkin patch when April was still in diapers. Hadn't she promised herself that she'd take them to Great Falls, just as soon as they could walk, to throw breadcrumbs to the ducks? Hadn't she planned on spending cold weekend afternoons visiting the Smithsonian, warm ones tossing a Frisbee across a field? Didn't she discuss with Shep her desire to take the girls on an overnight camping trip in the foothills of the Ozarks? What happened to those plans? The girls were old enough now to appreciate those things. They'd been old enough for years. Even a jaunt around the neighborhood with a butterfly net would have sufficed. The realization of this only strengthened her resolve. "A secret adventure," she said.

She'd toyed with the idea of going at it alone. But every time she imagined the girls coming home from school to a dark house, or sitting at the dinner table, being fed another TV dinner, or walking around the neighborhood with their pant legs hovering three inches above their ankles, every time she imagined them imagining her turning that key in the ignition, which always became tangled up with her own memories of scouring the blood stains off her mother's tub, every time she pictured her daughters tossing shovelfuls of dirt onto her coffin and saying Kaddish, if Shep would even let them say it, which he probably wouldn't, she knew she could not leave April and Lily here by themselves. Shep would adapt. He'd find someone to help around the house, to do the laundry and cleaning and grocery shopping. Maybe he'd even get remarried, although she doubted that Mavis would actually leave her husband. But the girls, they would never adapt. First they would suffer. Then they would be pitied. And avoided. And made to feel like lepers. Then, finally, the anger would sink in. After her own mother was wheeled out into the waiting ambulance, its bright lights flashing her family's shame across the Grand Concourse, the neighbors whispered at her approach. *That's the girl whose mother tried to kill herself . . . the father was schtupping his secretary . . . the mother did it for revenge.* Oh, she knew what they were saying! The lies, the truths, all bunched up together in the same suitcase. She knew what they were saying because she saw every word of it in their eyes. *Poor kid. Crazy mother. No love.* "It'll be the kind of adventure you'll remember for the rest of your life, muffin," she said, choking on the words. She kneeled down until she was at eye level with April, and then she kissed the top of her head. "But first we're going to visit Aunt Trudy in College Park to eat pizza. She's taking us to that Italian place you love."

"Famiglia's?" April said, pronouncing the word with the *g* sound intact. *Fah-mih-glee-ah.* Adele had explained that it had a silent *g*, the way they say family in Italy, but the girls insisted on pronouncing it the way it was spelled.

"Yes, muffin. That's right. Famiglia's," Adele said, enunciating the *g*, too. Family was difficult enough to master in English. "Then we're going to drive out to Gaithersburg to begin our adventure. Dress warmly, okay? Wear a long-sleeved T-shirt and a sweater, and tell your sister to do the same. I'll pack a suitcase with the rest of our stuff, but if you have any games or toys you want to bring along, just pack them in your school bag."

"We're sleeping over on our adventure?"

"Maybe."

"What about my school books?"

"You won't need them."

"Really?"

"Bring a chapter book, if you'd like. We'll read it if we have time. And maybe some small toys or activities for the ride. Checkers would be good. A deck of cards. Now hurry. Get Lily up and moving."

"Lily!" April yelled, dashing out of the kitchen. "Wake up! We're going to eat pizza with Aunt Trudy and go on an adventure!"

And while upstairs her daughters were excitedly putting on

their clothes and brushing their teeth, while they were giggling and packing their backpacks full of goodies *(Mad Libs,* an abacus, a set of magnetic travel checkers, and *Harriet the Spy* in April's bag; a Nancy Drew mystery, a sketch pad, a deck of cards, and a tape recorder with a cassette of Top Forty songs in Lily's bag), downstairs Adele Cassidy was studying the manual for the vacuum cleaner, trying to figure out a way to disengage its plastic hose without destroying the machine. Shep, after everything was said and done, would still need to vacuum.

2.

After lunch, their bellies full of pepperoni pizza and "Famiglia's famous" garlic bread, April and Lily climbed into the backseat of the family station wagon, which their mother had for some reason decided to wipe down with Lysol and water before leaving the house. They took out the *Mad Libs* and started working down their list of favorite words — *smelly, boogers, poop, farted.* Meanwhile, Adele stood on the sidewalk with her sister.

"Oh, Adele," said Trudy, giving her the kind of bear hug she'd perfected during her brief flirtation with EST. "You're doing the right thing. You know you are. Enough's enough. You gave it your best shot."

Adele was fiddling with a pebble with her big toe, rolling it back and forth between skin and flip-flop. "Remember when we got separated from Mom that day in Coney Island?" she said.

Trudy pursed her lips and turned her eyeballs skyward. "Vaguely. That wasn't Rye Playland?"

"No. It was Coney Island. I'm positive." She remembered exactly where they were standing, right under the Ferris wheel. In the line for the sliding cars, not the stationary ones. She was thirteen, which would have made Trudy three. She wrinkled her eyebrows, fiddled with the zipper on her housedress. The possibility of her sister not remembering this most seminal moment in their lives together had never even occurred to her.

"Anyway, it doesn't matter. Go on."

Of course it matters, thought Adele. *Memory matters!* She cleared her throat. "Anyway, so we'd been waiting in line to go on the Ferris wheel . . ." She took a deep breath, cleared her throat again. "We were in line to go on the Ferris wheel. Mom didn't realize she needed to buy tickets beforehand, so she stepped out of line to go buy them. But she didn't tell us she was going—she used to do that all the time, remember? just disappeared without explanation—and so we kept moving along in the line, just the two of us by ourselves—"

"—Oh, wait. I do remember. And I started crying."

"Yes! Exactly!" Victory at last. Someone to share the past, to prove she hadn't just dreamed it. "You started crying. So we got to the front of the line, but we still didn't have tickets, so we couldn't go on the ride, and you wanted to leave to go look for Mom . . ."

"I had to go to the bathroom," said Trudy.

"I don't remember that. Anyway, for whatever reason, you wanted to leave, and I kept saying, no, we have to stay here so she can find us again. But the people who were running the ride kept asking us to move out of the way and let the people with tickets through, and I kept saying that our mother would be right back. That she'd definitely come back for us, and then we'd go on the ride, even though I was starting to have my doubts." *I kept picturing her stepping into the surf and floating away,* Adele thought. *Or diving off the top of the Cyclone into the pavement.* "At that point we didn't even care about going on the ride anymore. Remember? We just wanted to be found. We just wanted our mother to come find us."

"So what does that have to do with anything?"

"Do you remember what you said—what you made me promise once Mom had come back, and given us our tickets, and we were stuck in that metal cage all by ourselves because she had another migraine and didn't feel well enough to go on with us?"

"No."

"You said, 'If Mommy's not there when we come back down, will you promise to stay with me forever?'"

"I did?"

"You did. Right at the top of the ride." *Even at your young age and at that great height,* Adele thought (feeling a sudden intensity of tenderness toward her little sister), *you could tell we were on shaky ground with our mother. That we'd always be on shaky ground. That it would mostly just be the two of us, rocking back and forth in the ocean breeze, holding hands in our metal cage.* "And I said of course. Of course I'll stay with you forever." Adele was starting to cry again, clinging to the parking meter for support, realizing she could no longer keep such a promise.

Trudy looked at her sister, perplexed. "Um, Adele? Two things. One, if I actually spoke those words—which I have no memory of having spoken—I'm sure I was just asking if you'd be my sister forever. You know, not understanding that once you're related, you're always related. But anyway it doesn't matter, because the second thing is that I know you're going through a rough time with Shep right now, and I love that you're still worried about my well-being, and I'm frankly, well, I'm just . . . *touched* that you think I still need you, but I'm a twenty-nine-year-old woman." Her voice was growing restive, hurt. "I'm seven months shy of my PhD! I pay my own rent, and I cook my own food, and I'm perfectly capable of taking care of my—."

"No, no, I didn't mean to suggest . . ." Adele was really making a mess of this, she knew. She wanted her parting words to her sister to be meaningful, deep, full of pathos and shared memory; instead she was pissing her off. "I just wanted you to know that I love you."

"Jesus, Adele, you sound like one of those after-school specials. You're going to Frederick. We'll see each other as much as we do now. Maybe even more so now that the . . ." — she peeked inside the car at the girls, who'd moved on to playing checkers, then lowered her voice, just in case — ". . . asshole's out of the picture."

"He's not an asshole, Trude. Please don't call him that. Don't even think that."

"Oh for Christ's sake, Adele. He is an asshole! Stop trying to defend him. He's a drunk and a cheat and a big fat bully, and he's never been a good father to those—"

"Stop! That's not true. He's always been a good father to the girls. He's always loved them. He may not love *me* anymore, but who can blame him? *I'm* the bad person. I'm the monster, Trudy. Me. Look at me."

And Trudy looked at her sister, thinking, *look what he's done to her, the schmuck.*

And Adele looked at her sister, thinking, *she'll never understand.*

And the two sisters kissed one another and said good-bye.

Then, as she pulled the station wagon away from the curb, Adele rolled down her window and yelled, "Wait! Trudy!" catching her sister midstride. "Where would I find the nearest hardware store?" And Trudy, assuming her sister needed nails or maybe some lightbulbs or a caulk gun for her new apartment, gave her directions.

3.

"Let's say I wanted to seal up a room," Adele was saying to the clerk in the red apron. "Like I was doing work in one room, you know, the kind of work that creates a lot of sawdust and mess, and I wanted to seal it off from the rest of the apartment. Make it so that no air or dust could go in or out. What would you recommend?" There. She'd said it. She'd taken the next step. She was surprised, as she spoke the words, to feel a burst of exhilaration mixed in with her anguish, a lump of sugar tossed in with the tar. She imagined that this is what it must feel like to hold up a store: dread and excitement, in dissonant stereo, a sense of power normally reserved for those who come by it naturally. Her heart was once more beating at twice its normal speed; she felt light-headed and agitated, in equal measure. She looked at her watch. 1:15 PM. She still had a few more hours before Shep would come home from his golf game and find the house empty. Clean, but empty. He'll think we're just out at the grocery store, she reasoned. Or shopping at the mall. She wondered how many hours would have to pass between his arrival home and the darkening of the evening sky before her husband would start to wonder where dinner was. The envelope, she knew, would take him at least a week to find. Sorting through the piles of mail, like most of the domestic chores, was her job.

"To seal up a room?" said the clerk. "Follow me."

She'd left the girls in the car in the parking lot, with the usual admonishment to keep the doors locked and not speak to any strangers. April had wanted to come in — she always wanted to come in — but Adele thought it best for her to stay with Lily. "But I love the smell of hardware stores!" April had said, her voice growing desperate. "*Please* let me come in." "No," said Adele. So she left her daughters there atop the defiled backseat, listening to a scratchy off-the-radio recording of "Crocodile Rock" on Lily's tape recorder.

"You can't come in with me, April, or else the surprise will be ruined," she'd lied, wondering what kind of object she might

bring back to them, a question that was answered the minute
she saw the bin of flashlights near the cash register. Perfect, she
thought. We'll need a few anyway. She followed the clerk to the
next aisle, passing rows of tiny boxes filled with nails and screws,
nuts and bolts, now past the garden hoses and household cleans-
ers, breathing it all in deeply. April's right, she thought. It's a
good smell.

"This here's plastic sheeting," said the clerk, a freckle-faced
teen with a distinct Southern twang. You never knew what kind
of accent you'd get in Maryland. The crossroads between north
and south, here and there, its voices ranged from the dropped *g*'s
of warmer climes, to the odd-sounding native *o* (rendering the
three-syllabled Potomac into the nearly four-syllable puh-*teh-o-*
mak), to the New York dialect of transplants like herself, who
still pronounced words like god and dog *gooawd* and *dooawg*,
despite all attempts to soften them. Your origins marked you,
thought Adele. In ways you could never escape. "You put a piece
of this here up with some duct tape, that should do the trick."

"Thank you," said Adele. "That's exactly what I need."

Her heart beating even faster now, she carried her purchases
up to the register, pulled three flashlights and a couple of pack-
ages of C batteries from the bin, and paid for all of it with the
cash she'd withdrawn from the drive-through bank window on
Friday morning, knowing that if she were to follow through on
her plan—which at the moment she'd pulled up to the teller
in her car, rolled down her window and said, Three hundred
dollars, please," she still wasn't sure she would—she'd want to
avoid using her credit card. She tried to look normal as she stood
there and waited for change, like a woman who just wanted to
seal up a room. But her hands were shaking as the bills changed
hands, and she made the kind of nervous, eye-contact-avoiding
small talk with the cashier about home improvement and saw-

dust he would have probably described as either suspicious or odd, had he ever been asked.

"I got you some flashlights," Adele said, as she opened the door of the car.

April breathed a sigh of relief. Her mother was back.

4.

"Where are we going?" April finally said, after they'd been driving in the car, around the Beltway, from Maryland to Virginia and back to Maryland again, until the gas tank was nearly empty.

Adele hadn't really thought through the where and when of her plan. She knew she needed to find someplace hidden from the road, where a car might sit, idling, without arousing suspicion. And she knew she had a better chance of success with this strategy after dark, when the roads would be emptier, her daughters sleepier. What she hadn't counted on in her calculations was the rain, which had begun to slam the windshield with the kind of biblical ferocity that rendered visibility close to nil. It would be impossible to make the necessary adjustments to the tailpipe without getting completely soaked. Or even to spot a proper venue for what she'd come to refer to in her head as *the big sleep*. "Camping," she said, over the slap of windshield wipers. "We're going camping. But not tonight. We'll have to wait until tomorrow night, because of the rain."

"So where are we going tonight?" said Lily.

A good question. She'd considered driving to New Jersey, where her mother had moved. But this was more of an instinctual impulse, misguided and useless, which she'd learned, by necessity, to repress. She was nearing the Maryland state line again, a GAS FOOD LODGING sign pointing the way. She turned on her signal. "We'll sleep in a motel tonight," she said. "That sounds like fun, doesn't it?"

"Yay!" the girls both shouted.

"Does it have an ice machine?" said April.

"And cups wrapped in plastic?" said her sister.

It took so little to excite a child. The promise of ice. *When does that part get lost?* Adele wondered. "Yes," she said. "It'll have an ice machine and plastic cups. Just like the Sea Esta."

What a dumb name for a motel. She'd always thought so. "Sea" she understood, and the play on the word "siesta," but what did "Esta" mean? It didn't stand by itself. A play on words could only work if each part could stand on its own. Like the OK Coral Shop, just down the road from the Sea Esta, where the girls bought those puka shell necklaces. That worked. Except, she thought, they were undercutting themselves by calling their merchandise mediocre. You'd never have the OK Burger Stand. Or the OK Crab Shack. No one wants crabs or burgers that are just okay, any more than one would want to have anything that is just okay. Unless, of course, the choice is between okay and miserable. She'd take an OK Life over the one she had now. She'd even settle for a Below-par-but-coping Life. Or a Boring-but-emotionally-steady Life. Anything but this.

The Sea Esta Motel. *Esta isn't a word.* Couldn't they see that? She tried coming up with a better name. Sea Sun, she thought: "season." No. No one would get it. They'd just say, "We're going to the Sea Sun Motel for vacation," without ever considering the elision. She pictured her own name. Adele. A Dell. As in "The farmer in the." She must have sung that song with the girls at least a thousand times. Two thousand, even. *The farmer in the dell, the farmer in the dell, hi ho the derry-o . . .* and the farmer fucks the wife and the wife slaps the child and the child scratches the nurse and the nurse kicks the dog and the dog bites the cat and the cat eats the mouse and the mouse shits all over the cheese and the cheese—oh, finally, the cheese, that lucky hunk of mold!—the cheese stands alone. Covered in mouse shit, but all by itself, with no responsibilities, no one asking it questions, no one to bother it or tell it to use old sponges instead of new because he couldn't stand to see anything wasted. His parents lived through the Depression, he'd said. They taught him the value of thrift. Depression? Fuck their Depression. She had her own, thank you very much.

She tried conjuring the brief happiness of that farmer-in-the-dell era. It was happy, wasn't it? She thought it was, she'd always told herself it was, with all those toddlers sitting around, gumming Nilla wafers, clapping their sticky hands, but wait, even then, she'd be sitting there in the circle, a kid on her lap, singing about doggies in windows or spiders on spouts, and her mind would start to wander back to the corridors of Holy Cross Hospital, back to the old colleagues she no longer saw, back to patients who no longer awaited her, back to a time when she was actually valued, instead of just needed.

Adele: Add El. Like some sort of misguided slogan for the elevated train in Chicago. Or a command in a game of Scrabble. See that word? Add *l*, and you'll have *shovel*. See? *Shove. Shovel. I* used a *shovel* to bury her.

Add Hell. Well, she nearly laughed, how appropriate. Like instructions for a recipe. Take one woman, throw in a couple of eggs, a teaspoon of sour cream, and then *add hell.* How prescient of her mother. And each word stood perfectly on its own.

How did that expression go again? *Hell hath no fury like a woman . . .* what? She spotted the metallic letters on the glove compartment—*Plymouth Fury*—at the same time she remembered the last word: . . . *scorned.* Some people would see this confluence, she knew, as a sign from God. These people were not her. Though sometimes she wished they were. How nice it would be to have faith in something. Anything. Even hell. But if you didn't buy the whole virgin birth story, it was impossible to swallow the rest. *Welcome to Maryland!* she read, crossing back over the state line. Mary-land. The land of Mary. Even her state was a lie.

"Just like the Sea Esta? Yay!" The girls shouted, which turned into a cacophonous medley of "Yay-yay-yay! Yay-yay-yay!" sung in 3/4 time, as they bounced up and down in the backseat, thinking about all those glistening ice cubes, just there for the scooping.

"Yay," whispered Adele, now feeling that familiar bulge of tears welling behind her eyes again. She took the next exit off of I-270.

5.

"Adele Levine," April's mother was saying to the man behind the counter, even though that wasn't her mother's last name. It was her *grandmother's* last name. Levine was her mother's middle name. Maybe everyone had to use secret code names for the adventure. Like 007. Or Maxwell Smart. She started thinking of her own secret name. Noreen was her middle name, but April Noreen sounded stupid. She could try to be April Levine, like her mother, but she'd rather be April Brady. She and Lizzie Burns (which used to be Bernstein . . . *another secret code)* were always talking about wanting to be one of the kids on *The Brady Bunch.* God. How great would it be to be a part of that family who was always laughing with each other and teasing Alice about Sam the Butcher and getting into the kind of trouble that only lasted a half an hour! How great would it be to have a mother whose smile matched the flip of her mullet and a father who taught you lessons like, "A wise man forgets his trouble before he lies down to sleep." That was a good one. She forgot what happened during the rest of the episode, but it didn't matter, because now she knew a smart thing, and she wasn't going to forget it. April was always trying to honor these words in her own life, like whenever Lily would cheat in jacks, and they'd get into a fight, she always tried to make up before they had to go to bed, even if she had to tell a white lie, which is a lie that doesn't hurt anyone. So she'd say, "Okay, Lily, you didn't cheat, and I'm not angry at you, because a wise girl always forgets her trouble before she lies down to sleep."

"Delle Vigne?" said the hotel clerk, in an Italian accent, pointing to his own nametag marked with the same name. He seemed excited to have found a member of his tribe. "From Firenze?"

"No. Adele Levine. From the Bronx."

"But Mom," April said, "That's not your—" She suddenly felt her wrist being squeezed tight enough to hurt. Her mother's secret signal for her to shut up, like the time when they were going on the Amtrak to visit her grandparents, and her mother told the woman she was four, not five, to save money, even though she was definitely five. "You lied!" she'd said to her mother afterwards, two little words that felt like fire coming out of her mouth. "I didn't lie," her mother had answered. "It was a white lie. Which means a lie that doesn't hurt anyone." To which April had countered, sobbing now, "Then I'm just going to tell everyone I'm a boy, because that's what I'd rather be, and no one will get hurt if I say it!" But her mother just said, "Forget it. Just do what I say, young lady, and do not contradict me." Her teachers had taught her to try to understand words in context; she decided "contradict" must mean "to tell the truth."

Today was turning into such a strange day. First her mother was in a medium mood, which is much better than a bad mood, even though she cut her leg, which would have made April cry.

But mothers were always crying when things were happy, and doing nothing when things were bad. When her dad hit her mom, which he did really not that often, even though you're not supposed to hit people ever, her mother would sit there, like those blow-up clowns you're allowed to hit because they're not people, and they don't get hurt, they just rock back and forth. But when April brought home a drawing of her family she'd done at school — and it was a really good drawing, with everyone smiling, and the sun behind them, and even a rainbow, nothing that would ever upset people who aren't mothers — her mother started crying so hard that she had to go to sleep for the rest of the afternoon, which meant frozen pizza again for dinner.

Then her mother said they were *going on an adventure,* which is something April had been dreaming of doing ever since she could dream. So far, she loved the pizza with Aunt Trudy, and playing *Mad Libs* and checkers with Lily, but not sitting in the parking lot while her mom looked for flashlights. How long does it take a person to look for flashlights? Her mother was always leaving them in the parking lot. "Don't talk to strangers, keep the doors locked, and don't let anyone in this car," she'd said. She and Lily had hidden below the window, crouched down on the floor of the car, petrified that one of the bad guys would try to push his way inside. What would he do, if he got in, she wondered? Give them Indian burns? Steal their tape recorder? There was no end to the horrible scenarios she could imagine.

6.

At the hotel, Adele ordered three hamburgers and two large French fries from room service and went into the bathroom to change her sanitary napkin, which, having forgotten to make provisions for such an occurrence, she'd had to scrounge at the last rest stop. What a hideous business, womanhood. Her uterus ached, her fingers were swollen, her energy sucked out and depleted. She pushed down on her pelvis to try to relieve the pain, but it was seized up with contractions and no more pliant than a basketball. As usual, the blood had flowed onto her underwear. She would have to clean them out in the sink.

Or . . . not.

She could, she suddenly realized, just toss them into the wastebasket. Another object left behind. Like April's school books. The stripped Hoover. The girls' lunch boxes. She would simply—how liberating—toss the whole mess into the trash. But instead of finding joy in this, she couldn't breathe.

A noise, she realized, was coming out of her. It sounded like a moan, only deeper, coming as it did from her diaphragm, not her throat. She held her head in her hands, her elbows digging into her knees. And soon she was crying again.

"What's wrong, Mommy?" April said, rushing into the bathroom, which Adele had neglected to lock. "What happened?" She stared down at her mother's underwear and froze.

"It's nothing. It's just . . ." *Everything's black. A ten-ton elephant, crushing the bones of my back. Every day, the waking up, the crumbs on the table, the trash piling up.* "It's just . . ." What a sight she must be, her thighs puckered over the porcelain, her stained underwear halfway down her legs, her eyes bloodshot and rheumy. "It's just women stuff, sweetheart. Nothing for you to worry about."

"Are you dying?"

In the background Adele could hear Walter Cronkite, counting the dead. "No, I'm not dying. Why don't you change the channel, sweetheart? I bet ZOOM is on." She could see Lily sitting on the edge of the bed, one eye glued to the screen, the other staring at her with what appeared to be contempt. By eight years old, one knew. If not consciously then somewhere inside. An eight-year-old knew other mothers were not spending their days in a fog. That they were not sleeping through the afternoon, or staring at the walls, or wailing at the sight of their own blood. They were crying for reasons a girl could forgive: a son sent home in a body bag; a husband shipped off to war. April, with only six years under her belt, may still have been giving Adele the benefit of the doubt, may still have believed a real mother lay under all those layers of sludge and lard, but Lily had already moved on, already made promises to herself about the kind of mother she would be when she grew up. And that mother looked nothing at all like her own. If anyone could understand such thoughts it was Adele. She'd made the same promises to herself, when she was her daughter's age.

Yet another reason to end the farce. Because, really, where would it end? It was a chain of despair, stretching infinitely from past to future. Why put her children through it? Why make them experience any of it? The sting of an unrequited crush, the pain of childbirth, the sudden appearance of a gray hair; the standing by, helplessly, as the world burned. Why make them reach for the dangling carrot of love only to find out, after biting down hard, that the soil in which it grew was rife with poison? Why give them any hope that their daughters could have happier childhoods, better fates, richer lives?

And she was crying once again.

7.

April knew it. Her mother was dying. First it was her leg. Now her vagina. It was only a matter of time before her whole body would bleed, like that kid on the poster at the Deli Den, who had that disease with the *ph* that sounded like an *f* and made you die from a paper cut. You were supposed to leave your extra quarters for him in the tiny slots underneath his picture, even though it said March of Dimes, not March of Quarters. Or, wait. Maybe it was Easter Seals.

So *that's* why her mother had been crying so much. Of course. It all made sense now. April suddenly felt guilty for all the times she'd been bad. Her mother was bleeding to death and here she was, arguing with Lily about who got to shuffle the cards. Who got to sleep in the side of the bed nearest the window.

From now on, she decided, she would be good. Better than good.

So when she heard her mother moaning in the bathroom, she jumped off the bed — the side nearest the window, which now seemed an empty prize — and offered it to Lily, who was by now getting used to April's pre-bedtime, *Brady Bunch*-inspired shows of largesse. Then she took the three flashlights and C batteries out of the Value Hardware bag, and, following the tiny diagram pasted inside the flashlight, loaded two of them into each barrel, nipple-side up. She had trouble screwing on the tops, though, because you had to press down on the exact center *and* screw on the top at the same time, which was impossible, but Lily, who was now kindly predisposed toward her, on account of her new proximity to the motel window, helped her do it during a commercial.

Now she needed a pole. Finding nothing of that size and shape in the room, knowing her mother would remain sitting on the toilet crying for at least another half hour, maybe more, she told Lily she was going down the hall to get some ice, which was another white lie, something she did all the time these days, even to her friend Lizzie, because once you start lying it's hard to stop, especially when you have something to hide, like a mother. But that was okay, because not only would she not be hurting someone this time, she might even be helping, which she decided should be called a silver lie.

A few minutes later, she walked back into the room carrying a mop, which she'd found—okay, stole—from one of the maid's carts in the hallway, after remembering the use of an unscrewed mop pole to play limbo at a recent birthday party. Lily said, "Where's the ice? What's that?"

"It's a mop," said April. Lily rolled her eyes and shook her head and went back to watching her show. *Let her think I'm stupid,* thought April. *That I can't tell the difference between ice and mops. She'll change her mind when she sees what I've made.*

Then April went to work, pulling the comforter off the bed, unscrewing the handle from the mop head, the latter which she threw into the trash because it smelled, and sliding the stick, perpendicularly, under the sheets. She tried tucking in the sides of the sheets between the box spring and mattress to make the pole stand up straight, but it kept falling down, so she simply crawled between sheet and mattress and held it up herself.

It was magnificent under there, exactly as she'd imagined, and by the time her mother reemerged from the bathroom and she'd turned on both flashlights, it was ready for its unveiling.

"April, what have you done?" said Adele, her voice tinged with irritation, which was at least better than silent.

Lily stayed on her side of the bed, waiting to see where such irritation would lead.

"It's a tent," said April, sticking her head out. She could barely contain her excitement. "I made it for you."

"For me?" said Adele.

"So we can camp. So the rain won't stop us," she said, which, once again, made her mother cry. But not the scary kind of crying, like when she'd brought home the picture of her family with the rainbow, or when Lily asked her why Lenny never stopped by anymore with his jump rope and fruit. It was, as far as she could tell, a good cry, the kind the contestants sometimes did on *The Price Is Right,* when they won a new car.

And then, because Lily felt bad about rolling her eyes at her little sister, and because April wanted her mother to experience camping before all the other parts of her started bleeding, and because Adele wanted her daughters to have one lasting memory of a pleasant moment with their mother, even if only for a day, they crawled under the tent together.

8.

"Does the flashlight make the dust, or is the dust already there before you turn on the flashlight?" April was asking. "Lizzie says it's already there, but I told her she was wrong. You only see the dust when you shine something on it."

"Who's Lizzie?" said Adele. She'd been on her back, a girl tucked under each arm, their heads warm against her chest, their flashlights dancing over the surface of the sheets above them in time to the Carpenters' "Top Of The World" on Lily's tape recorder. It had been decided that Adele would hold the pole between her legs, to keep the tent up, so she lay there with her three-foot erection, a broomstick Atlas, holding up the fragile dwelling.

"She's my *best friend,*" said April, sounding perturbed that this fact would not be common knowledge to everyone.

"Oh, right," said Adele, faking it. "Your best friend." *She?* When had April made a girlfriend? She was twice the size of most of the girls in her class, preferred hunting imaginary animals to hopscotch, and had, as her kindergarten teacher once admonished during a parent/teacher conference the previous year, significant issues with "boundaries." Which was why, the teacher said, April only played with boys, whose equally prodigious lack of boundaries—or "friskiness," as she referred to it in their case—matched her own. The girls in her class not only didn't appreciate her, they shunned her. Made fun of her "boy" body and Toughskins. Didn't invite her to their birthday parties at Shakey's. Called her fatso. Adele had wanted to rip every strand of hair from their skulls when April broke down one night and cried over that one.

But now she felt a sudden rush of pride at her daughter's accomplishment. A friend. A best friend, even. How . . . hopeful. And what if she left her here then? What if she were to drive them home, tell Shep she had to run an "errand" and then just never return? Maybe they'd be okay. Maybe they'd thrive.

No. Without a mother, they wouldn't. They couldn't. She knew that as well as anyone. The muscles of her thighs were starting to tremble. She'd been anchoring the pole for nearly thirty minutes, and she didn't think she could take it much longer. It was too hard, holding up the world.

What was she thinking, bringing two creatures into it? Imagining she could shelter them from everything ugly, everything bad. They would see it all soon. Rivers of shit. Cauldrons of fire. A parched desert atop an icy core. Lily was already starting to see it on the six o'clock news, all those boys zipped up in bags. Now April would, too. It was only a matter of time.

"You and Lizzie are both right," she said. "See?" She turned the flashlight on and off, on and off, on and off. A cone of dust. Black. A cone of dust. Black. A cone of dust. Black. Then, apologizing for her weakness, kissing her daughters good-night, she let the pole drop.

9.

Sunday morning, after driving around Gaithersburg for several hours, Adele found the perfect spot to hide a car. It was just off

I-270 in Martinsburg, where a small stretch of woods abutted a cornfield, whose stalks had recently been stripped.

"Are we there yet?" April asked, for perhaps the tenth time.

Adele had told the girls that she was looking for a place to set up camp. That they would be sleeping in the car, most likely with the heat on, as it was too cold this time of year to sleep outside. That they should trust her. It didn't matter whether or not Daddy would be joining them, or why they were camping on a school night, or who would be collecting their homework for them during the days they would be missing. No, she didn't know Lizzie Burns's telephone number; no, they couldn't stop at a phone booth to call information or Daddy; yes, other kids' parents let them camp on school nights, too; no, killer bees did not live in the woods where they'd be camping; and yes, the tooth fairy does visit children who lose teeth far from home (as April had just done, biting into a pretzel stick). "Almost, April. We're almost there." She turned left onto the dirt path heading into the woods, the twin beams of her headlights guiding the way around trunks and leaves, branches and saplings, as twigs gently snapped under her tires.

"I'm hungry."

"Me, too," said Lily.

"Have another pretzel."

"I want a Twinkie," said April.

"So have a Twinkie," said Adele. So what if they spoiled their appetites tonight? What would it matter? A smile overcame her. "Have two."

"Really?"

"Really."

"Me, too?" said Lily. "Can I have two Twinkies, too?"

"Have three," said Adele. "Go ahead. Dig right in."

She caught a shadowed glimpse of her daughters in the

rearview mirror, staring at one another with a mixture of puzzlement and elation. Then, with a shrug at their good fortune, they ripped open the box of Twinkies and started devouring them one by one, sucking out the sweet cream with tongues and little fingers, emitting groans of delight after every bite. "Oh my god," Lily said, pointing at her little sister and giggling. "Your mouth has whipped cream all over it."

"Look at yours!" April squealed.

"Let me see," said Adele. She stopped the car, shifted into park, and turned around to look at her children. "Oh, April Noreen," she said, seeing the sorry state of her daughter's face, "you win. You definitely win the messiest child award. Followed in a close second by Miss Lily Ann Cassidy. Here . . ." She reached out her hand. April squeezed it with delight. "No, silly," she said, smiling. "I don't want one of those. I want one of *those*." She pointed to the box of Twinkies. "Give me one."

She removed the Twinkie from its plastic wrap and took a slow, luxurious bite into its creamy center before shifting back into drive. Oh, it was good. So good. The spongy softness of the cake, the smooth sweetness of the filling, all melting together, filling her mouth with, with, well, if not happiness itself, then with some close facsimile thereof.

Then, wiping her hands clean on the hem of her dress, she pressed on the gas and drove deeper into the woods.

10.

This was the best day ever, thought April. She woke up in a motel with an ice machine, her tooth fell out, she ate three Twinkies at once, and now she was going camping overnight in the woods with her mother! She couldn't wait to get back home to tell Lizzie.

II.

"Here, drink," said Adele. She held out a shaking spoonful of cough syrup. They were all three crouched together in the back-seat of the station wagon—or the back-back, as the girls liked to call it—with the middle seat collapsed for added room. Adele had spread out blankets and pillows and given each daughter a pair of pajamas to change into, as well as a free pass on the brushing of teeth. She could have made a show out of crawling over the front seat, fishing the thermos, toothpaste, and toothbrushes out of the suitcase, making the girls spit out the back window, but why bother? If nothing else, the last few moments of their lives should be free from all things specious and obligatory.

"But I don't have a cough," said April.

Amnesty from fraud, however, was another story. "Just drink it," said Adele, trying to steady her hand. "It'll . . ." The chorus from that new song on the radio came into her head. Lily had wanted to tape it, planting herself in front of the clock radio, faithfully tuned to WPGC, for three afternoons in a row. *That's okay,* April had said, on the evening of the third day, when Lily was bemoaning her bad luck. *It's a silly song anyway. There's no such thing as killing someone softly. Is there, Mommy?* Adele, who was busy loading the dishwasher, pretended she hadn't heard. *Is there, Mommy?* she repeated, adding, *I mean, you can't kill someone softly, right? Because if you kill them, then they're dead.* At which point Adele dropped a handful of knives into the silverware caddy with a loud clang and said, *Do your homework, you two, right now,* putting an end to the conversation. "It will make you have good dreams," she now said.

"Cough syrup makes you have good dreams?"

"Of course."

"Is that a white lie?"

No, thought Adele. *It's a black one.* "Just drink it, okay? I don't have all day."

"Okay," said April. And she opened her mouth wide.

12.

April's eyes felt so heavy. But she didn't want to go to sleep yet. There were activities they could still be doing, important logistics still to consider. "Are you sure the tooth fairy will find us here?" she asked her mother.

"Of course she will, sweetheart. Now close your eyes. Look at Lily. See? She's already fast asleep."

Oh, no. Her mother was crying *again.* Just from watching Lily sleep. And she was still bleeding from down there. April knew, because of her stealth mission into the motel bathroom, where the evidence in the trash can was piling high. Her mother pretended this was normal, but April knew it was a white lie. And the tooth fairy would definitely not find her here, in the middle of the woods. Sometimes white lies were annoying. People wanted to know the truth. Even if it hurt.

Maybe this wasn't turning out to be the best day ever. And not only because of the tooth fairy. Her mother was acting even weirder than usual. Not making them brush their teeth. Giving them cough syrup when neither of them had coughs. Not calling Daddy for two days. Hugging her and Lily too tight and asking them strange questions. Of course she would love her forever, no matter what. Why would she even ask such a silly question?

This wasn't how she'd imagined camping. Where were the s'mores? The tent? "Can we make s'mores?" she asked.

"Yes. Tomorrow. We'll buy everything we need at the store," said her mother.

"Promise?"

"I promise."

She removed from her coat pocket the tooth she'd carefully wrapped in rest-stop toilet paper and placed it under her pillow, which was actually a guest pillow, not her own. "I want to go home," she said, or perhaps whispered, or maybe she just thought it. Her eyelids felt heavy. So heavy.

13.

It took more than an hour after the girls had fallen asleep for Adele to finally work up the courage to wipe her eyes with the collar of her housedress and crawl over to the front seat of the station wagon. She'd watched them sleep, their little chests moving in and out, in and out, their eyes darting around under their eyelids, which reminded her, a bit too intensely, of the subcutaneous movement of a fetus.

Now, however, her resolve returned, she rummaged inside the half-opened suitcase for her supplies, locating almost everything she needed by feel. She unzipped the suitcase completely and then turned on a flashlight to find the duct tape, shining its beam through the gaps between her suddenly translucent red fingers and onto the loosely packed clothes. *Ah, there it is,* she thought, retrieving the tape from under a shirt.

She stepped out of the car into the brisk air and shut the door gently behind her. The ground was still moist from the previous night's rain, and as she walked the short distance from the front of the car to the rear, her flip-flops sank into the bog. She envied the trees their roots and hard sheaths, their inert grace and self-reliance. She did not believe in reincarnation or even in God, but she thought that if she ever were to come back to life, if such a thing were actually possible, it would be nice to do so as a tree.

That way she could just exist, tall and impassive, without ever uttering another word.

Because that was the problem, really, wasn't it, with being human? You couldn't just be, couldn't just stand, couldn't just live and exist without dragging your feet through the mud. You had to communicate, congregate, collaborate, cohabitate. You had to corroborate. Copulate. You had to co-this, co-that, co-bloody-everything, and if you weren't co-operating you were operating without the *co,* which was a declaration less of independence than of relativity. You could only really exist in relation to others. No matter what she did, Adele would always be her mother's daughter. Her daughters' mother. People clung to you, like burrs.

Even her planned escape, that most solitude of acts, would create as many new ties as it would sever. No longer her husband's wife, she would become his late wife; in addition to her children's mother, their murderer. But while the former had little to no effect on her determination, the latter ripped at her, made her reconsider several times over the past two years, until finally she had to leave, with or without them. But wasn't death better than desertion? The question was one of compassion. The deserted know they've been left. The dead do not. People would understand this. Hadn't her job as a nurse always taught her to alleviate pain, to mitigate suffering? The rules of triage were both simple and brutal: save those who can make it, leave the hopeless to die. Her husband would be fine without her. Her daughters would not.

Crouching low behind the car now, gripping the flashlight between her thighs and pointing it up under the chassis, she attached the vacuum hose to the end of the tailpipe, wrapping several long pieces of duct tape around the seal. It had to be tight, with no possibility of a leak. The delivery system might be primitive, but it could not be inefficient. She knew, from having treated several close calls of carbon monoxide poisoning, both accidental and intentional, that you didn't want to do such a thing halfway. The inhaled fumes could take up to three hours to generate enough carboxyhemoglobin in the bloodstream to permanently inhibit the transport of oxygen. Once the levels were high enough, the oxygen low enough, the body simply stopped. Without pain. Without suffering. Without violence. All because carbon, the building block of life, could also be the instrument of its demise. Like a mother, thought Adele. Like me.

The end of the hose in place, she stood up, unrolled the back window a hand's length, and began covering the gap with plastic sheeting. The noise of the billowing plastic seemed to rouse April, causing Adele to suddenly freeze, but the girl was only switching positions in her sleep, her hand still clutched to the tooth under her pillow. Adele gulped and continued taping the edges of the plastic to the car, pulling the surface taut. When she was sure every edge was tightly sealed, every square inch of that gap between window and frame covered, she punctured a small hole into the surface of the plastic with a twig and twisted the other end of the hose into this tiny aperture, like a screw into an anchor.

She stepped back from her creation to admire it.

She walked back around the car, this time in the direction of the driver's seat, and snuck in quietly. The seat felt cold against her thighs. Winter would be coming soon. All that snow, all that ice. Like clockwork every year. How was it that most people scraping a windshield on a frigid dawn could find solace in the anticipation of spring? She'd tried to be like those people. She tried, she really did. When Lily was born, Shep had wanted to call her Joan, but Adele demurred. No, she said, no names of martyrs. Martyrs die. Flowers live. She willed herself to face the sun, to have faith in the promise of renewal.

But then came April. And then, instead of spring, more darkness. And then the ice returned, once again.

She reached into her pocket and removed her keys, noticing their heft and coldness and cragginess of edge as she stared out into the darkness beyond the windshield. *If you exist, God, then send me a sign!* she pleaded, her tears once again flowing freely. *A reason not to stick this key in that hole.*

14.

In the distance, too far to be detected without headlights, a doe and her two fawns crossed in front of the car, their gait synchronized and full of grace, like ballerinas on tiptoe. Had Adele seen them, had her headlights actually been turned on that night, she might have woken the girls to show them. Look, she would have whispered. Look at those deer! Lily would have rubbed her eyes and begged to get out of the car. April would have started spouting everything she'd learned about mammals from school. How mammals are warm blooded and furry. How they feed their babies milk from their own bodies. Then Lily might have even insisted, feeling the boldness of her eight years, despite the late hour and the darkness beyond, *Let's go find them!* And April, tracker of imaginary animals, who believed in the depths of her soul that all troubles *could* be forgotten before sleep, who fancied herself just as wise and as brave as her big sister, would say, *Yes, let's! Let's go follow the deer.* They might have even put on their Keds then, over footed pajamas, ignoring Adele's protestations that it was time to go to bed, time to close their eyes. Then they would have pushed open the back door of that blue Plymouth Fury, ripping hose and plastic sheeting from their fragile moorings.

15.

Adele held the car keys in her hands and waited. One minute passed. Then two. She could hear the ticking of her watch, felt the coursing of blood in her chest. She strained her eyes to try to see, but nothing stirred in the darkness beyond.

She slipped the key into the ignition with a soft click. She was about to turn it when she remembered the unsealed letter she'd composed earlier that morning. She'd woken up two hours before the girls to give herself the proper time and space to say everything she wanted to say in it, to finally describe, once and for all, the blackness inside, but when she actually sat down with the blank sheets of motel stationery and a pen, only the most absurd clichés popped out. *I can't go on. I feel like I'm drowning. I'm living in a kind of hell.* After throwing out several aborted attempts, seeing that the girls had started to stir, she finally settled on a simple admission of guilt. If she couldn't say what she wanted to say, at least she could say what she needed to say. The last thing she wanted was for someone else, after she was gone, to get blamed for her death for lack of evidence.

She pulled the envelope out of her purse, the note out of the envelope and read it:

October 22, 1972
Dear Shep,

This is not your fault. It's mine. You know what I've been living through these past few years. You've seen it up close, even if you haven't really understood it, but I would hope you could understand why such a life would be untenable for me and for our children. I'm sorry for taking them with me, I really am, but I'm sure you'll come to realize, as I have, that this was the only way. Do not hate me for what I've done.

Love,

Adele

Pathetic! she thought, reading it over. Totally insufficient and devoid of answers. Her toes curled inward. Her shoulders tensed. But what else could she write? Some things were beyond words.

Her chest heaved. She leaned over the steering wheel and held on tight, sobbing silently into her arms so as not to wake the girls. *God,* she thought, *please forgive me.*

With a brisk flick of the wrist, she turned the key clockwise in the ignition and stepped firmly on the gas. The fumes burst in, acrid and foul. She revved the engine twice more, then floored it a third for good measure. Nauseated and growing dizzy more rapidly than she'd expected, she quickly hoisted herself over the headrest and fell into the backseat, where she lay down between her slumbering children, her knees tucked up underneath her. Finally, she thought. The big sleep. In her mounting confusion, she suddenly remembered the tooth under April's pillow and panicked. She fumbled in her pocket for a quarter, but by the time she had it in hand, it had already slipped through her fingers.

"Did you get the s'mores?" April said, struggling to open her eyes. She reached for her mother's hand.

Exhaust filled the car.

CHAPTER 22

MARK SHOWED UP early Sunday evening. I'd passed out on the couch as the sunlight began to fade, my papers scattered around me, the fire I'd lit and stoked continually for the past thirty-six hours reduced to a gray pile of smoldering ash. The girls were making snow angels outside when he arrived, the sound of their giggles mixing in with the crunch and whir of his car wheels on the frozen driveway.

I heard the car door slam. Daisy's muffled voice shouting, "Daddy, you're here!"

Tess shouting, "Shh! Mommy's working."

I put on my boots and stepped outside. The dusk-kissed sky was now filling with the stars, the storm having finally come and gone, leaving two feet of snow and a thick coating of sleet in its wake. *Shoveling it by hand would be hard,* I thought, *but not impossible.*

Mark was hanging back ten yards or so, standing tentatively in front of the car he must have rented that morning, staring down at the ground and kicking away at a patch of ice with the tip of his left snow boot. *"Business or pleasure?"* I imagined the woman behind the Hertz counter asking him. I wondered how he answered.

"Did you finish, Mommy?" said Daisy, when she saw me emerge.

"Nope." I kissed her on the nose. "But I think I got off to a good start."

"That's good."

"Are there any Pop-Tarts in the house?" said Tess. "Daisy said last time we were here Astrid gave her Pop-Tarts."

"As a matter of fact, I think I saw a box of them in the pantry. Do you want to go inside and check?"

The girls eyed one another conspiratorially: the verboten pastry, stuffed with preservatives and refined sugar, offered without even the minutest of moral struggles; to what do we owe this great pleasure? "Yes!" said Daisy, running toward the house, not waiting for me to change my mind.

Mark was still standing back, still kicking away at the ice, clearing a hole until he'd finally hit dirt. "I wasn't sure if . . ." he started to say. "You said in your note you—"

I walked toward him to bridge the distance between us. "I said in my note not to come find me."

"I wasn't sure if you meant it."

"I did."

I saw the pain creeping into his expression. His jaw growing stiff. He didn't want me to have meant it. "Do you still?"

I grabbed his hands in mine, rubbed the back of his jagged knuckles with my thumbs, and sighed. "I don't know. I need some time to mull it over."

He clenched his mouth before attempting a slight smile. "Are we talking like a few minutes here or more like a week, because it's freezing out here and I've got to pee."

I smiled, despite myself. Then I invited him inside.

IT WOULD TAKE a couple of years, in fact, to come up with a proper answer to Mark's question, but by then much about our lives would have already changed. I would lease a small office up in Harlem, where I would go during working hours to write. Some of these days would be difficult, most of them would be lonely, but they were mine, they paid the rent, and I looked forward to them. I would try to remember which Friday of the month to bring in cupcakes, but sometimes I'd forget, and I no longer mistook either outcome as proof or indictment of my competency to mother. The girls loved me, I loved them, and with each new batch of cupcakes baked the needs and boundaries of our relationship changed anyway. Motherhood was not something one could plan. It just happened, candle by candle.

Mark would resign from Lortex, giving up stock options and promises of riches in exchange for his old job back at CUNY, where he would keep working on mathematical models of mortality, but on his own terms. Within his own parameters. And with a bevy of smart grad students to help him structure the equations, allowing him to come home from work in time for dinner most nights full of stories and hours to spare. Eventually, he and his team would create an actuarial chart that could be fine-tuned beyond anything that had ever been used before, and they would sell these findings to Aon. Not for millions, but for enough to give each one of his engineers a little breathing room that year, a vacation they wouldn't normally have taken. We'd take our portion of the profits and book a month-long trip to Italy. The first week we'd spend in Rome, showing the girls where we'd met and fallen in love, but they would be far less interested in the specific narrative of their parents' courtship—*And here's the restaurant where we had our first meal! Oh, and sweetheart, here's the piazza where you once kissed me in the rain, remember?*—than they were in seeking out, along those ancient, cobbled streets, the perfect cup of gelato. After awhile, we would agree with them. There was only so much memory a place could hold. Only so much power the past could wield over the present. Time moves on. Piazzas fill with new lovers. Children get born. Chapters come to a close.

I would also take the opportunity, during that same sojourn, to make a pilgrimage to the Paloma DiMarco Gallery, where Renzo's photographs from Iraq were being shown. It didn't make sense for me to stand in line, Mark said, in the hot Roman sun, waiting for three hours to get into the Vatican. "Go take some time for yourself," he'd tell me. "Put your feet up, like the doctor said. I can handle the kids on my own." I would drop the three of them off in a taxi near the entrance to the museum and continue on to the gallery, where I would make my way, one by one, from photograph to photograph, starting with the endless line of American tanks, trailing like a miniature serpent through the empty, brown landscape on the first day of the war, and ending with the photo that had caused yet another stir when it was published a few years later in several magazines, above a caption reading, "The last image of war he ever saw."

This last one would be, ironically, a fairly pedestrian panorama when compared with the others: a market, on the outskirts of Baghdad, the object of interest small and poorly framed in the dead center of the image, with nothing notable on the periphery to counterbalance the composition. Even the focus was slightly off. I would sense that Renzo had probably just been setting up the camera on his tripod at the time it was taken, trying to decide whether and what to shoot, when the woman suddenly appeared. When he must have realized he was out of time. In fact, aside from the small halo of light and debris extruding out from her waist, the black nylon of her *hijab* caught in the first microseconds of ignition, the image was almost embarrassingly mundane: just a woman in a market, pressing a button on her cell phone. I couldn't help but wonder if Renzo had survived that particular 1/125 of a second, if he'd gone on, like his colleagues, to spend many more years of his life in and out of that hellhole, whether he would have even included its consequent remnant in the show.

Despite its lack of artistry, I found myself immobilized in front of it, unable to look or walk away. I must have stood in front of that photograph for nearly ten minutes, feeling my lungs expand and contract, wondering what Renzo's final thoughts were as the shrapnel pierced his sternum. Was he thinking about Paloma, how he'd never get to meet the child growing inside her? Was he thinking about his mother, how he'd found her dangling from the rafters of her father's barn? Was he thinking, for even the tiniest fraction of that fragment of a second, about me?

"It is an interesting image," a voice behind me would say, in a thick Italian accent, "even if it lacks the compositional rigor of the others." I would turn around to see a beautiful woman, with smooth, dark hair and a high, regal forehead. She would be wearing a suede skirt with a cream silk blouse, holding a clipboard with the prices for the photographs attached, clearly wondering whether I was a buyer or just passing through. "You are American, yes? British?"

"American," I would say, suddenly embarrassed by my ugly sandals, the only ones that would fit around my swollen ankles, knowing that they must have been the dead giveaway. "And yes. I agree. It is interesting. How did the film survive the blast?"

"This is the crazy part of it," she would say. "The camera, she came out fine. Not a single scratch on the lens. Can you believe it?"

Yes, I would think, *I can.* "That's wild," I would say. "Do you know the photographer?"

"Did," she would answer. "I *did* know him." She would glance up at the black, stenciled letters painted on the wall, spelling out *Renzo D'Aubigny, 1962–2007.* But before she could elaborate, the woman's daughter would come bounding out from the back office, a blur of pigtails and white smocking, her heart-shaped face the spitting image of Renzo's. *"Mamma, ho fame,"* she would whine. I am hungry. And the woman would excuse herself—the babysitter had called in sick that day, she was so sorry, but if I had any questions about purchasing any of the photographs I should speak to her assistant, Fabrizio—to take her daughter out for lunch. "So when are you due?" she'd ask, before turning to leave.

"End of August."

"How wonderful," she'd say, sweeping up her daughter into her arms and planting a kiss on her cheek. *"Si, Mona Lisa?* Isn't it wonderful? *Andiamo, mi amore. Mangiare."*

The space inside my chest would seize up. "What did you just call her?"

The woman, already halfway out the door, would look slightly embarrassed. "Mona Lisa. I know, pretentious, no? At least her stepfather think so. But it was her father's choice, so we honor it. We call her Mona, for short."

"It's a beautiful name," I would say. A flash of Renzo's face hovering above mine, contorted, ecstatic, reappeared. As it would, now and then, for the rest of my life. I'd tell the woman maybe I'd come back later, though I knew I never would. Then I'd find a deserted bench on the banks of the Tiber, where I would sit, and I would cry, feeling the new life stirring inside me, watching the waters of the river flow.

• • •

A week later, arriving home from Italy, I'd sort through the month's worth of mail and find a package addressed to me from Shep Cassidy, containing the copy of the manuscript I'd sent him plus the following letter:

Dear Ms. Burns:

I can't say I enjoyed reading this, and I didn't understand the point of *The Inferno* or why you included all that extra stuff from your own life. But never mind. If someone wants to turn it into a book, that's their business. It's not what happened, and it's not how I would have written it, but I'm not the writer. I'm just grateful you respected my privacy and made it up.

And no, I don't mind if you keep April's initials in the "in memory of" part. I guess if she'd lived she might have liked that.

Cordially yours,

Shepherd Cassidy

Before folding it back up, I would read the last line again: *I guess if she'd lived* . . . And then again: . . . *if she'd lived* . . . Realizing I'd never conjugated her fate in the conditional. If she had lived? But she hadn't. She'd disappeared, suddenly and soundlessly, and it was the absence that took up permanent residence inside me, not her presence. In fact, had April Cassidy actually made it past her seventh birthday, had she grown up and grown breasts and gone trudging off toward her own horizon, red shorts ablaze, she would have probably slipped out of my basket of friends the same way most childhood friends do: not with a loud crash, yolk and shell lying in a puddle on the ground, but so quietly and imperceptibly I wouldn't have even realized she was missing.

ACKNOWLEDGMENTS

FOR HARBORING BOTH this author and her manuscript when no one else would: David McCormick and Kathy Pories.

For sparking the flame: *Infanticide: Psychosocial and Legal Perspectives on Mothers Who Kill,* by Margaret Spinelli; *Mothers Who Kill Their Children: Understanding the Acts of Moms from Susan Smith to the "Prom Mom,"* by Cheryl Meyer and Michelle Oberman; *Women's Moods: What Every Woman Must Know About Hormones, the Brain, and Emotional Health,* by Deborah Sichel and Jeanne Watson Driscoll; *Night Falls Fast: Understanding Suicide,* by Kay Redfield Jamison.

For tending the fire: Dr. Gloria Stern.

For explaining data mining to a word person: Chris Wiggins, Associate Professor in the Department of Applied Physics and Applied Mathematics, Columbia University.

For rescuing an old file from the shredder: Mike Fry, Montgomery County Police Department.

For its amalgamation of commentary on *The Inferno:* The Princeton Dante Project (http://etcweb.princeton.edu/dante/pdp); and for his translation: John Ciardi.

For providing the time, space, and audience for the first reading: Tim Ransom and The Naked Angels Theater Company.

For eggs with a chance of Coke: Meg Wolitzer.

For the cabin in the woods: Anne and Kipp Sylvester.

For further acts of midwifery: Abigail Asher, Elizabeth Beier, Nora Ephron, Leslie Falk, Tad Friend, Sarah Jane Grossbard, Courtney Hodell, Brunson Hoole, Gillian Linden, Patty Marx, Samantha Miller, Janet Patterson, Martha Parker, Francesca Schwartz, John Burnham Schwartz, Jennifer Steinhauer.

For childcare: Bonnel Mercado and the staff at Park West Montessori Day Care.

For grandchildcare: Margie and Dick Copaken, Marcy and Maurice Swergold.

For love, every day: Paul, Jacob, Sasha, and Leo Kogan.

Between Here and April

Reading and Discussion Guide

READING AND DISCUSSION GUIDE

1. Lizzie tells her shrink she feels "lost" (page 9). Is it personal? Societal? A combination of both? In what ways are both Lizzie and Adele representative of the gender politics of their times? In what ways are they simply human?

2. Lizzie and Mark have some unresolved issues in the bedroom. How do themes of human bondage inform the rest of this story? At the end of the book, we're left in the dark as to whether these issues get resolved, either in the master bedroom or in the marriage. Is bondage, whether explicit or implicit, an inescapable element of love? When you imagine Lizzie and Mark's marriage five years, ten years, twenty years down the road, what do you see?

3. The year 1972, the historical setting of this book, was the golden age of journalism, but in 2007, the modern-day setting of this book, journalism has entered a period of crisis. Celebrity culture has all but drowned out the news. Newspapers and magazines are foundering. How do these issues affect Lizzie's life and career? Should Lizzie have gone to Iraq? Why or why not? If she were a man and a father, would your response be the same?

4. Consider Renzo: should he have gone off to war and left a pregnant girlfriend behind? How has Renzo, in his own work, dealt with the issues facing the modern-day journalist? "No more close-ups of the crying widows," he tells Lizzie, "and the

bleeding soldiers and the little child with the shrapnel stuck into the skin on his face in the hospital bed. We have seen these pictures too many times, in too many places. They have become meaningless" (page 155). Is he right? Have we, as a society, become inured to the pain of others?

5. Eyewitness accounts — of an event, of a life — are inherently inaccurate. When Lizzie sets out to discover the *why* of Adele's crime, she talks to several eyewitnesses, each of whom give her versions of the story based on their own particular lives and biases, none of whom provide the kind of answers Lizzie's hoping to find. "You think you need facts to write truth?" Renzo exhorts on page 174, and by the end, she accepts that he's right. She must settle for the musings of her own imagination to get to the truth of the story. What are the limitations of such novelistic inquiry? What are the limitations of journalistic inquiry? Is one "better" than the other, "truer"? If so, how?

6. How does the repression of painful memories and events influence both Lizzie's life and the plot of this novel? Are some things better left repressed, or should they be brought to the surface in order for the psyche to right itself?

7. All the main characters in this novel — Adele, Lizzie, Mark, Renzo — are dealing, in one way or another, with the fall-out from maternal wrath and/or abandonment. How are their situations similar? How are they different?

8. Dr. Rivers asks Lizzie what Renzo represents. Lizzie responds, "Oh, I don't know. All the normal cliché things, I suppose. Freedom. Love. The path not taken" (page 191). Is this a cop-out or the best possible answer Lizzie is able to offer? What do

you think Renzo represents to her? What does he represent to the story?

9. If Lizzie had married Renzo instead of Mark, what would her life have looked like today? Do you fault her for her adulterous behavior, or did you see her actions as inevitable, understandable within the confines of her situation?

10. Is Lizzie a good mother? If so, how? If not, what advice would you give her? What about Adele? Were you able to empathize with her actions in any way, or were they completely anathema to your way of thinking about motherhood and, therefore, indefensible? If Adele could talk from the grave today, what would she say, how would she defend her actions? Would she consider herself a good mother?

11. Trudy Levine teaches a class called Misogyny in Literature. When Lizzie asks her which novels she studies, Trudy replies, "All of them" (page 89). Is this a fair assessment of literature? If you were designing such a class, which authors and novels would you include? Is this novel misogynistic in any way? If so, how? Does the author treat her male characters fairly? Empathetically? Cruelly?

12. When Lizzie tries to find the woods where Adele killed herself and her children, she finds instead a new development of McMansions. "Refugee camps I'd visited in Somalia had more joy in them that that house," she narrates, "yet there it was (I zoomed out until the whole house was in the frame): The American Dream" (page 96). How does Lizzie feel about this American Dream? In which ways might the house represent those feelings?

13. "Revenge! It's built into our RAM just as surely as hunger," Lizzie muses on page 169, when she frets over the future legacy of Iraq. Is a desire for revenge part of our genetic makeup? Is Lizzie driven by it? What about Adele? What makes you believe this?

14. When Lizzie takes her own children into the frigid woods, she hits rock bottom, the icy center of hell. Why is she able to snap out of it, to find her way back out into the starry night, while Adele was not?

15. At the novel's end, Lizzie goes to Italy, where she stands, pregnant and immobilized, in front of the last photograph of war Renzo ever snapped: a female suicide bomber, at the moment of detonation. How is this photograph a proper coda, not only for Renzo's life, but for the novel as a whole? What about Lizzie: why is she so moved by that image, unable to look away?

Deborah Copaken Kogan is the author of *Shutterbabe*, the bestselling memoir of her years as a war photographer, and the just published *Hell Is Other Parents*, comic essays she has performed live onstage with both the Moth and Afterbirth. Her work has appeared in the *New Yorker*, the *New York Times*, *O: The Oprah Magazine*, *Paris Match*, *Newsweek*, *Time*, *Elle*, *Géo*, *L'Express*, and *PHOTO*, and on *ABC News* (for which she won an Emmy), *Dateline NBC*, and CNN. She lives in Harlem with her husband and three children.

Other Algonquin Readers Round Table Novels

Every Last Cuckoo, a novel by Kate Maloy

In the tradition of Jane Smiley and Sue Miller comes this wise and gratifying novel about a woman who gracefully accepts a surprising new role in life just when she thinks her best years are behind her.

Winner of the ALA Reading List Award for Women's Fiction

"Truly engrossing . . . An excellent book club selection."
—*Library Journal*

"A tender and wise story of what happens when love lasts."
—Katharine Weber, author of *Triangle*

"Inspiring . . . Grabs the reader by the heart."
—*The New Orleans Times-Picayune*

AN ALGONQUIN READERS ROUND TABLE EDITION WITH READING GROUP GUIDE AND OTHER SPECIAL FEATURES • FICTION • ISBN 13: 978-1-56512-675-6

Mudbound, a novel by Hillary Jordan

Mudbound is the saga of the McAllan family, who struggle to survive on a remote ramshackle farm, and the Jacksons, their black sharecroppers. When two men return from World War II to work the land, the unlikely friendship between these brothers-in-arms—one white, one black—arouses the passions of their neighbors. In this award-winning portrait of two families caught up in the blind hatred of a small Southern town, prejudice takes many forms, both subtle and ruthless.

Winner of the Bellwether Prize for Fiction

"This is storytelling at the height of its powers . . . Hillary Jordan writes with the force of a Delta storm."—Barbara Kingsolver

AN ALGONQUIN READERS ROUND TABLE EDITION WITH READING GROUP GUIDE AND OTHER SPECIAL FEATURES • FICTION • ISBN 13: 978-1-56512-677-0

Water for Elephants, a novel by Sara Gruen

As a young man, Jacob Jankowski is tossed by fate onto a rickety train, home to the Benzini Brothers Most Spectacular Show on Earth. Amid a world of freaks, grifters, and misfits, Jacob becomes involved with Marlena, the beautiful young equestrian star; her husband, a charismatic but twisted animal trainer; and Rosie, an untrainable elephant who is the great gray hope for this third-rate show. Now in his nineties, Jacob at long last reveals the story of their unlikely yet powerful bonds, ones that nearly shatter them all.

"[An] arresting new novel . . . With a showman's expert timing, [Gruen] saves a terrific revelation for the final pages, transforming a glimpse of Americana into an enchanting escapist fairy tale."
—*The New York Times Book Review*

"Gritty, sensual and charged with dark secrets involving love, murder and a majestic, mute heroine." —*Parade*

AN ALGONQUIN READERS ROUND TABLE EDITION WITH READING GROUP GUIDE AND OTHER SPECIAL FEATURES • FICTION • ISBN-13: 978-1-56512-560-5

Breakfast with Buddha, a novel by Roland Merullo

When his sister tricks him into taking her guru, a crimson-robed monk, on a trip to their childhood home, Otto Ringling, a confirmed skeptic, is not amused. Six days on the road with an enigmatic holy man who answers every question with a riddle is not what he'd planned. But along the way, Otto is given the remarkable opportunity to see his world—and more important, his life—through someone else's eyes.

"Enlightenment meets *On the Road* in this witty, insightful novel."
—*The Boston Sunday Globe*

"A laugh-out-loud novel that's both comical and wise . . . balancing irreverence with insight." —*The Louisville Courier-Journal*

AN ALGONQUIN READERS ROUND TABLE EDITION WITH READING GROUP GUIDE AND OTHER SPECIAL FEATURES • FICTION • ISBN 13: 978-1-56512-616-9

Saving the World, a novel by Julia Alvarez

While Alma Huebner is researching a new novel, she discovers the true story of Isabel Sendales y Gómez, who embarked on a courageous sea voyage to rescue the New World from smallpox. The author of *How the García Girls Lost Their Accents* and *In the Time of the Butterflies*, Alvarez captures the worlds of two women living two centuries apart but with surprisingly parallel fates.

"Fresh and unusual, and thought-provokingly sensitive."
—*The Boston Globe*

"Engrossing, expertly paced." —*People*

AN ALGONQUIN READERS ROUND TABLE EDITION WITH READING GROUP GUIDE AND OTHER SPECIAL FEATURES • FICTION • ISBN-13: 978-1-56512-558-2

The Ghost at the Table, a novel by Suzanne Berne

When Frances arranges to host Thanksgiving at her idyllic New England farmhouse, she envisions a happy family reunion, one that will include her sister, Cynthia. But tension mounts between them as each struggles with a different version of the mysterious circumstances surrounding their mother's death twenty-five years earlier.

"Wholly engaging, the perfect spark for launching a rich conversation around your own table." —*The Washington Post Book World*

"A crash course in sibling rivalry." —*O: The Oprah Magazine*

AN ALGONQUIN READERS ROUND TABLE EDITION WITH READING GROUP GUIDE AND OTHER SPECIAL FEATURES • FICTION • ISBN-13: 978-1-56512-579-7

Coal Black Horse, a novel by Robert Olmstead

When Robey Childs's mother has a premonition about her husband, who is away fighting in the Civil War, she sends her only son to find him and bring him home. At fourteen, Robey thinks he's off on a great adventure. But it takes the gift of a powerful and noble coal black horse to show him how to undertake the most important journey in his life.

"A remarkable creation." —*Chicago Tribune*

"Exciting . . . A grueling adventure." —*The New York Times Book Review*

"Gripping . . . Echoes the work of Cormac McCarthy."
—*The Cleveland Plain Dealer*

AN ALGONQUIN READERS ROUND TABLE EDITION WITH READING GROUP GUIDE AND OTHER SPECIAL FEATURES • FICTION • ISBN-13: 978-1-56512-601-5